# The Stone of Orinn

*Book II of the Beyond the Elderwood Series*

D1565317

## By Michael Greenleaf

*For my mother, who always encouraged my imagination.*

Map illustration by Michael Greenleaf

Cover design by Monica Haynes of The Thatchery
(thethatchery.com)

Please visit the series website at
www.beyondtheelderwood.com

# Author's Note

The *Stone of Orinn* is the second book in the *Beyond the Elderwood* series. Once again, we journey to the kingdom of Angard to find Ryan settled in his new home. As in our own lives, just when you think things are set and all is right with the world, life has the uncanny ability to disrupt your best laid plans. The time will come when we all must face an even greater challenge than we ever have before.

Each of us will stand at these crossroads and decide whether it is easier to take the less risky path, or forge ahead and brave the unknown. While the latter will be the more difficult, the rewards can be great. In the end, we may come to realize that the previous journey was only meant to prepare us for what lies ahead.

After all, there's an entire world out there, beyond the Elderwood.

The Vicar of Orinn walked the perimeter of the nave. The lowering of the lamps might be considered a task for an initiate, but the aged priest found a certain solace in completing the last chore of the day himself. He walked up the short flight of broad steps and bowed his head as he approached the sanctuary. Above the altar of polished marble, rose a tall sheaf of grain fashioned of hammered gold. Set amid the stalks, the Stone of Orinn gleamed in the lamp light.

Forged by the god of the harvest and surely imbued with the power to heal the land, the vicar pause a moment to reflect on its mysterious discovery. It had been rescued out of the Darkwood shortly after the Goblin Campaign ended, as he understood it. How long had it been in goblin hands? What evils were they able to work by twisting its god-given power?

Any other abilities lay dormant, unknown. He would not be the one to meddle with the gemstone. It best served right where it was. Comforted by his beliefs, the vicar departed, closing the doors behind him. With a nod to the guards, he headed for his comfortable bed.

The nave doors had scarcely closed when a thick rope dropped from the narrow skylight. It swayed wildly as its length abruptly ended a foot above the floor beside the altar. A slim figure began his descent as his accomplice watched from overhead. Once on solid ground, Karsten wasted no time. He gave no thought to the majesty of the marbled altar, nor was he tempted by the other religious trappings of silver and gold. The god Orinn meant nothing to him. Only the gemstone.

The Stone of Orinn glittered, catching the low lamp light and returning each flicker with a flash of emerald green. Karsten's hand wavered as he reached out for the walnut-sized gem. He held an involuntary breath, half-expecting to be struck down on the spot. Was it his imagination, or was the gemstone warm to the touch, even through his gloved hand?

Karsten exhaled. His other hand flew to his pouch and produced the tool needed to gently pry the precious relic from its mounting. To his relief, the stone came free with less effort than he had anticipated.

Out in the vestibule, the cough of a guard broke the silence.

Working quickly, Karsten secured the end of the rope to the harness he wore. Up on the roof, Derric planted his feet and adjusted the pulley so the rope would feed smoothly. He tugged at the length that disappeared over the side of the roof to signal all was ready. It was all about timing now.

On the street below, Adran blended with the shadows, hidden among the tall evergreen shrubs that lined the south side of the temple. Karsten and Derric had extinguished the nearby streetlamp, aiding in his concealment. Adran felt the tug on the rope as a horse turned onto the lane.

"Come on," he whispered impatiently.

Wrella slowed to a halt and Adran broke cover to fasten his end of the rope to the saddle horn. They would only have a moment before the next pass of the city watch. With a slap on the rump, he sent the horse on its way. The rope tightened, but the stolen animal hesitated under the strain.

"Get moving," Adran ordered. "Did you have to pick the most stubborn one in the stable?"

"Next time, I'll check with the owner first!" Green eyes flashed as Wrella shot him a burning glare. She kicked the horse forward.

With a lurch, Karsten was plucked from the floor. He grunted in protest as the handmade harness tightened in all the wrong spots. He raised his eyes to see the ceiling of the sanctuary rapidly approaching. Much faster than they had talked about, he was sure. His body contorted as he shifted, trying to settle into a position of least pain.

From a pouch, one of his lock picks slid free. It fell to the floor below to land with a metallic ring. One hand closed over the gemstone to protect it from falling as well. Karsten braced himself for a painful impact with the stone above. Then with another jolt, his rapid ascent ended. Wrella stopped the horse at the exact spot they had marked earlier.

Karsten scrambled through the slit of a window and joined Derric at the edge of the roof. A low whistle signaled they were ready. Adran repeated the whistle and Wrella turned the mount around, guiding the horse back in their direction. Derric and Karsten clung to each other, as they slid over the side of the temple roof and were smoothly lowered to the ground.

Harness and rope were bundled and hastily secreted within the green foliage. Wrella set the horse loose with a slap. The stolen animal was not a complication they needed. Booted feet down the lane was their cue to depart. The four sped around the corner and hunkered behind a storehouse. They listened with hands on weapons as the men of the city watch kept to their usual patrol route. Derric let out a breath as the sounds of footsteps receded.

"After all this trouble, tell me you have it," he grumbled at Karsten.

"Of course I do! What kind of—"

"Never mind that now," Adran interrupted. "We're sticking to the plan and getting out of the city as early as possible. Drynas will be in an uproar come morning and anyone even spotted near the temple will be questioned. That means all four of us for sure."

"And if things go south?" Wrella asked. "We don't have much of a head start. Maybe I should stick with Karsten."

"We part ways and meet where we agreed," Adran instructed. "Keep your heads, and in the end, we'll all be rich."

The deep knell of the temple bell shattered the quiet summer night. All four jumped.

"Or we'll all be dead," Derric growled.

# ∽ Chapter 1 ∾

Ryan's breath fogged in the morning air. An early winter had settled upon the territory of Galanthor and snow dusted the gentle hills. Birds flitted among scattered patches of leafless trees. The brown-haired youth drew his heavy cloak tighter about his five foot, nine inch frame as he scanned the rolling grassland. Sometime during the night, one of the horses he had acquired that summer must have escaped the paddock and wandered off. Having arranged a trade with a farmer for winter supplies, he was anxious to see the animal returned. He urged his steed onward.

As Ryan ascended the next rise, he sighted hoofprints in the thin layer of snow. He brought his mount to a faster gait and followed the tracks into a sparsely wooded dell. He was surprised to see a pair of riders with his mare and called out a greeting as he drew near. The men glanced at each another. Both appeared unkempt and gave no response. Ryan reined in his mount before them.

"You have my thanks. I've been on her trail since sunrise," he motioned toward the mare.

"It seems we've done you a service," the shorter of the men replied. "If this be your horse."

"I can assure you it's mine," Ryan insisted. "In fact, we can ride into Llerwyth if you require proof."

The look he received gave Ryan the impression that he was being sized up.

"I can tell by the pommel, you carry a fine sword," the taller of the two grinned. "We should get a reward for our troubles." The men edged their horses closer.

Ryan studied them in turn. "Reward?"

The smaller man was bearded and wore a ragged cloak. He drummed his fingers on the hilt of a short sword. The taller bore a long-handled axe and held onto a rope, which they had managed to get around the neck of the mare. He leaned forward and waved the other end of the rope before Ryan.

"Finders keepers, boy. Take our steed if you can," he challenged.

"*Your* steed?" Fear gave way to anger. How dare they rob him!

Ryan's hand shot out. He grasped the man's wrist instead of the rope and whip his mount's head in the opposite direction. Ryan used the animal's strength to pull the surprised thief from the saddle.

The shorter fellow cursed his fallen partner and fumbled for the weapon at his side. Ryan snatched the rope dangling from the mare. With a shout, he whipped the man's steed on the rump before the short sword cleared his scabbard. The animal's flight instinct took over and it charged from the dell, its rider bouncing wildly. He swatted the taller man's horse as well, and it chased after them, leaving its owner behind.

Ryan held onto the rope, allowing some slack in the line. With a kick, he set off in pursuit of the mounted rogue, the mare following on his flank. His horses were swifter and Ryan inched closer until he could reach out and place a firm grip on the ruffian's billowing cloak. Ryan reined in his horse and pulled on the heavy garment with all of his strength. The man was yanked from the saddle and tumbled backwards onto the ground.

Shaken by the unexpected encounter, Ryan raced on toward Llerwyth. He kept the horses at a gallop, and did not allow them a rest until he was satisfied he was not being followed. He slid from the saddle to inspect the mare as the horses chewed on short stalks of winter rye.

"Who were those guys?" he wondered aloud. "Bandits, no doubt. I'll definitely report the matter."

Satisfied the animal was unharmed, Ryan swung up into the saddle of his dark bay. He clicked his tongue and gave a light kick. His horse did not budge.

"You serve me well when it counts," he patted its neck, "but you're sure stubborn between times." He had not yet given the black-maned horse a name. He supposed one would eventually come to him.


Later in the afternoon, Ryan rode into the small hamlet with the mare in tow. He steered his horse past the handful of shops, humble temple and cluster of homes that made up the center of Llerwyth. He arrived at Corbyn's farm to find others also in need of supplies, to one extent or another. He was not surprised. However, he chalked up such shortcomings to the late summer blight and an early winter. The occurrence in Drynas surely had nothing to do with the poor harvest across most of Galanthor. It was pure coincidence that these events followed the disappearance of the Stone of Orinn.

Ryan found the notion that a missing relic, even one of this importance, could somehow be responsible for everything from sour milk to sickness a bit absurd, despite prevailing opinion. His circumstances were certainly not the results of anything supernatural. Having recently reclaimed his family land, the fields lay bare and no garden had yet been planted. And his friend and mentor, Thadius, would soon return to Galanthor with his younger brother, Darien.

Ryan pondered how much he should tell his brother about his adventures since leaving Othgard. Darien was ten, and should he repeat tales of wizards and warlocks and lost treasures, it was sure to attract attention. With Thadius' status with the king and Trenn's wizardly pursuits to consider, there were just too many secrets that should remain . . . secret. His newfound wealth could be explained away as a long-lost inheritance from their father. He would take the advise Thadius had given him and leave out the interesting parts.

"Ryan!"

Corbyn's son, Elias, greeted Ryan with a wave. He was a red-haired lad, a few inches shorter and four months younger than Ryan. The boys had met as the summer ended. Ryan and Thadius still labored on restoring the house and Elias' visits had allowed them some normal conversation — devoid of any magical escapades.

"Da says to help you get this mare in the barn. Have you heard the news? King Trevin has died," Elias exclaimed. "His oldest son, Daven, now rules Angard."

"I hadn't heard," Ryan returned.

"Everyone's talking about it. That and bandits."

"Bandits?"

"Ya, a whole band of 'em. There've been robberies on the road to Drynas. Farms have been raided. Luckily, no one's been killed."

"I think I've met a couple of them. Let's tell your father."

With the mare at home in its new stall, the boys found Corbyn and his wife speaking with a group of men from the hamlet. Elias' father was a robust man, his hair a deeper shade of red than his son's and starting to gray on the edges. With the conversation already centered on bandits, the tale of Ryan's encounter was added to the accounts.

"Something should be done," one of the men commented.

"There's been talk of forming a militia to hunt down the criminals," Corbyn hinted, casting a sideways glance at his wife.

Corbyn's wife scowled in disapproval. "Best to let Lord Varis handle this problem."

"I'll gladly join in the defense of the hamlet if needed," Ryan promised.

"Me too," Elias offered.

All business concluded, Ryan accepted an invitation to dine with Corbyn and his family. Afterward, as he guided his stubborn bay home through the darkness, he felt less brave than before. Once in bed, Ryan's thoughts lingered on the death of kings and roving brigands as sleep overtook him.

Ryan rose with the dawn to water the horses and refill their feed bins with flakes of fresh hay and a scoops of grain. His own mount stepped over to investigate, then turned its head with a snort.

"That's a perfectly good breakfast," Ryan pointed out. The animal nudged him in the arm with its nose.

"You think you're getting a treat before your meal?"

The horse whickered in answer. Ryan shook his head. Human and horse eyed one another.

"Fine," Ryan relented. He reached into his coat and produced a bright red apple. He held out the fruit and his horse ate it greedily.

Ryan wiped his hand on his pants and picked up a pair of empty buckets on his way out of the stables. "I should name you something that fits. Mule-headed comes to mind," he called over his shoulder.

With no well dug as yet, Ryan made due with filling buckets from the shallow creek at the bottom of the hill. He topped the rise on the return trip to see a dozen horsemen in the distance. Ryan dropped the buckets and dashed for the house. Inside, he strapped on his sword belt and grabbed his bow and quiver. His heart pounded as he sped out the door. As Ryan ran for the stable, he recognized men from the hamlet. The horsemen drew up as they neared the house. Elias and his father dismounted.

"I see you're someone who meets trouble head-on," Corbyn observed. The man looked every bit the warrior in his thick leather jerkin and broad blade at his side, but Ryan knew him to be a farmer at heart.

"I'm relieved you weren't a band of thieves," Ryan confessed. All bore a weapon and even Elias traveled with a stout club secured to his saddle.

The middle-aged farmer bellowed with laughter. "Lucky for us, you might have cut half of us down!"

"He is good, Da," Elias cut in. "I've seen him and Thadius at practice."

Corbyn's smile faded. "Can I convince you to join us? There have been more robberies. We mount a force to deal with them — on our terms this time."

"I'll go," Ryan volunteered without hesitation. "And I've extra mounts we can use." Corbyn waved some men forward and all helped with preparations to depart.

While a rider was dispatched to request aid from Lord Varis, the men of Llerwyth refused to wait idly. All were determined to see these outlaws brought to justice. Corbyn was voted their war leader and his plan was simple enough. Those men with horses would patrol the northern trails, straying into the countryside and confronting any strangers they came upon. Those without horses would stay behind in Llerwyth to defend the hamlet.

Ryan swung up into the saddle. Besides his camp gear and bedroll, he rode with his bow and quiver strapped to his mount. At his left side hung the sword retrieved from the lost citadel. On his right hip hung a dagger acquired during the same adventure. Its twin was carried by Arlena, who was now apprenticed to the wizard Trenn. Ryan's thoughts often wandered to the dark-haired girl. Perhaps come summer, he could pay a visit to the southern Elderwood.

Over the next few days, the sun shone brightly and gradually melted away the snow on the open ground. The company stopped at other settlements and isolated farms to discover word of bandit activity had spread. The number of volunteers increased to sixteen, limited by the number of dependable steeds available. Ryan was excited to be included as a member of the host, made up of ten men and five other boys of about his age. However, he soon noticed that he and the other teenage boys were assigned lesser duties. They cared for the mounts and gear and attended to other camp chores. Only the men ranged afield or rode ahead to challenge any riders.

His suspicions were later confirmed, when a pair of riders approached the band. Corbyn signaled some of the men forward. Ryan and Elias attempted to join them, but he waved them back. "A crowd will make them nervous. Best to stay here with the others," Corbyn directed.

"This isn't fair," Elias complained as his father rode off. "We're nothing more than baggage handlers."

Ryan was of the same opinion. "Easy, Elias. We may see some adventure yet. At least you're out of the hamlet for a couple of days."

This did not put the impatient youth at ease. He shifted in the saddle and drew his heavy cloak around him. His father and the others returned with the riders after a brief exchange.

"We ride to the west," Corbyn declared.

The pair of riders turned out to be the sons of a nearby farmer. While the brothers were trading in Aldwyn, the brigands had struck, beating their father and making off with the family cattle.

The brothers joined them and guided the company through the sparsely wooded countryside. Ryan found himself at the rear of the line, with the other boys. If they did locate the bandits, would the outlaws surrender? The farmers might find themselves outnumbered, and with the teens forming a third of the band, Ryan feared casualties could be heavy. Few of the men owned a proper sword. Most were armed with spears and axes, although half of them did carry a bow and plenty of arrows. Ryan was convinced none had seen any real combat.

Further along the path, they passed barren fields before a farmhouse came into view. A broken section of fence and trampled earth told of how the beasts had been led away. Corbyn drew the men together and held a hasty council.

"We'll follow their trail," he decided.

"Corbyn, we're but a day's ride from Aldwyn. Maybe we should send for the garrison," a man from Llerwyth spoke up.

"The bandits will have fled the area. They're hindered by livestock and won't be waiting around to get caught," he answered.

The company left the farmer and his wife in the care of their sons and rode onward. They pressed their mounts, seeking to gain as much ground as possible. When darkness hid the tracks, Corbyn stopped them. Scouts were sent out and the remaining men and boys rolled out their blankets for a brief rest.

"I can't wait to pound on one of those robbers with this." Elias patted his club. "I'll beat him black and blue. I'd do more if I owned a fine sword like you've got."

"We may have to fight, but only if forced to." Ryan tried to impart a bit of wisdom, as Thadius had done with him.

"Aren't you the least bit anxious for a scrap?"

Not wishing to encourage him, Ryan sought to draw Elias off the subject. "Never mind all that. Let's get some rest."

The boys slept restlessly and woke when the last scout returned.

"We're in luck," Corbyn informed them. "The bandits' camp is just inside the Darkwood Forest."

"It's a wonder our scouts weren't caught!" Ryan whispered to Elias.

"Are you sure it's them?" Elias blurted.

"It's them. They have the stolen cattle and horses penned nearby, and besides, no sane person would camp within those wild lands."

The eastern Darkwood was a former haunt of goblins, where strange creatures were rumored to still lurk. None but the king's soldiers and the bravest hunters dare enter its depths. And even then, never alone. There was a hushed discussion on how to proceed from here. In the end, the men looked to Corbyn for his decision.

"We know their strength and location. It's best we take them before daybreak, unawares. Let me make it clear — we will accept the surrender of any who do so."

Ryan expected a bit of grumbling. He was astonished to hear none and was further impressed with the farmer's tactical assessment and strategy as he laid out his plan.

"One last thing," Corbyn addressed them. "A rider will be sent to Aldwyn to notify the garrison of the situation."

The men went quiet as Corbyn's gaze swept over the group. Heads lowered and some inched backward. At last, Corbyn said the name of the youngest boy in the company. The lad was downcast as he swung up into the saddle.

The host moved out and their route took them south of the camp, to avoid an approach from the open grasslands. The men of Galanthor intended to pick their way through the woods and surprise the sleeping bandits. Ryan was thinking on how to convince Corbyn to include him, when the farmer brought them to a halt before the fringes of Darkwood Forest.

"We'll dismount and leave our horses here," he explained. "The boys will keep them ready, should we need to make a speedy retreat."

"I knew it!" Elias echoed Ryan's thoughts. There were many complaints among the boys.

"This undertaking is risky enough without worrying about your necks," Corbyn scolded. "The five of you will stay here as rear guard. This is as important a task as the men's. I'll hear no more grumbling about it."

The matter was settled and the men handed their reins to the boys. Ryan took the reins of Corbyn's steed. He recalled the last time he and his companions had tried to take an armed camp unaware.

"Sir," he caught Corbyn's attention, "they may have posted sentries."

"I've considered it, and I appreciate you speaking your mind. I know you're disappointed, but this is a man's work. You're not far off from that responsibility, lad. However, this is not the day."

Ryan fought to hold his tongue. He had fought ferocious trolls, creatures of stone and magic and a host of the undead. How could Corbyn exclude him?

"I want to ask a favor of you, Ryan."

Ryan nodded in silence.

"Watch out for Elias. I've heard you have some skill with the sword. Keep him by your side and safe from harm, if you are able. I make this request as a father, not as a leader."

"I'll do my best," he promised.

Corbyn clapped him on the shoulder. The men set out, and the boys positioned the horses in a loose line. A length of rope secured them, and with the pull of a knot, the mounts would be freed to carry them away to safety.

"At least all is set at this end," Ryan sighed. His breath came out as a fine mist in the cold air. He turned to find Elias gone.

# ❦ Chapter 2 ❦

Ryan cast about and glimpsed a figure disappearing into the shadows. So far, no one else had seen Elias sneak away. Ryan edged his way further into the forest. He did not want any of the others to leave their posts as well.

"I'll wring his neck!"

Ryan sped after him. How could Elias be so thick-headed? Then he remembered how eager he had been to prove himself to Thadius.

Within moments, he caught up with Elias, who stopped to stare at the sight before him. As expected, the bandits had posted a sentry. Arrows protruded from the sprawled body. A short sword and a signal horn lay next to the dead man. It was apparent he had given Corbyn's men no choice. Elias breathed rapidly.

"I-I've never seen a man slain," Elias' voice trembled.

"Don't feel ashamed if you've no stomach for this," Ryan laid a hand on his shoulder. "This is the reality of battle. It's very different from the tales and the songs."

"I suppose that's the truth of it." Elias cleared his throat and straightened. "The men will need us."

"No," Ryan stated. "We need to—"

The shrill note of a hunting horn blared. The attack was on. Elias bolted forward.

"Elias, wait!"

Ryan overtook him as the boys broke into a clearing. Campfires burned low and men wrenched from their sleep scrambled for weapons. Corbyn called for them to surrender as he led most of the farmers into their midst.

The others positioned themselves at the edge of the wood and held arrows at the ready.

While some bandits raised their hands, a number of them regrouped near an enormous tent in the center of camp. A man with long hair, armored in a leather cuirass and brandishing a longsword, rallied them. Ryan assumed him to be the leader of the thieving band. His heart raced and a rush of adrenaline surged through him. There would be a fight after all.

"Stay here," he said to Elias as he continued on.

The groups clashed, and Corbyn exchanged blows with their leader. Ryan arrived just in time to intercept a wild-eyed man, who thrust at Corbyn with a spear. Ryan deflected the tip of the weapon and slashed the bandit in the arm. Before the wounded man could retaliate, he was struck by an arrow and fell to the ground. Corbyn's archers had evened the odds.

"In the name of the gods!" Corbyn spotted Elias, and was plainly more panicked by the appearance of his son than he was of fighting outlaws. He redoubled his assault and hammered at the armored man with his sword.

Ryan fought alongside a fellow farmer from Llerwyth. The tall man wielded an aged broadsword with surprising skill, and their combined efforts forced those before them to retreat. As they pressed the attack, a resounding clap thundered in the midst of the camp. Bewildered, men cast about for the source. The sides of the canvas tent billowed, and Ryan was certain the sound had emanated from within.

In the confusion, the bandit leader tripped on the tent ropes and fell into the canvas structure. Corbyn and his men took advantage of the unusual distraction. With his sword at the fallen leader's throat, the majority of the band raised their hands in surrender.

At the far end of the tent, a knife pierced the collapsing material and tore open a slit. Ryan's jaw dropped. He recognized the wiry man who scampered from beneath the folds.

Karsten.

Dumbfounded, Ryan could only stare. The last time he had seen the thinly framed thief, the man was running off with the rest of his mercenary friends. They had intentionally used Ryan as a decoy to escape the king's soldiers. The thief and murderer bolted for the trees as riders burst into the clearing, horns blasting. The boys had not waited patiently at hearing the din of battle. Thinking them a lord's war band, the handful of bandits who still resisted dropped their weapons. With everyone else occupied, Ryan pursued Karsten into the woods.

Ryan chased the sound of snapping twigs and crunching leaves. Patches of snow remained, sheltered beneath the trees, and the occasional boot print indicated that he was on the right track. Then ahead, he sighted Karsten between the trees. The wiry thief came to a halt as a goblin dropped from the lower branch of a towering oak. It landed before him, scimitar already in motion. Karsten was slain in one fell swoop.

Ryan froze as childhood memories surfaced to haunt him. Clutching his baby brother tightly as he hastened through the streets of Drynas . . . The gates of the keep scarcely shutting before goblin warriors reached them . . . The death of his parents. Unable to move, he watched the green-skinned creature hunch over Karsten and search the thief's body. It pulled something from his coat and held it aloft. A walnut-sized gem flashed an emerald green in the early morning sun. The goblin shoved it into its rough leather coat. Ryan hardly registered footfalls behind him.

"It's a goblin!" Elias arrived with a gasp. Ryan shook his head to clear away the past.

"Get help," he pushed Elias away.

The goblin whipped about to face them. A full foot shorter than the average man, it eyed the boys with a malicious glare and sprang at them. Before Elias could react, it lashed out at Ryan with its scimitar. Ryan leapt back and avoided decapitation by inches. The sinewy goblin proved agile and dodged Ryan's swing. Human and goblin circled each other.

"Ryan!" Elias shouted.

A second goblin crept from the cover of a nearby tree. The crooked-nosed goblin bore a curved blade as well. Ryan lunged at them, hoping Elias could escape. But the opportunity was gone. The second goblin circled around to cut Elias off, while the first launched into Ryan. He was unable to bring his blade about in time and barely grabbed hold of its sword arm at the wrist with his free hand.

Ryan grappled eye to eye with the snarling goblin. He turned away from its foul breath as it snapped at him with discolored teeth. Seizing hold of its coat, he planted a foot against the goblin's stomach and rolled backwards, flipping it over him. Both lost their swords in the exchange. As they jumped to their feet, Ryan drew his dagger.

The goblin swiped at him with thick, sharp nails. Ryan dipped below its reach and slashed it across the thigh.

The goblin yelped and dropped a hand to the wound in an attempt to stem the flow of dark blood.

Meanwhile, Elias was not faring well with the other goblin. His arm cut and his club splintering, Elias cried out for help. He could not keep up with the goblin's speed. Ryan rushed to his aid and sent the goblin sprawling with a kick to the ribs. The goblins hesitated when a horn sounded and the men of Llerwyth called out. They snatched up their weapons and disappeared into the woods.

"That was close!" A pale Elias clutched his wounded arm and blood welled between his fingers. "I thought we'd be killed for sure."

"Let me see your arm."

Reluctantly, Elias withdrew his hand.

"It's not as bad as it looks," Ryan encouraged him. "I'll need to tear some cloth to make a bandage. Keep pressure on it."

As he wrapped his arm, Ryan noticed an object lying where he had flipped his opponent. The goblin must have dropped it.

"What is it?" Elias wondered aloud.

"I've no idea." Ryan examined the patch of leather. About four inches square, it bore the branded profile of a tusked boar. The meaning of the image was lost on the boys. Without further thought, Ryan placed the piece of leather in his pouch.

"Let's get you back to camp. We've more work to do on your arm."

They met up with Corbyn, who was relieved to see his son safe. The big farmer threw his arms around him.

"Da," Elias protested, "not in front of the others!"

"Ha! My son, the warrior!" he bellowed.

"I've healing salves and bandages in my gear," Ryan offered.

"Come, Ryan, let's tend to this scratch and see how he likes the warrior's ways after seeing his flesh stitched on."

As they treated the wound, Ryan apologized for letting Elias come to harm. However, the boy spoke up and admitted that it was he who ran off, ignoring Ryan's counsel. Corbyn shook his head.

"Thanks be to every god who protects fools," he muttered. "And goblins on this side of the Cimrinn? What's Ilsgaard up to?"

Ryan was shocked to find the farmers so calm after the fight and already binding one another's injuries. He lent what aid he could, especially to Corbyn for his numerous scrapes and bruises. Though one man of Llerwyth had momentarily lost consciousness, he would fully recover. It was miraculous to Ryan that no other members of the company had received life-threatening injuries.

Many of the bandits, a quarter of their number, lay dead. Ryan was told that Lord Varis would send men to collect them for burial. Another group sat tied at the wrists in a semi-circle before a fire. Few of the thieves had escaped. Ryan spotted the men who tried to make off with his horse several days earlier among the captured. Both avoided his condemning gaze.

Once his own men received attention, Corbyn allowed for the care of the wounded bandits. He looked the sullen group over and ordered the most nervous pair of the bunch taken aside for questioning. The rest would be lashed together with a long rope for the march to Aldwyn, where the nearest garrison could be found. Ryan followed, along with some of the others, curious as to what Corbyn could learn. Already shaken, the men did not require much prodding before they talked.

"We was just robbin' and such, my lord," one whined. "Never did we harm no one."

"It's the honest truth," the younger man swore. "We only joined for the fact we was half-starved."

Corbyn glared at each. "You be truthful and I'll see no harm comes to you. My men are vicious when roused and seek revenge for the farmer you lot beat," he threatened. Ryan knew this was not exactly true, but the bandits took it as fact.

"We had nothin' to do with that business," the first insisted. "We was here in camp all day." The other nodded in agreement.

"So you saw those goblins? What business did they have hanging around?" Corbyn demanded. "And no whimpering, straight out with it!"

"S-swords, my lord. The goblins was lookin' to trade for human-forged arms and such," the younger admitted.

"You'd deal with those animals, knowing that sooner or later, those weapons could be used against your fellow man?" Corbyn spat and shoved the younger one down.

"Corbyn," Ryan interrupted, "I need to ask about the man named Karsten. I had the misfortune of crossing his path in the Elderwood. The last I saw of him and his cohorts, they were on the run." Ryan turned to the prisoners. "But what was he doing here?"

The younger of the men regained his feet and half-hid behind the other man. Neither spoke until Corbyn balled up a meaty fist.

"Karsten knew the man who led us," the younger man let out. "Joined us last month. Promised us we'd be rich if we stayed on."

The bandits exchanged a subtle glance, confirming Ryan's suspicions.

"Tell us about the green gemstone. It must be the one Karsten and company had stolen this past summer. Was it also for sale? One of the goblins knew to look for it. I saw it steal the stone from Karsten's body."

"What's this?" Corbyn stepped forward.

"Did you say a green gemstone? The biggest you ever seen?" a farmer asked.

"Huge," Ryan answered, "and now the goblins have it."

"It couldn't be," another whispered.

Corbyn grabbed the older bandit by the shirt. "Is this true? Is the Stone of Orinn in goblin hands?"

"It-it be true," the thief stammered. His response set everyone speaking at once.

"What does this mean?" Ryan raised his voice to be heard. Corbyn leaned closer.

"It may mean the ruin of the land."

# ❧ Chapter 3 ❧

The revelation threw the men of Galanthor into an uproar. Accusations of treason flew and some seized the bandit leader, jerking the man to his feet. Corbyn was quick to step in and separate them before matters got out of hand.

"It was Karsten who arranged for the sale of the gem," the leader hastily confessed. "And it wasn't to the goblins."

Corbyn hushed the agitated men. "To who then?"

"It was a wizard."

"Was this wizard in camp?" someone demanded.

"If he was dealing with these outlaws, he was no wizard," Ryan stated. "He was a sorcerer."

"Wizard or sorcerer, what's the difference?" Elias questioned.

"A wizard uses his powers to benefit and protect others. A sorcerer follows an evil path," Ryan clarified. "Of course! The thunderclap during the battle was the mage escaping by way of a spell."

"He simply disappeared?" Elias marveled.

"You seem to know an awful lot about magic and mercenaries," Corbyn observed.

"I traveled briefly with Karsten and a company of mercenaries this past summer," Ryan explained. "I discovered that they had stolen a sizeable gem but had no clue it was from the Temple of Orinn in Drynas. Is what you said about the stone true?"

"The Stone of Orinn is considered a gift to the people from the god of the harvest. Many see it as the heart of the land and the source of its fertility," Corbyn related.

"I believe it," one of the farmers affirmed. "I saw what it did for the land with my own eyes. When we broke them at the battle of Drynas, the goblins burned crops and tainted streams with their poisons and filth as they retreated."

"Their shamans worked wicked spells, and disease swept the region like a foul wind," another added.

"It was a dark time," Corbyn sighed. "Priests from the holy orders accompanied the king's warriors and lent their skills to counter goblin magic. In the second season after the war's end, the Stone of Orinn was found."

"Found? By who?" Ryan was not familiar with this tale.

"The story goes, that following a vision, a priest of Orinn ventured deep into the Darkwood Forest. The priest and his party faced deadly perils before locating the gemstone. They brought it to Drynas, to the newly built temple, and placed it on the altar. Galanthor began to heal. Streams were cleansed, disease faded and for seven seasons, the land has produced in abundance. Until its theft this summer."

Ryan knew the people took the stone's loss seriously. The head of the northern pantheon, Orinn was more than the god of the harvest. His influence was felt in every aspect of life, from the general welfare of the population to the weather. He was also father to the goddess Shariss, the patron of the order that had raised Ryan. With the farmers' testimonies, Ryan better understood how the absence of the gemstone might be blamed for any hardship — the late summer blight, the early winter and the poorest harvest in years. Perhaps the recent sickness in some of the livestock was no coincidence. And goblins had reappeared on this side of the Cimrinn River . . .

"Corbyn, I owe you and all of my neighbors an apology," Ryan announced.

"How so?"

"I'm ashamed to admit it, but I assumed you all simple farmers. I had no idea there were veterans of the Goblin Campaign among us."

Corbyn surveyed the men of Llerwyth, and each stood a bit taller. "Most here served as foot soldiers for King Trevin and settled in Galanthor after the war. But don't feel bad, lad, you didn't misjudge us," he clapped Ryan on the shoulder. "We *are* simple farmers."

They learned nothing more from the bandit leader. Their mission accomplished, the men of Llerwyth left the Darkwood behind. They marched the captured men and cattle toward Aldwyn, the nearest town. Ryan rode at the end of the line with Elias and the other boys, this time without complaint. Halfway to Aldwyn, they encountered a war band of twenty riders under Lord Varis' banner. Corbyn gave a full account of their deeds to the captain and reported the news concerning the Stone of Orinn. With the prisoners turned over, the farmers agreed to return the stolen cattle to the rightful owners on their way back to Llerwyth.

\*      \*      \*

Bare branches whipped at the young thief as he raced through the woods. Hale stumbled over roots and rocks as he dashed amid the trees at a full run. He was sure that the men who raided the camp were the local militia and would soon be on his trail. A lengthy prison sentence lay in store should he be caught, or worse.

Hale was nearly spent. His breath came out in great misty clouds in the cold morning air. He cast a backward glance and was dismayed to see his footprints in the lingering patches of snow. He mumbled a prayer to Lazum, the mischievous god of stealth and thievery, for the sun to melt them away.

After a moment's respite, Hale set out once more. He reached the edge of the woods, and as he thanked his outlawed god for his escape, he was suddenly grabbed from behind. His right leg was kicked out from under him and aided in the quick takedown. Before Hale realized he was still alive, he was flat on his back and a woman straddled his chest.

The first thing he noticed was her beauty. Her auburn hair held a dark red tint and was pulled into a ponytail. Her lips parted into a slight smile and her green eyes flashed with menace. The next thing he noticed was the dagger at his throat. Hale waited for her to speak first.

"What are we running from, boy?" she asked in a pleasant voice and nudged his throat with the dagger.

Hale swallowed hard. He was a skinny youth, neither a strong nor particularly good fighter, and was shaken at being taken so unaware. "M-m-men raided our camp." He stammered whenever nervous.

"Bandits?" The woman rose and stood over him. She looked to be in her mid-twenties and wore a heavy woolen jacket and loose-fitting pants. To his surprise, she bore a sword in addition to the dagger. She studied him as he lay there.

"Of course. *You* were the bandits." She held out her hand.

Hale froze, unsure of her intention.

"Take it," she ordered.

Hale accepted her hand. She helped him up and strode to a stand of trees, where she picked up her gear. The woman donned a hefty pack with a bedroll, water skin and a leather quiver. She also carried with her a sturdy short bow.

"Who are you?" Hale was leery. Was she some kind of bounty hunter? He was sure she was no soldier.

"We'll put some distance between you and whoever is probably putting your friends into chains — those still living, anyway. Along the way, I want you to tell me all about them."

"I d-don't know anything about them, miss."

"Not the men who attacked you, boy," she responded with measured patience. "I'm interested in the surly company you've been keeping."

No, he decided, she was not interested in him, just information. She might be an outlaw too.

"What can I tell you? The others of the band were either killed or captured."

"You see, I've been on the lookout for an old friend," she said. "He fell in with a group of rogues, last rumored to be working this area."

"What's your friend's name?"

"Karsten. He's shorter than I, about your height in fact. Black hair and smells bad to boot," she described.

"Ya," he admitted. "A man named Karsten joined us."

"Was he in the camp during the attack?" She stopped in her tracks and grasped Hale by the shoulders. "Answer me!"

"Y-yes, lady."

She regained her composure. "You must tell me all about him, everything. And young man, leave nothing out," she added ominously.

Hale talked. He did not mean to tell her everything at first, but her eyes danced with an unknown mischief. It was not the kind of playfulness the young man wanted to see. It was a darker, more menacing look. Out of fear, he told her all, from Karsten's arrival, to the events of the morning. He even spoke of the anonymous mage and the goblins that appeared in camp the day before. Hale tried to be vague about the attack. His new companion would have none of it.

"Tell me about the battle," she coached. "What happened to Karsten?"

"It happened so fast. We were set upon by men on foot, then m-mounted warriors surrounded us. I saw Karsten as I ran. He was d-dead." Hale nearly flinched and half-expected the woman to strike him for bearing the news. Instead, she laughed and shook her head.

"So much for my plans," she let out with a sigh. "It seems this was not meant to be. Never go against the gods, boy."

Her relationship with this Karsten was a mystery. However, he did not care. She apparently was not going to kill him. He began to fantasize about the two of them starting their own outlaw company. He was thinking of how he might bring up the subject, when her questions continued.

"So then you fled?"

"Yes, my lady. We were t-terribly outnumbered."

"Had you run far before I found you?" she soothed. If she was about to suggest a rest, he was all for it.

"Perhaps for half an hour," he reckoned. "In fact, we should get moving. I'm sure the woods will be searched."

"Let's be on our way." As they resumed their walk, the woman opened her belt pouch and handed him a small flask. "A bit of whiskey?" she offered. "It'll take the bite from this cold. It's Karganthian. Harsh but does the job."

He took the flask and hesitated at the sour smell.

"You are old enough, aren't you?" she teased. "I like a man who can handle his drink."

"I'm nineteen years this summer," he proclaimed. Hale raised the flask and drew a long pull from it. He almost choked and coughed several times. She patted him on the back and retrieved her flask with the other hand.

"You know it's good if it takes you like that!" she exclaimed.

"Q-quite smooth," he squeaked.

A moment later, a wave of exhaustion washed over him. He needed to rest, and not merely for a few minutes, for an hour. He was dizzy and came to a stop as the ground swirled beneath him.

"W-what's wrong, honey?" she asked innocently.

"I n-need to sit . . ." Hale knew no more. He staggered and collapsed into a deep sleep.

"You lie here until the militia, or whoever they are, chances upon you. That way, they won't range too far afield and stumble across me as well. I don't want to be mistaken for a common bandit. Thieving and a little misadventure is one thing, but throwing in with rogues who deal with goblins?" She shook her head disapprovingly at the sleeping figure.

The green-eyed woman relieved him of his meager funds, then left him laying there to return to Drynas by a roundabout route.

"Karsten!" she steamed. "The Stone of Orinn has been recovered by now and will be on its way back to the temple . . . and after all our hard work. You may have been spared my sword, but at least you met a deserved end."

As she walked, Wrella contemplated her next move.

# ✢ Chapter 4 ✢

On the day of their return, the men of Llerwyth rode into a hamlet abuzz with news. The territory of Galanthor had been proclaimed an Earldom. In addition, King Daven had named Malikar of the House of Rhuddlun, as the land's first earl. A distant relative to the crown, Earl Malikar was said to be en route to Drynas with a full entourage.

"If we're just hearing about this now, he must be halfway here," Elias chimed in. "We may see our new earl sooner than expected."

Corbyn chuckled. "One of the disadvantages of living so far away from the king's city is information often moves at a caravan's pace."

Ryan tarried longer than he intended, entertained by good conversation and a last look at Elias' wounded arm. It was late in the evening when he bade them farewell. The first thing he noticed as his house came into view was the light. The lamps burned brightly and a fire was lit. Ryan urged his mount into a gallop. He brought his energetic steed to a halt before the door and drew his sword.

"Come out, you brigands!" he challenged in his deepest voice. The door flew open and Darien burst out. Thadius appeared on the threshold behind him.

"Ryan, it's us!" Darien shouted with joy.

Ryan broke into a wide grin. He leapt from his horse and sheathed his blade. "Well-met, both of you!" He ran to hug his brother and shake Thadius' hand. "I didn't expect you until next week."

"The road was good to us," Thadius returned his smile.

Darien had turned eleven the previous month and Ryan swore he was taller than when last he saw him. Leaner, and with a lighter shade to his hair than Ryan, Darien had more of his mother's look about him, especially in his bright blue eyes. Ryan could see it more than ever, but perhaps it was because of their time apart. As they led Ryan's horse to the stables, Darien began a thousand questions about his brother's adventures since leaving Othgard.

Ryan let out a laugh. "Did you quiz Thadius like this all the way from the southern Elderwood?"

"On the contrary, Darien was an excellent traveling companion," Thadius interceded. "He never led us into any mischief or unwanted adventures, unlike some persons who I'll not name."

Darien helped Ryan unsaddle his horse and hang the tack and other gear. He placed the saddle blanket over the rail and offered to brush the animal down. Ryan was impressed with all that Darien had learned and complimented his younger brother as they finished their tasks. Once completed, the three retired indoors.

"I can't believe how things have changed for us," Darien shook his head, "what with Da leaving us this fine house and gold as well."

Ryan caught Thadius' wink. It was as good a story as any to explain away their current circumstances. They laid their blankets before the fireplace and sipped on hot tea as they talked into the night.

The boys stayed up quite late and were in no hurry to rise in the morning. The chill of the room kept them bundled in warm woolen blankets until Thadius rose and coaxed the fire to life. Ryan and Darien rode together after breakfast.

"I'm sorry I missed your birthday," Ryan said to Darien.

"It was odd without you there. Elise baked a cake. Lowen enjoyed himself, no incidents with fire this year. And I'm glad we made it in time to celebrate yours."

Ryan's fifteenth birthday was a mere two days away. How ironic, he mused, it would also have marked the end of his days under the order's care. Reminiscing on their years spent at the temple orphanage, the brothers steered their mounts toward the stable.

Ryan was envious of Darien's close partnership with his tan-colored horse, which he had named Mythas. On the other hand, his steed definitely had a mind of its own. He often repeated commands or signals before the horse obeyed. Ryan commented on his predicament to Thadius upon their return.

"Do you spend a lot of time with him?" Thadius asked.

"I suppose I don't—"

"That's your problem," Thadius pointed out. "Darien would have brought Mythas into every inn along the way if he could have. The two have been inseparable since Othgard."

"I'll try to spend more evenings in the stables," Ryan replied wryly.

When the winter provisions arrived, the brothers worked to unload and store them away. Although Corbyn's farm also provided them with fresh milk, eggs and certain vegetables, Ryan voiced a need for a wider variety of fruits and other perishables not grown locally.

"I assume you're hinting at a visit to Drynas," Thadius gave him a sideways glance.

Darien's eyes brightened. "Could we?"

"I'll leave that up to Thadius," Ryan said with a bit of a somber tone. Though Thadius had accompanied Ryan into Drynas for building supplies during the summer, Ryan was always nervous about him entering the city.

Two years before Ryan had met him, Thadius served in the king's elite scouting force, the Huntsman Legion. However, he had disobeyed orders and come to the aid of women and children under goblin attack. He could have been executed for such an offense. Instead of death, King Trevin had forever banned Thadius from any of his settlements. No merchant could knowingly accept his coin, no temple his prayers. He could greet no one with an open hand, for a large "X" was branded into his right palm as a means of enforcing his banishment.

To hide the mark of his fate, the woodsman wore a thin, fingerless glove of worn leather. It was simply accepted as part of his attire, as many men who rode or carried a bow wore such gloves. The guards at the city gates had never given him a second glance.

"I think I can make time for one last trip before I depart." Thadius' slight nod assured Ryan that all would be okay, and the three were soon on the road to Drynas.

Their first destination was an inn with a stable. For a couple of bronze dyra, their mounts were boarded, cared for, and most importantly to Ryan, guarded. A lad about

Darien's age took the horses' reins as Thadius handed the coins to the stout fellow on duty. With a generous amount of pocket money from Ryan, Darien hurried them out and onto the street, impatient to explore the city. He formed a list during their journey of all the things he wished to do and see. He reminded Ryan that a visit to a weaponsmith was among them.

"You have no need to bear arms," Ryan told him.

"Isn't it my right according to the law?" Darien shot back.

"Not the law of common sense," Thadius interjected.

Darien would not give up. "I should at least have my own dagger."

"We'll talk about it later," Ryan promised.

As they walked along an avenue of merchants, conversations around them centered on the missing Stone of Orinn. Many were convinced that the goblins of Ilsgaard had long-planned the theft, and the Red Moon Clan was the primary suspect. Ryan could feel an underlying current of apprehension in the air.

"I'm amazed at how quickly word of the stone has spread."

"Good news travels fast and bad news faster," Thadius quoted an old adage.

On a row of smiths, they stopped before a shop and joined a growing crowd to watch a husky man hammer delicately on an ornate helmet. Ryan recalled how he had once longed for a fine suit of chain mail armor. A helmet might make a fine addition. A nudge from Thadius brought him out of his reverie.

"It will double the weight of your head and mess up your hair," Thadius teased.

"I wish I'd worn a chain hauberk when we battled against—" Ryan caught himself before he said too much, "—that legion of ogres."

"You're making it all up," Darien accused.

"He might be, somewhat," Thadius smiled.

The smith and his apprentices labored steadily and men lined up to view their wares or place orders. Judging by the exchanges about him, the reason for the increase in business was apparent. Those gathered spoke of war. Governor Varis had already ordered garrisons on alert and smiths all around the city had been put on notice. Their services may soon be needed by the king. Most believed that an army would be assembled to cross the Cimrinn River.

Talk of war excited Darien, yet it worried Ryan. Had he provided them a safe home only to be uprooted by a long, drawn-out conflict that might involve all of Ilsgaard? He did not think the other goblin clans would sit idle if a human army crossed into the western Darkwood.

They paused before the Temple of Orinn to admire the beauty of its mighty bell tower. Darien stared upward in awe. An immense sheaf of grain, symbol of the god, adorned the structure. Fashioned of hammered plates of gold, it sparkled in the sun as if waving in the wind. The temple doors stood wide open, and while many of the people discussed goblins and gemstones, not all of Drynas swirled with rumors of war. Earl Malikar was to arrive in the city by the end of the week. From what Ryan overheard, few knew much about the new earl.

"It has to be gossip," Thadius voiced. "No relative of the king, no matter how far removed, could be in such a hurry to take up residence so far from the comforts and intrigue of the royal court."

To Ryan, Malikar's seeming eagerness to assume control of Galanthor was but one more event that brought with it unknown change. Though they ate at the best vendors and visited numerous shops and sights, he could not shake his darkening mood.

The three shared a comfortable inn room on the east side of the city. Worn-out from the afternoon of sightseeing, Darien fell fast asleep soon after they ate dinner. Ryan slept fitfully and was in no better spirits the next day. Despite the fact that it was his birthday, he was anxious to be home. During their ride, Thadius announced his imminent departure for his own home in the southern Elderwood. Ryan understood that Thadius could not linger in Galanthor forever, yet the news was a further burden to his spirit. When at last they were inside and out of the cold, Thadius and Darien surprised him with gifts.

"You shouldn't have troubled yourselves," he scolded them half-heartedly.

"Open mine first," Darien pleaded. "I'm sure you'll like it."

"All right," Ryan gave in with a grin. "We'll see if it's worth my trouble," he joked. Ryan untied the cord and unwrapped the cloth to reveal a thick shirt in a russet hue, as well as a new belt pouch.

"Thanks, Darien. A warmer shirt is exactly what I need."

"You really like them?"

"I do. And I appreciate both."

"And here is mine," Thadius offered. "It may ease one of the things on your mind."

Ryan opened the package to uncover a stack of blank parchment. A well of ink and quills accompanied the high quality paper. "This must have been expensive, Thadius. You shouldn't have gone to this trouble."

"No trouble at all. Besides, writing Arlena will raise your spirits. I'll deliver your first letter myself," Thadius added with a wink.

"You don't really have to go, do you?" Darien pleaded.

"I've already delayed the inevitable for too long. My cabin will be overrun by squirrels and chipmunks by now," he mused.

"We understand," Ryan acknowledged, his tone melancholy.

"Let's forget about that tonight. It's your fifteenth birthday and we have a feast of your favorite foods planned."

When Ryan rose, Thadius waved him back. "Darien and I will cook. You sit and write that pretty girl you're always thinking about."

"I'm not *always* thinking about her," Ryan protested with a blush. He settled at the table and tried to organize his thoughts into a letter. He did miss her. And it was all true — she was quite often on his mind. Still, he could not articulate his feelings into words. Making no progress, he switched tasks and dumped out the contents of his old belt pouch. Out spilled the leather patch with the tusked boar's head branded on it. He showed it to Thadius.

"Where did you find this?"

"One of those goblins dropped it. As a matter of fact, it was the same one that made off with the Stone of Orinn. Do you recognize this symbol?"

"Yes, from other Huntsmen." Thadius held the patch closer. "It's the mark of an outcast band of deserters, renegades and other exiles from Ilsgaard. They menace the Lost Hills, a stretch of land north of the Darkwood."

"They're the ones who have the gemstone?" Ryan asked. "Then attacking the goblins of the Red Moon Clan won't recover the Stone of Orinn. They don't have it!"

# ❧ *Chapter 5* ☙

Ryan leapt to his feet. "We have to tell somebody. War with Ilsgaard can be avoided!"

"We'll depart for Drynas at first light," Thadius decided.

"I'll be going too . . . right?" Darien joined in.

"We'll be riding with all speed, Darien. Besides, it won't be any fun at all," Ryan tried to dissuade him.

"It's true," Thadius affirmed. "This information must get directly to Varis. Earldom or not, he's still in charge of Galanthor for now. But it might be days before we can see him."

Further convincing silenced Darien on the matter, though the lad brooded for the remainder of the night and his mood did not improve until the next day. Nevertheless, Darien helped Thadius ready their gear while Ryan enlisted Elias to watch over things during his absence. Corbyn was more than happy to see his son set to work and kept out of mischief.

With a final farewell to Darien, Ryan and Thadius brought their mounts to a gallop. Thadius wanted to reach Drynas before sundown. The morning air was cold and the brisk ride warmed both man and beast. When they finally slowed, Ryan pulled alongside Thadius.

"Did you mean what you said to Darien, about waiting days to see Lord Varis?"

"It's likely. We're not in the company of a nobleman this time. We'll be prohibited from entering Varis' hall with weapons of battle and we'll wait our turn to speak, like any other commoner. You may have to show a little patience."

"Patience?"

"Varis will be occupied. I presume he's already gathered the other lords of Galanthor for a council of war. They'll have come from their country estates, and of course, Aldwyn. Maybe a dozen noblemen altogether."

"That's not many."

"It's hard to get nobility to settle in a territory still half-wild. But with Galanthor a full-fledged earldom, and an heir to a prestigious house installed as earl, you can bet on a new tide of settlers."

"And this war council?"

"Varis and the other noblemen will take stock of their resources — men, mounts, weapons, equipment, food stocks — you get the idea. I think they'll wait and see what this Malikar will do. These noble lords do nothing in a hurry. They weigh each option like a miser weighs a flake of gold, royalty in particular."

The two arrived at the gates of Drynas before nightfall. Extra guards scrutinized the incoming traffic, checking everything from carts to pouches. Ryan supposed that between missing gemstones and bandits abroad, the extra vigilance made sense. Those departing the city received nothing more than a gesture to keep moving. The line crept forward, and when at last it was their turn, Ryan held his belt pouch open.

"State your names and the purpose of your visit," the gatekeeper instructed as a guardsman sifted through their belongings.

"Ryan and Torin. We're from Llerwyth, here for winter supplies," Thadius declared. He never divulged his real name to a stranger, especially to any soldier who may have heard of him.

"Supplies? What kind?"

"Foodstuffs for the larder. Not much of a harvest this year," Thadius answered with a half-truth.

"That's a common story," the gatekeeper nodded. "How long will you be in Drynas?"

Ryan was not accustomed to the additional questions. The guard's gaze lingered on the glove Thadius wore on his right hand. Ryan grew nervous, conscious of his friend's sentence.

"We'll find an inn and some dinner and visit the markets in the morning. I expect our business will be done by noon," Thadius shrugged.

"Enjoy your visit." Satisfied, the gatekeeper motioned them along.

"Is our mission so secret?" Ryan asked when they passed beyond the gates.

"Let's just say I want to ensure it gets into the right ears. I also want Varis to see this evidence with his own eyes. We can't leave this to chance."

"Our message is vital," Ryan insisted. "Surely he'll see that. We can save the kingdom from another war with the goblins!"

"We will. One way or another, we'll get the message through."

Ryan was not sure such measures were needed but was inclined to trust his friend.

They had not arrived in time to call upon the provincial governor without first telling their tale to everyone from the gatekeeper to the chief steward and entrusting that Varis received an accurate account.

However, it was Varis' custom to hold an open audience during the latter part of the week, and this would take place tomorrow. Resigned to wait until morning, they stabled their horses at the Oaken Shield Inn and Tavern and went inside for a meal.

Ryan and Thadius seated themselves at a small table and listened to the conversations around them. Some had come in for the food, others for the latest gossip on the affairs of the new earldom. A lass served them a hearty meal of roast lamb, potato, a wedge of cheese and a round loaf of bread. As patrons enjoyed their food, the innkeeper announced that a traveling bard would play songs to raise the spirits and ease digestion. He received some chuckles from this remark and stepped aside as the young man came forward.

Ryan found the bard's spiky hair an oddity. It was cropped short by northern standards and nearly as white as a summer cloud. The man stood just shy of six feet in height, a few inches taller than Ryan, and looked to be in his early twenties. The bard also sported a golden earring in his left earlobe.

"A Vyrenan lute," Thadius pointed out, "a rarity in these parts."

"How can you tell?"

"Northern lutes have more of a squat shape and a shorter neck."

The musician warmed up with an ascending scale of chords. As he strummed his lute, he joined his voice with the melody. The bard's accent was strange to Ryan, with its elongated r's, though not quite rolling, and peculiar inflection occasionally placed on a vowel. But its nuances lent itself to the music, and his songs were uplifting, with no mention of war or lost gemstones. This set the crowd in a good mood and there was a round of applause when at last he stopped for a break. Many tossed coins into the bucket set before him.

After he collected his earnings, a young woman with flowing black hair glided onto the floor. Clad in nothing more than a series of colored veils, she was accompanied by a piper and a drummer. As the music started, she began an exotic dance that held the complete attention of the audience. To Ryan's amazement, she shed a veil as she whirled about.

"Are you going to finish your lamb?" Thadius gave him a nudge.

"Huh? Oh, I'll get to it in a bit," Ryan responded without taking his eyes from the dancer. He did not notice Thadius skewer a slice of meat with a fork and take it from his plate as another veil floated to the floor.

"Do you think she'll remove all the veils?"

"You'll find out soon enough, I imagine," Thadius teased. While nudity would not be permitted in such a fine establishment, Thadius took advantage of the dancer's distraction to slice himself a piece of Ryan's smoked cheese.

The rhythm of pipe and drum reached a crescendo. The dance abruptly ended with a final beat. The dancer held her pose as the innkeeper reappeared and clapped his hands.

"A most delightful performance!" he exclaimed. The patrons applauded and some threw coins. Others pleaded for her to continue.

"She still had three veils to go!" Ryan joined in.

"Our good bard will return in a moment to raise your spirits," the innkeeper promised. "And speaking of spirits, a keg of our finest house ale has just been tapped."

As requests for service rang out, Ryan picked up his fork.

"This place must have rats. They got half my cheese." He gave Thadius a sideways glare.

"I see the dancer's spell has been broken. Maybe it should serve as a lesson."

"Keep an eye on your dinner companion?"

"Keep your mind on the task before you. Or, beware the tempting charms of strange women."

"More like beware of hungry friends. Can't we forget the lessons and enjoy ourselves?"

"You're right. We've plenty of time for business tomorrow."

Ryan cast his gaze toward the door to see a group of armed men file in. All six were armored in chain mail and each bore the familiar emblem of a griffin on their yellow surcoats. Ryan remembered running wildly through the woods, hunted by the king's soldiers. He turned his face away as they occupied the next table and called for ale.

"Thadius . . ."

"Relax. They're only here for a meal."

Ryan's apprehension faded. After all, the unfortunate incident with Adran and company was several months ago and far to the south. He meant nothing to the garrison in Drynas, and besides, he was a law-abiding landowner now.

The bard returned to the floor, and with a somber tone, began a familiar ode from a hero's saga. The soldiers frequently shouted out the best lines, sometimes before the bard could recite them. Ryan was irritated by their behavior. He had often recited this ode to the other children at the temple. No doubt, it irked the bard as well. With any luck, they will eat and be gone, Ryan hoped.

The Oaken Shield became more crowded as the hour grew later. Thadius left to circulate about the room, interested in learning what news he could. Ryan sat alone and listened as the bard finished his last set of songs. Across from him, the king's men wolfed down their food and drank liberally. The serving lasses avoided the table when they could, tired of the swats to their backsides. This did not improve the temperament of the men, who grew drunk on strong ale.

"Quit that squallin' and play the warrior's dirge!" one yelled.

"Before we make better use of that lute — as kindlin'!" another added. The musician was in the middle of a song and paid no heed to the rude outburst.

Irritated, one of the men threw an empty mug at the bard. With a well-timed step, the spiky-headed songster dodged the flying cup by mere inches. Without missing a beat, he changed the words of his tune. He played the same chords, but now his song spoke of drunken soldiers who could not hold their ale. Patrons laughed and he was another stanza into the impromptu version before the men realized he mocked them.

More insults were hurled, along with another mug half-filled with ale. While the innkeeper attempted to restore order, the bard slipped from the stage. Ryan decided it was better to retire for the night. He did not wish to be caught in the middle of the inevitable clash between the magistrate's men and the out-of-control warriors. He was sure the magistrate would not stand to see a bard treated in such a manner.

Ryan weaved through the throng of people in search of Thadius. He had nearly completed a circuit of the common room, when he caught sight of yellow surcoats. He was relieved to see that the three rowdiest of the soldiers had collected their cloaks and helms. However, the men were not heading in the direction of the main doors. Ryan traced their path and saw a flash of white hair as the bard exited via the side door. Ryan set out after the soldiers.

Outside, he spotted them stagger into the stables. Ryan crept past the open doors. The stalls within the long building ran in twin rows on either side of a central walkway. An oil lamp burned on opposite ends, bathing the rectangular structure in a dim, flickering light. The bard led his mount from a stall near the far end and a young stable hand hastened to help him saddle the horse as the three figures closed in.

"There he is," the tallest of the three pointed a wavering finger.

"Lesh hear that clever tune now," another slurred. He stumbled and almost fell, his helmet slipping from his grasp. His friends pulled him upright.

The third man jerked his thumb toward the doors. "Git yourshelf gone, boy."

As the stable hand made a hasty exit, the bard maneuvered his horse between them. "Now, gentlemen, surely other duties await you?"

The one who had lost his helmet balled his fist and cocked his arm back. "How 'bout we jush beat you to a pulp instead."

The taller of them threw an arm over his comrade's shoulder. "Thash a fine idea."

Ryan had the feeling that any encounter with the king's men would likely go against him. Yet he had to act. He picked up and donned the fallen helmet and grabbed a saddle blanket off a nearby rail. It was almost the same shade of black as their cloaks, and he draped it over his shoulders.

"That will be quite enough." Ryan deepened his voice and addressed them as sternly as he could muster. All three wheeled about, unsteady on their feet.

"Who the blazes are you?" The taller regarded him with a wobbly stance.

"Is this how you address a captain? Stand down and clear out of here."

The men hesitated. Each swayed as they regarded one another.

"That's an order. Or would you care to see our new earl's dungeons?"

The men filed past Ryan, reeking of alcohol and grumbling in protest. The last man in line paused.

"Yer lucky day, Sour-Note," he glowered at the bard. His squinty gaze turned to linger on Ryan's borrowed blanket, then wandered up to inspect his headgear.

"Thash *my* helmet!"

"This one?" Ryan snatched it off and swung the helmet around, crashing it into the side of his head with a dull clunk. The warrior collapsed in a heap. The others stopped in their tracks and turned at the sound. Vengeful glares settled upon Ryan. As the men lurched toward him, the stable darkened. The bard had extinguished the nearest lamp, leaving only a faint glow from the other end of the building. Ryan ducked into an empty stall. He threw the blanket over the back rail and balanced the helmet atop it, hoping to distract them. In the next moment, the men stumbled inside.

Ryan slipped into the adjacent stall and joined the bard in the central walkway, prepared to fight the soldiers when they re-emerged. But grunts, groans and the thuds of pounding fists erupted. Horses stamped and snorted at the disturbance. Then all was silent. The bard relit the lamp to reveal both men sprawled out on the ground.

"They knocked themselves out cold," Ryan shook his head in amazement.

"I see they got the fight they were looking for. I'm in your debt, friend." The bard smiled and shook Ryan's hand vigorously. "Even in their condition, I fear they would've managed to deliver at least half the beating they promised. I'm Crispen, from Vyrena." The bard's accent was heavier in his regular speech than in his singing voice, but Ryan followed his pronunciation with no trouble.

"I'm Ryan, recently moved to the area, and I need no thanks. I was glad to help. What brings you so far north, if you don't mind me asking?"

"Just visiting the northlands, to see what there is to see."

Together, they dragged the other unconscious warrior into the empty stall. Crispen fetched a long rope, and bound the men together. Ryan cocked an eyebrow when he covered them with hay and topped them with the saddle blanket, tucking them in as if in their beds.

"I'm not going to let their bad attitudes change my own. I believe the gods see our good deeds," the bard explained.

Ryan helped him ready the horse and Crispen secured his lute, making sure the instrument was safely tucked away. "Let's be gone from here," he urged, "before more trouble comes along."

As they led the bard's horse from the stables, two more of the king's men stepped out from the tavern.

"Look who it is," one nudged the other.

"You'd best be on your way, bard. If our companions see you, they'll make short work of you," the other advised.

"My thanks," Crispen gave them a bow. "I'll certainly avoid being roughed-up if I can prevent it." They watched as the soldiers staggered away.

"Thanks again, Ryan. Maybe someday I can repay you. I'm off to find another inn. I think it best if I'm gone from Drynas on the 'morrow."

"May the road be good to you," Ryan wished him.

"And to you as well."

Thadius emerged from the tavern as the bard disappeared down the lane. "I've heard of some possible trouble in the stables."

"If it involved some drunkards getting what they deserved, then I heard the same thing." Ryan faked a yawn and stretched. "Well, I'm turning in."

Thadius shook his head. "I'm afraid to ask."

# ☞Chapter 6☜

Ryan and Thadius ate a hurried breakfast and walked to Varis' fortress as dawn broke. They took their place among the first to gather before the tall gates. Ryan remembered the simpler keep from his childhood, before the outer walls encompassed a manor of dual wings and many more buildings.

"I wish we could just make our report and go," Ryan complained with a yawn.

"Last night, I found out that those warriors you tangled with are part of a new garrison assigned to Drynas," Thadius told him. "Another full garrison comes with Earl Malikar and is intended to reinforce Ardan."

"I guess the new king means to settle quickly with the goblins."

"Think on this: news of the gemstone is hardly days old. It takes weeks to raise, arm and equip a garrison. And that doesn't take into account the time to train them. Judging from the conduct we've seen, I'd say Daven's not particular as to the quality of man who bears his device."

"So, he already commissioned garrisons for Galanthor, even before hearing that goblins were involved with the gemstone."

"Something's not right. My gut tells me we need to ensure the right ears hear us."

The growing crowd parted as a pair of riders thundered down the lane and drew up to the gates. Ryan and Thadius were close enough to learn that Earl Malikar should arrive before noon. Only the most pressing business had the chance of being heard now, as the court of Governor Varis would be in a frenzy with last minute preparations.

The morning dragged on, and while Thadius was content to lean against the wall and listen to the conversations around them, a fidgety Ryan paced with impatience. News spread quickly that Drynas would soon see its new earl. Before long, people began lining the streets, hoping for a good view.

As it turned out, the earl reached Drynas earlier than expected. Before the noon hour, a grand procession wound its way onto Governors' Lane. From the eastern gate, all the way to Varis' manor, common folk lined the paved road. Some did so to honor Angard's nobility, though the majority did so out of curiosity. As was the way of the time, Malikar could make himself at home within Varis' gates until a proper manor was raised for him. Rumors already abound concerning the structure, ranging in size from a walled manor built within the city, to a full castle constructed in the surrounding hills.

Ryan stood in awe as the parade of men and mounts passed. In the lead was a mounted war band, forty men strong, the griffin of Angard emblazoned upon their yellow surcoats. These men were armed with both sword and lance.

Following the horsemen was the earl's fine coach. It was a huge, lumbering thing, black in color and pulled by six white horses. The mighty vehicle was as large as a caravan wagon, its intricate trimwork painted with gold. A squad of soldiers rode in both front and rear seats. The crest of the House of Rhuddlun adorned each wide door. The windows of the great coach were of thick, smoked glass. Ryan imagined an ample interior within, furnished in luxury reserved for the richest of guildmasters, or perhaps even a king. Next came the earl's entourage. This consisted of a train of lesser coaches, wagons and carts, carrying household goods, personal attendants and servants.

Behind all of this marched a force of about one hundred men. If Thadius was correct, they were bound for the fortress Ardan on the Cimrinn River. These men wore armor of ringed mail instead of chain. Each wore a sword and dagger, and hefted a wooden shield. The last five ranks of men bore no shields. These warriors carried longbows and wore short swords. Strapped to their backs were leather quivers filled with yellow-fletched arrows. Supply wagons brought up the rear, a dozen in all. The garrison veered off to establish a temporary camp in a field to the east of the manor. With Malikar's arrival, Ryan feared their chance to be heard might disappear.

"Maybe we should relate our information to the sergeant of the guard," Ryan suggested. "We can always check later, to make sure it was passed on."

Thadius let out a sigh. "I prefer our local officials hear it from us first hand."

Shortly after the earl's company was within the gates, the sergeant stepped out and addressed those assembled.

"Listen up, you lot!" he shouted. "I'm only going to say this once." The man paused for the throng to quiet. "Those who wished to come before Lord Varis will be seen within the hour by Magistrate Allen instead." With that, the sergeant returned to the gatehouse.

Ryan remembered his last experience with the magistrate's office. If Trenn had not used his family's noble name to intercede, Ryan might not have been able to claim his father's land. He wished they could simply give their statement to the sergeant. But he suspected Thadius was correct. The story might change by the time it got to Varis' ears, or may not reach him at all.

Ryan paced for the better part of another hour, before they were admitted inside the gates. They followed the crowd through an open courtyard lined with sculpted hedges and now barren fruit trees. Buildings of varying sizes and purpose surrounded the landscaped grounds, stretching from the outer walls to the grass lawn that bordered Varis' manor. Ahead, the two-story manor incorporated much of the original keep. Situated in the eastern wing was the Magistrate's Hall. Ryan and Thadius were ushered inside the main doors and took their seats on one of the hard, wooden benches.

The court of Magistrate Allan grew crowded, as this was also the day of the week he judged criminal cases. Noble lords who ruled big towns or cities appointed a magistrate to mediate the numerous grievances of the common folk. Though a man of lesser nobility was usually placed in such a position, common men of good standing or renowned reputation sometimes attained this station.

A magistrate was responsible for more than their judgment based on the king's law. The majority maintained their own force of constables who patrolled the streets and answered to the immediate needs of the citizens. In rural areas, a magistrate's scope of responsibility could include a number of towns or villages.

The law in these times was swift, and a case heard by the magistrate was judged without delay. Only extreme circumstances or a lengthy wait on testimony could postpone the inevitable decision. When Magistrate Allan finished these criminal cases, he would attend to the common folk in Varis' stead.

At last, a page entered through a side door and announced the magistrate. A hush fell over the room, and all rose as a man in his middle forties strode in. Clothed in a robe of black and bearing the scepter of his office, Allan stepped onto a raised floor and seated himself in an ornately carved high-backed chair. A pair of guardsmen stood close at hand, while others flanked the door at the side of the hall.

"The Court of Magistrate Allan is now in session," the page declared. "The assembly may be seated." The guards stationed at the main doors closed them. However, before the magistrate could summon forward the first of the accused, a commotion turned heads. Earl Malikar, with Lord Varis at his side, appeared with a small entourage on the upper landing that overlooked the hall.

This was the first view Ryan had of the Earl of Galanthor, and he was amazed to find him so young. Malikar could not be much older than he was, Ryan judged. His black hair was cut neatly above his shoulders, and the effort to grow a mustache showed on his angular face only because the fine hairs were dark against his pale skin. In his embroidered vest and fancy shirt, Ryan thought Malikar quite out of place among the rougher northern lords. Especially Varis, who contrasted the younger earl's slim build with his bearded and bear-like frame. The two powerful figures took their seats to view the proceedings.

Thadius grunted. "I suppose Malikar wants to see how justice is served in Galanthor."

Once all were settled, Magistrate Allan called for the first case. Most of the men brought before the court had been arrested for minor offenses. These ranged from drunken brawling to petty thievery. Their crimes could bring them from a few days in the stocks to several months in Varis' dungeon. Ryan recognized the last men brought before the court. They were the very bandits he had helped capture. A lengthy list of the charges was read aloud. The men's heads hung low, and all wore shackles.

In the end, the brigand leader would face the axe man. Each of his men received a sentence of twenty years, to be spent at hard labor. For many, it meant long days working to repair and maintain the walls that surrounded the city of Drynas. With the new earl in need of his own grand manor, there would be more than enough labor for all the prisoners in the earldom. Malikar rose at the conclusion of the criminal proceedings.

"My good people, Galanthor will not become a land of bandits and goblins. I vow to you that my men and I will scour it clean. I'll not rest until every such enemy of the king has been put in chains!" The people broke into cheers. Malikar sat and held his smile until the applause died away.

"The land is in no need of scouring," Thadius whispered. "He's making a big fuss over one band of thieves and a couple of rogue goblins."

"What if there are more goblins in Galanthor?" Ryan asked. While the clans of Ilsgaard may not have been involved with the bandits, the goblin outcasts surely were. Given his family history, Ryan had mixed feelings over Malikar's proclamation.

The time allotted to hear the people in Varis' place had come and the magistrate called for any citizen with a plea to make to come forth. Some came forward in groups, with urgent needs to do with sewage or trash. Others had brought their disputes before the nobleman because all other efforts had failed them.

Ryan was convinced that no other matter brought before this court was as important as the information they carried. Thadius was correct about war with the goblin clans. Hundreds would die in even a short war, and it would still not return the Stone of Orinn to the land. But as he was not a citizen of Drynas, Thadius was the last to be summoned before the magistrate.

Thadius came to stand before the noble lord. From his high-backed chair, Magistrate Allen nodded for him to begin. Thadius spoke well, to Ryan's surprise, considering the company they found themselves in, for Varis and Malikar remained to see the audience until the end. Thadius began by relating the tale of how simple country farmers banded together to come to the aid of their fellow man and ended the bandits' raids.

"Of course," Allan interjected when Thadius paused, "the brave men of Llerwyth will be recognized as heroes. Those who escaped will be brought to justice."

"There is more to the tale, Magistrate," Thadius resumed. "It involves the goblins discovered in the brigands' company." He drew forth the leather patch with the goblin symbol branded on it and handed it to a page, who passed it to the magistrate.

"I fail to see the meaning of this item," Allan confessed.

"The patch was dropped by the same goblin that seized the Stone of Orinn. The emblem is the mark of a goblin band, made up of those cast out of their clans."

"Goblins are goblins, wherever they are spawned from. Our army will march into the western Darkwood," Malikar proclaimed. "The Stone of Orinn will be recaptured if every goblin must be slain."

"The band I speak of is made up of exiles and renegades. It is they who have the Stone of Orinn in their possession, not the goblins of Ilsgaard," Thadius explained. "Angard need not go to war with all of Ilsgaard."

Malikar shot to his feet as the room erupted. It was a moment before Magistrate Allan could restore order. When the assembly quieted again, Allan addressed Thadius.

"This is a significant revelation, if true. You're evidently familiar with these so-called outcasts. Tell us how you've come to know about them." His tone was almost accusatory and Ryan could hear some openly speculate about Thadius' possible involvement with goblins.

"I have on occasion come across these beings and take note of any emblems or devices worn. I've never been in the company of a goblin who bore this sign but have spoken with other woodsmen who have crossed their path."

"Maybe he's done more than he lets on," someone alleged. Again, murmurs of secret meetings with goblins circulated. Ryan could not allow such rumors to gain a foothold.

"This is not true!" He jumped to his feet. "Thadius is an honorable man and does not deal with goblins."

"And your name, lad?" Allan asked him.

"I am Ryan, son of Branic, my lord."

At the mention of Branic's name, the magistrate's eyebrows raised in recognition. However, his stern expression returned as he studied Ryan.

"Ryan rode with the men of Llerwyth. He crossed swords with the very goblins that made off with the Stone of Orinn," Thadius reported.

"You speak as if you were not among the men of Llerwyth," Allan directed the statement at Thadius. "How is it you came by this goblin article?" The magistrate glanced over the patch of leather.

"It was Ryan who found it and showed it to me," Thadius answered.

"These thieves were captured a week ago," Varis interjected. "Why wasn't this brought to our attention before now?"

"This piece of evidence was only recently shown to me. When I saw it for what it was, we made for Drynas straightaway."

"Who are you to know so much about creatures few have ever seen?" Malikar sneered down at Thadius.

"With all due respect, my noble Lords, these are matters of little consequence compared to the facts. The goblins of Ilsgaard do not possess the Stone of Orinn. War can be averted."

Ryan scrutinized the earl's face. Instead of realization, he read frustration.

"Are we to surmise that the theft of the greatest religious artifact in Galanthor amounts to one lucky goblin being in the right place at the right moment?" The magistrate shook his head. "I find it a remarkable coincidence."

"Please, sir, it's the truth. War with Ilsgaard is not necessary. The gemstone can be recovered if this rogue band could be tracked to their camp," Ryan pleaded.

"Tell us, where is this camp?" Allan requested.

"Well, I couldn't tell you exactly . . ." Ryan looked to Thadius. It seemed they had not yet convinced the magistrate to accept the facts of the matter.

"You, Thadius, come clean and tell us of your connection with these goblins," demanded Allan.

Ryan could feel the man slipping back into his role as a judge, refusing to accept their story at face value. Was he that stubborn, or did he suspect them of some kind of trickery?

"My connection is one of a woodsman, who on occasion encounters these beings on the frontiers of the kingdom," Thadius replied.

"For eight years, I have sat as Magistrate of Drynas," Allan responded. "For all these years I have trusted my instincts for rooting out the truth. There's more to you than this simple tale." His hazel eyes locked onto Thadius. "On what basis are you expert enough to tell us Ilsgaard has no involvement in this affair? The truth may prevent a long and bloody war."

Commoner and magistrate held each other's gaze. The chamber was silent as all awaited the outcome that could change the course of future events.

"I know of what I speak, for I once patrolled the borders as a member of the Huntsman Legion."

Exclamations of astonishment preceded a boisterous clamor. Allan banged the scepter of his office on the wooden floor in a call for silence. An aide leaned forward to whisper in Malikar's ear.

"The testimony of a Huntsman carries much weight," Magistrate Allan acknowledged.

Ryan did not like the term "testimony". It sounded as if they were on trial. This was not how their news was supposed to be received.

"As a Huntsman, you are one who has learned more than most about these creatures. I'm inclined to agree with your opinion as to who may actually possess the Stone of Orinn," the magistrate concluded. Ryan breathed a sigh of relief.

"Magistrate Allan," Malikar interrupted, "if I may confirm one last thing?"

Thadius faced the young earl, his jaw set and his eyes narrowed.

"I've been told that there is only one man alive who *once* served in the Huntsman Legion but now does not. That man is Thadius of Corin." Malikar's eyes smoldered. He motioned the guardsmen on the floor forward. "Remove his glove."

Ryan froze. His mind screamed for them to escape, yet he could not move. Thadius stood his ground as one guard grabbed his left arm and shoulder. The other secured his right arm and peeled off the fingerless glove.

Thadius did not resist as his hand was held up for all to see. Burned into his right palm was the clear mark of an "X".

The hall was sent into an uproar and could not be silenced so easily this time. Earl Malikar shouted to the guards below.

"Seize the criminal! Seize him and put him in chains!"

"Go, Ryan," Thadius urged. Ryan was shocked, frozen in place as Thadius was roughly manacled, hand and foot. His dagger was taken and his clothes searched. Malikar and Varis emerged at floor level. Some semblance of order had been restored by then, and four guardsmen surrounded Thadius. A fifth rushed over from the main doors and laid a hand on Ryan's shoulder, ready to detain him if ordered.

"Your sentence banishes you from the king's settlements and you dare enter this court?" Malikar accused with a pointed finger.

"If it will save Angard from war, it is my duty," Thadius countered.

"I leave him to your judgment, for the law has been willfully broken and the guilty stands before you." Malikar cast a haughty glare at Allan.

Although the magistrate appeared to wrestle with his conscience, he did not ponder the judgment long. Thrice he rapped his scepter and announced his decision.

"The law has been broken and with willful intent," Allan said heavily. "Despite the valuable information laid before this court, the fact remains that Thadius is guilty of violating a royal decree. There is but one judgment to be made for those who disregard the king's will." The magistrate raised his voice for all to hear.

"Thadius of Corin will join those to lose their heads by the axe in three days."

# Chapter 7

Thadius offered no resistance as he was jostled toward the door at the side of the hall. Many voiced their protest at the magistrate's decision.

"Thadius, you can't let them do this!" Ryan cried out.

Thadius halted, unmoved by the guards' prodding. "Leave while you can, Ryan. You cannot help me."

One of the men slugged him in the stomach. Another landed a blow to his side. Thadius gritted his teeth and straightened to his full height. Chains scraped against the wooden floor as he walked away in half-strides.

"Lord Varis, you can't allow this," Ryan pleaded. "The evidence he has given can stop this war."

"Seize the boy as well," Malikar commanded. "He's obviously in league with the outlaw."

Ryan's eyes burned with hatred for the earl. Regardless of the warrior's grip on him, he would have recklessly drawn his sword had he worn it.

Varis turned to Malikar. "Your Lordship, if I may be granted a request."

"A request, Lord Varis?" Malikar's brow wrinkled.

"This boy is the charge of a noble family. I believe he's fallen into bad company and wasn't aware of the former Huntsman's standing."

"Your request, Varis?" Malikar snapped.

"Free the boy. I'll see to it he's returned home, where he belongs."

Although Varis was a brawny man and towered above Malikar, the young earl spoke to him as if he had already ruled Galanthor for years. "Very well. The boy is free to go, but I don't want to see him in the city again."

Lord Varis took Ryan by the shoulders and guided him out of the main doors. He did not speak until they were outside.

"I remember you, lad. I know who your father was and that you're a friend of Squire Trennan's. This may be all I can do for you."

"Thadius risked everything to bring you the evidence to prevent this war," Ryan appealed. "Shouldn't it count for something, king's decree or not?"

"I'll see what can be done on behalf of your friend, but the fact is, he willingly disobeyed the king. It will be almost impossible to keep his neck from the block."

"Thadius was right about our new earl. And I see how justice will work now," Ryan seethed.

"Go in peace, Ryan. Don't come back to Drynas until you've received permission to do so. I cannot protect you from arrest again, if it's the earl's will."

Ryan bit his tongue and left without another word.

Varis watched as Ryan stormed off. "Stay away, lad. I've the feeling Drynas is about to see dark times."


Ryan marched straight for the inn where their horses were stabled. He saddled their mounts, secured their gear and left the city. Leading Thadius' horse, he rode with all speed. He switched horses often and pushed himself long past dark, sometimes dozing in the saddle and trusting that his horse knew the way. His faith in the animal was rewarded, for at last he arrived bleary-eyed at home.

"Thank you, boy. Without a doubt, I'll have to name you soon," he patted the steed's neck.

Ryan was near exhaustion as he stabled the horses. Darien and Elias came out to lend a hand. Ryan was pleased Elias could stay over while he was gone, for though the brigands were captured, he realized even life in a remote hamlet could prove dangerous.

"Where's Thadius?" Darien asked.

"He's still in Drynas," Ryan answered.

"Drynas? What's going on, Ryan?"

Ryan let out a breath. "Thadius is in trouble."

"What happened?" Elias added his own question.

"There was a . . . misunderstanding with the earl's men. It's all I can say." Neither boy was aware of the sentence that Thadius lived under and Ryan did not wish to explain everything to them. "I can tell you this; we delivered the news that the goblins of Ilsgaard do not have the Stone of Orinn. Perhaps now, there will be no war." They pressed him further, but Ryan remained tight-lipped about what had occurred in Drynas.

"I'm worn-out," he staved off further questions as they walked to the house. "Let me get some sleep and we'll talk in the morning."

With winter settled in, the boys camped out before the fireplace. Ryan's thoughts swirled, and he battled to control his emotions as he readied his bedding before the fire. He could not believe the day's events, yet they replayed in his mind over and over. Ryan had another battle to fight. He must hold off sleep until his brother and Elias dozed off. There was only one person who might be able to help Thadius now, and he needed absolute privacy to contact him.

At last, conversation died away as Darien and Elias drifted off to sleep. Ryan moved silently as he slipped from his blankets and crept into his bedchamber. He fumbled about in the dark until he laid his hands on his leather pack and fished about inside for the small red pouch the wizard Trenn had given him that summer. He donned a warm shirt, and collected a few other items, before stealing out the back door.

The night was clear and chilled him to the bone, but he was glad there was no snow on the ground. Ryan stopped by the woodpile and gathered an armful of firewood and kindling. He walked down the leeward side of the hill and faced to the south. Fully awakened by the biting cold, he prepared a fire.

Before long, Ryan warmed himself within the orange glow and prayed this would work. He rehearsed the incantations in his mind, and when he felt ready, drew close to the flames and chanted the strange words. After reciting them a third time, he tossed the pouch into the fire. Though he knew a flash would follow, he was startled all the same. As the flames deepened from shades of amber to a ruby hue, he concentrated on a mental picture of the faraway wizard.

Ryan recalled Thadius explaining how sometimes other practitioners of magic could overhear these conversations. Therefore, he addressed Trenn as Thadius had done earlier in the summer.

A wispy smoke swirled about as Ryan invoked, "Old friend, heed my call."

All was still, there were no other sounds save for the crackle of the fire.

"Old friend, you must hear my call!"

Moments crept by and Ryan worried he had not recited the incantations correctly. Then gradually, an image of the blond-haired mage formed within the flames. Amazed, Ryan was struck speechless. The visage of Trenn yawned.

"Are you aware of the hour?"

Ryan found his voice. "I need your help."

"I can see something is amiss. Take a breath and tell me what has happened."

Ryan wasn't sure how much he should say through this means of communication. He decided to keep things as simple as he could.

"It's our mutual friend, he's been discovered."

"Where is he now?"

"At the end of our summer's journey," Ryan reported. There was a pause, and for a second, Ryan feared he had lost him. "Can you come? He'll lose his head within three days!"

"I am unfortunately obligated to matters that require my complete attention, it pains me to say."

Ryan's heart sank.

"Do not despair," Trenn seemed to read his mind. "There is someone whom I trust and I will direct him to you."

"Who?"

"Visit the Temple of Orinn in Drynas before the evening service tomorrow. He will find you."

"I'll leave at first light," Ryan promised.

"Get some sleep," the wizard advised. "And do not worry yourself. Our friend will be returned to us."

Trenn's image dissolved. The fire burned low and the translucent blanket of smoke wafted away on the wintry breeze. Ryan scooped up his tinderbox and flint striker. He kicked dirt onto the embers and headed to the house. He hardly made a noise creeping back inside. Darien snorted in his sleep as Ryan slid beneath the warm blankets. Elias was undisturbed in his slumber.

Ryan was unsure of his faith. The few instances he had prayed were under dire circumstances. And it was not always to the familiar gods of his childhood. Yet, as he reflected on those times, had not each prayer been answered? Did a greater something exist out there? As he settled in, he made his plea to Orinn, god of the harvest and patron of the land. After all, it was one of his artifacts that had caused all of this mess. Somewhere in the midst of his prayers, sleep overtook him.


Ryan half-woke, his mind in a fog. He was vaguely aware of someone speaking, perhaps to him, but he was in no hurry to rise. He was safe at home. Later, he would tell Thadius about his terrible nightmare. However, as he rose through the layers of consciousness, the bad dream stayed with him. At last he was wide awake, with the realization this was no dream. His friend faced the axe and he must take to the road.

"We have potatoes and onions cooking," Darien greeted. "We can leave—"

"Darien, listen. I've no time to eat. I have to get back to Drynas," Ryan said as he slipped on his shirt.

"I can go with—"

"No, you're staying here."

"You might need us," Elias cut in from the kitchen.

"I appreciate the offer, both of you. But I must do this myself. Alone," he added. "Elias, do you mind looking after Darien for a bit longer? Consider it a paying job, and you'll be well-rewarded."

"I will. Can you tell us how much trouble Thadius is in?"

"It could be very serious, and I don't want either of you involved. In fact, if any of the earl's men ask, don't tell them I've returned to Drynas. It would mean trouble for me too."

"That doesn't sound good, Ryan. At least eat some breakfast first, then we'll help send you off," Darien stated. "I'll saddle your horse. Should I see to Thadius' horse too?"

"Yes," Ryan answered. "Elias, can you put together some provisions? I'll pack some winter gear and supplies."

Within an hour of waking, Ryan was on the road and riding toward Drynas. He bore his sword, as well as the dagger Arlena had given him. His bow, along with Thadius' weapons, were concealed, wrapped in a blanket. He chose to enter the city through the less traveled western gate and arrived well before dusk. He recognized none of the sentries on duty, and they gave no sign they knew him. Nevertheless, he was stopped and asked to state his business in the city. Ryan was prepared for the possibility that his name may have been left at the gate.

"I am Ursig, servant of the Order of Shariss. I bear missives for our brothers in Drynas," he tried to sound convincing.

One of the guards eyed his sword. "Since when does the Order of Shariss bear arms?"

Ryan had to think fast. Maybe he should have risked the eastern gate after all.

"I meant that I serve the order as a courier and sometimes I'm entrusted with a hefty amount of coins. Besides, with rumors of goblins about, one can't be too careful."

"Goblins . . . They wouldn't dare show their green faces around here," the guard boasted. "Earl Malikar's declared a bounty on any found within Galanthor." He stepped aside and waved Ryan on.

"Shariss' blessings upon you," Ryan smiled as he passed.

He made for an inn close to Varis' keep and paid careful attention to the route between the two. Once the horses were stabled and their belongings locked in a storage bin, he gave a generous tip to the man on watch. Satisfied the mounts and gear were guarded, Ryan raised the hood of his cloak and set out for the Temple of Orinn.

Twilight settled over the city as people gathered for evening services. Ryan blended into the crowd and entered the temple. Great lamps, suspended by sturdy iron rings, provided abundant lighting from high above. He marveled at the number of people in attendance, for services never attracted many worshippers at the temple in Othgard. Of course, this was a proper city, not some small and obscure township. He worked his way through the throng and wondered if he should have waited outside.

After completing a circuit of the vast vestibule, Ryan decided to do exactly that. There was no point in trying to find a man he did not know. Curse it all! Why hadn't Trenn told him how to locate this friend of his? As he neared the doors, he halted dead in his tracks. Magistrate Allan strode into the building.

Ryan turned aside and brought his hand up to scratch his head, briefly obscuring his face from the magistrate. Allan passed him with no notice and was soon lost in the crowd. With a sigh of relief, Ryan waited until the temple bells rang out. The service would begin shortly, and as worshippers flowed into the nave, Ryan remained behind. It was not long before he stood alone.

All was quiet, save for the murmur of the masses within. Then the temple's immense bell rang out once more and silenced those assembled. Surely he was not to meet this man in the service itself? Should he enter the nave now, all eyes would turn on him and Magistrate Allan could not miss him.

The shuffle of sandals against the stone floor echoed throughout the vestibule. An elderly monk emerged from a side hall and walked straight for him.

"I say there, young man," he greeted, "you should be inside, not dawdling about out here." The monk wore the robe of an initiate, yet he was the oldest initiate Ryan had ever seen. Perhaps he had joined the temple late in life.

"I'm waiting for a friend," Ryan replied.

"Well, he's late! We can't have you miss the service. The Magistrate of Drynas himself is here. He always comes the night before an execution," the man added with a wink. He placed a hand on Ryan's shoulder and turned him toward the tall doors of the nave.

"I really should wait—"

"Nonsense, let's get you inside. I'll send your friend along, just give me his name."

"His name?"

"His name, lad. Your *old* friend's name."

"You may have heard of him," Ryan said in a lowered voice. "His name is Trenn."

"Trenn?" the monk repeated much too loud for Ryan. He glanced about, afraid they might be overheard.

"Let me see if that rings a bell." He scratched the short gray beard on his chin, then startled Ryan by snapping his fingers. "I know a Trenn. Says he's friends with a young man who might be in a bit of trouble."

"I knew it!" Ryan exclaimed. "You *are* the one he sent to help me."

"Since we're the only ones out here and not in there, that's a good guess," the elder man chuckled.

"You're not really a monk?" Of course, if he was a friend of Trenn's, the man must be a fellow wizard in disguise.

"I aid the temple on special occasions as a volunteer, not a full initiate. Now, let's be on our way. We've a lot to talk about and precious little time."

Ryan followed as the man strode out into the chill of the night.

# Chapter 8

"Sorry to rush you off, lad. It's better we're away as quickly as possible."

"No apologies needed," Ryan returned. "With Magistrate Allan in the temple, the faster we're away, the better."

"I'm Ephram." He offered his hand and owned a surprisingly strong grip. "Trennan has explained the gist of the matter. You'll have to fill me in on the details, but not here in the street."

"I'm Ryan," he introduced himself. "I assume you're a wizard as well?"

"Of course."

"I thought so. I've seen Trenn use this trick."

"Trick?"

"Yes, the spell that changes your appearance. I've got to say, the wrinkles on your face are even more convincing than Trenn's."

"Really?" Ephram's brow furrowed. "This *is* my face."

The gray-haired mage was spry and set off at a fast pace. They made a number of turns onto side streets before Ephram lead them to the end of a row of single-story, whitewashed houses. Ryan had kept silent during the remainder of their brief journey. Unable to hold them in, his questions resumed as they walked through the door.

"When did Trenn contact you? How much was he able to tell you?"

"We'll get to all that in a bit." The wizard bent to rekindle the fire.

"But Thadius will go before the axe tomorrow!"

"I already have some ideas and a spell book full of tricks." Ephram straightened. "We'll get the job done."

"Can you take us into the dungeons by magic?" Ryan asked. "Trenn speaks of traveling the netherways . . ."

"Whisk us in by spell? You do understand something of our art. Have you ever considered an apprenticeship?"

"Not seriously," Ryan admitted. "I'm more curious than anything."

"Curiosity generally leads to trouble. As far as the netherways, I cannot. A special sigil is required, created at the destination. I've never seen the insides of the place, and never expected to either."

Ryan knew something of what Ephram meant. He recalled the magical sigil Trenn had created in the cavern beneath the citadel of Arakronis.

Ephram poured some fresh water into a kettle. "Let's get some tea and biscuits on and we'll make plans."

The two were soon immersed in planning the rescue of Thadius. Before they finished a kettle of honey-sweetened tea, a scheme was conceived. Ephram blackened Ryan's brown hair and tucked it up into a tight-fitting cap. Ryan donned a loose leather cuirass, borrowed from the wizard's stores to complete his cover as a man-at-arms. Ephram scowled as he evaluated his work.

"Somehow, it seems incomplete."

"Perhaps a spell to change my face?"

"It would fade too rapidly." Ephram's green eyes suddenly brightened. "I've got it!" He dabbed his finger into a small jar and dotted Ryan's cheek. As Ephram rolled a bit of doughy biscuit between his fingers, Ryan raised a hand to his face.

"Don't touch it," Ephram stressed. "It feels sticky. However, it wipes away easier than you think."

Ephram formed a round, flat shape and pressed the bit of material into the sticky substance. The wizard stepped back and nodded in satisfaction. Ryan picked up a mirror and brought it to his face. A hideous, wart-like growth appeared to spring from his cheek.

"Ephram, I look horrible. This is not a good disguise."

"On the contrary, what will the guards remember? Merely some young warrior with a . . ."

"With a horrible affliction."

"Exactly. Nothing at all like Ryan of Llerwyth. Now, let's get ready."

As they left Ephram's home, a temple bell rang out somewhere in the night. Ryan was not sure from which temple it came. If he knew, he might have been tempted to take it as an omen, for good or ill. Shortly after, Ephram rapped on the window slit of the gatehouse. The wooden panel slid open and the narrowed eyes of a sentry peered out to see an aged man and his man-at-arms.

"State your business," a voice demanded.

"I have authorization to visit the prisons. Fetch your sergeant," Ephram insisted with authority.

When the sergeant of the watch arrived, his eyes glared at the unexpected visitors. "What's this about authorization?"

Ephram drew closer. Ryan could not make out his words but was familiar with their strange rhythm. He kept an eye on the lane, worried they might be discovered before getting into Varis' fortress.

"We're here to see one of the condemned prisoners. We have the permission of the magistrate," Ephram intoned. A single finger swayed before the sergeant like a candle in a breeze.

"Permission of the magistrate . . . I'll have you escorted in."

The panel slid shut and Ryan broke into a grin. "It worked."

"Of course it did," Ephram whispered.

With a metallic squeak, the stout door was unbolted and swung inward. The sergeant beckoned them inside. Ryan and Ephram were escorted through the gatehouse and into the dimly lit courtyard. Ryan looked about nervously. There were a few servants about, and he was fearful that he might be recognized in spite of the change to his appearance. They passed the rows of sculpted hedges, following the sergeant along a paved walkway, and into a door at the side of the Magistrate's Hall.

Two constables sat behind a squat desk in a well-lit chamber. Both stood as the sergeant announced the purpose of Ephram's visit, then departed. Ryan held his breath. So far, so good.

The taller of the men opened a bulky, leather-bound book and dipped a quill into a well of ink. "Prisoner's name?"

"Thadius of Corin," Ephram responded.

"And your names?" The man filled out an entry in the logbook.

"Vallus and Solith, both of Canton."

"You're far from home," the other constable commented, staring at Ryan's mole.

"Yes, I'm afraid business takes us away from our fair city for most of the year," Ephram sought to redirect his attention.

The taller man rose and withdrew a thick key from the desk. "You'll have to leave your weapons here," he glanced at Ryan as he unlocked the opposite door.

Ryan undid his sword belt and laid it on the desk. Unarmed, they were led into a corridor and down a flight of steps. Beyond a stout door reinforced with iron bands, they were confronted by another guard post. A trio of imposing men sat about a table littered with coins, dice and clay mugs. Judging by their uniforms, these men served the new earl. All stopped their game of dice to glower at the intruders who interrupted their gambling.

"What's this all about?" their leader questioned.

"These gentleman are here to speak with the prisoner, Thadius of Corin, by order of Magistrate Allan," their escort motioned to Ephram.

"Thadius the condemned? At this hour?" a warrior with tattoos on the sides of his bald head spat.

"I'll hardly have the chance tomorrow, will I?" Ephram shot back.

With a scowl at the men, the constable left Ryan and Ephram to return to his post upstairs.

"All right," the leader relinquished. "You've got ten minutes and not a second more." The men resumed their dice game.

"Come, lad. We've not much time."

Ryan and Ephram hurried down the row of darkened cells. Each peered through the small window of bars until they found Thadius.

"I thought I heard your voice, old one."

Thadius sat cross-legged on an earthen floor covered with dirty straw. His hair hung before his face and when he raised his head, Ryan gasped. His bottom lip was split and an eye was blackened. Otherwise, he appeared to be in one piece. From the guards' table came crude laughter.

"You must remember him lookin' prettier," the bald man mocked. More laughter followed.

"I wanted to make sure you were here," Ephram told Thadius. "I'll be back momentarily." The wizard turned on the earl's men, a spell on his lips.

"What do ya got to say about it, old man?" the leader challenged.

"He's babbling about something," the third guard remarked.

"Your time is up," the leader ceased his laughter and his eyes rolled. "Get outta . . . my prison . . ."

All three slumped over onto the table.

"The key, lad," Ephram prodded Ryan.

Ryan rushed to the table and recovered a ring of keys from one of the sleeping men. He tried half a dozen in the lock before finding the one that let them into the cell. Unlike some of the other prisoners, Thadius was chained to the floor. Ryan searched several more seconds for the key that unlocked the manacles about his feet. Thadius rose stiffly and limped out of the cell.

"I'll be fine." Thadius straightened to his full height and waved Ryan off as Ephram ushered them to the table of sleeping men.

The wizard positioned Thadius next to one of the spellbound guards and produced a small round mirror from a pocket in his cloak. "If you would, lift his head so I can see his face."

Thadius returned a dubious expression.

"Don't worry, it won't hurt a bit," Ephram promised.

"Comforting. What am I in store for?"

"I'm going to make you the spitting image of this gentleman."

Thadius grunted. "Not him. He's the ugliest of the lot."

"Fine, your choice."

Thadius rounded the table and jerked the leader's head up by the hair. Ephram held the mirror before them, catching the reflection of both. "We're halfway out," he winked at Ryan.

Thadius stared at Ryan's homemade wart as Ephram worked his spell. "You might want to get that thing looked at."

"Ya, because *I* look bad."

Ryan watched in fascination as Thadius' features slowly altered, until he was the twin of the man beside him. As the incantations came to an end, the surface of the mirror swirled and clouded until it was opaque.

"This will have to do," Ephram eyed the results with a shrug of his shoulders. "It won't last long, let's be on our way."

On the way out, Thadius collected his belongings, as well as every last coin from the table.

"This is the cost of mistreating your prisoner," he rebuked the sleeping men.

Ephram halted them before they re-entered the guard post upstairs. "Tell them you'll see us to the gates, you're on your way out anyway. Say as little else as possible," the wizard advised. Thadius nodded and opened the door.

Ryan picked up his sword belt and buckled it on as Thadius made his announcement to the constables seated behind the desk. As he neared the opposite door, the taller of them cleared his throat with a loud "ahem".

"Where do you think you're going?"

Ryan started to perspire. He felt something fall from his face. He looked down to see the dried lump of biscuit on the floor.

"You need to leave those keys," the man pointed out in irritation. Ryan's stomach sunk. He still held onto the key ring taken from the guards downstairs.

"My fault," Thadius spoke up in a gruff voice. "Told him to give 'em back when they were done."

Both constables frowned in unison. Ryan placed the keys on the desk and the three strode out into the night. As they crossed the courtyard, the magical disguise faded away. Ryan noticed it first and was relieved nobody else was about to see the change.

Thadius stopped them. "Did you count on this spell to get us past the gatehouse?"

"We planned to pass you off as a warrior going off duty and into the city," Ryan explained. "Ephram, can you change him back?"

The wizard drew forth the mirror and shook his head. Its surface was still clouded and dull. "The material component of the spell requires time to recharge."

Ryan groaned in frustration. "We can't get him past the gates."

Ephram ushered them past a row of bare fruit trees, into the shadows of the eastern wall. "Let me think."

"We don't have long," Thadius stated. "There are a couple of serving girls who bring strong drink to our sleeping friends after hours."

"We'll be away from here momentarily," Ephram assured them.

"I can't ask you to risk yourselves any more than you already have. Go on, you two can get past the gates. I'll find another way out," Thadius suggested.

Ephram shook his head. "No, my friend. We'll all get out of here. Come along."

The wizard led them to the foot of the wall and motioned for them to stand together. "This will feel odd at first, but I promise it's harmless. Before I begin, may I say I'm glad to see you again," he clasped Thadius' hand. "Give Trennan my greetings and tell him we have much to discuss when next we meet." He took Ryan's hand. "Good luck to you, lad. I'm sure we'll see each other again." The mage began the words of yet another spell.

"I didn't know Ephram was a friend of yours," Ryan murmured.

"Trenn is not the only wizard in my acquaintance."

"He never mentioned—" Ryan was seized by a force that seemed to lift him from everywhere. With a peculiar sensation of weightlessness, he rose higher and higher. He and Thadius were smoothly levitated to the ramparts above. Once both had a firm seat on the cold gray stones, Ephram released them from the spell.

"There's a soft place to land on the other side. I have another means of escape should I need to use it."

"You have my gratitude, Ephram," Thadius thanked him.

"Farewell, my friends." The wizard disappeared into the darkness.

Ryan and Thadius crept among the parapets. In the field outside the fortress, the campfires of a full garrison spread out below and they were careful to stay low, lest someone spot their silhouettes in the moonlight. With a bird's eye view of the courtyard, they witnessed a guard burst from the doors of the Magistrate's Hall and run for the gates.

"Tell me that's not for us already," Ryan moaned. As they hurried along the wall, thunder crackled and Thadius told him that Ephram had made his escape. Ryan leaned over the parapets and could make out heaping mounds beneath them. The odor wafting upward was awful.

"Soft place to land? Those are garbage piles!" he let out. "Why couldn't it have been hay?" Then a horn blasted in the courtyard.

"It won't be long before they search the streets for us," Thadius warned. "Don't think about the smell." He swung a leg over the wall and lowered himself as far as he could, before dropping onto the garbage below. He landed with a thump and a rustle.

"It's safe," he called up.

Ryan hung from the parapets and dropped. He landed with a squish.

"Fish heads and cabbage," he uttered with disgust. "I'll smell like this for a week!"

"You'll smell worse if we don't move fast."

They walked briskly through the darkened side streets of Drynas, all but deserted due to the late hour.

"Have I thanked you for coming to my rescue?"

"You'd have done the same for me." Ryan beamed with pride.

"Nevertheless, you shouldn't have risked your life to free me. Allan is no fool. He might connect you to this jailbreak."

"It's not likely anyone will have recognized me in all of this." Ryan removed his cap and freed his dyed hair. The pealing of a bell interrupted the still of the night.

Thadius quickened their pace. "That's the knell to assemble. Allan's constables will spread throughout the city, and you can bet Varis' men will join them."

"The inn is just ahead," Ryan said.

Booted feet sounded. From around the corner, four constables turned onto the street, heading straight for them.

# Chapter 9

"Relax, they're reporting to the garrison and haven't heard anything yet," Thadius assured.

Ryan was anxious. The constables looked them over and the scrutinizing gaze of one lingered as they passed. He wanted to know what they were about, Ryan was sure. To his relief, the men marched down the street.

"The irony is, they're in a rush to answer the call to assemble, or we probably would have been questioned," Thadius remarked once the men were out of earshot.

"Because of my smell, or your lurking?"

Thadius' chuckle was cut short by a painful wince. "Please, save the jokes. At least until it doesn't hurt to laugh."

At the stable entry, Ryan led the way past the snoring watchman. "The service was not worth the extra coin," he whispered.

"We better hurry. The gates of the city will soon be closed."

Ryan's horse snorted and stepped away at his approach. It took a few more attempts before he was able to saddle the animal. From the locked bin, he and Thadius retrieved their weapons and gear. The two worked with practiced hands to mount and situate their equipment. When at last he sat ready to ride, the horse turned with an expression Ryan read as indignant.

"Yes, I smell awful. I promise to bathe at the first chance."

Ryan tossed the key to the watchman, who woke as they departed. "Perhaps the day shift is a better fit for you."

Outside, they urged their steeds through the nearly empty streets at a canter, mindful that riders may have already been dispatched to the city gates. Ryan prayed that they would remain open, just a bit longer.

"Oh, thank you," he said aloud. They turned a corner to see the western gates ahead. One side stood wide, and in the lamplights, Ryan counted six men on duty. Thadius stopped before the men on guard duty.

"And where might you be headin' at such a late hour?" The sergeant in charge grabbed hold of the horse's harness.

"I must return this boy to his father in Aldwyn by midday tomorrow," Thadius replied. "He's a runaway and I've been given the task to see him home."

A hard-looking fellow drew near and snorted at Ryan, much like his horse had. "The boy stinks of rotten food. Where's he been, hiding in the garbage with the rats?"

"Or in the company of some mongrel dogs?" another added his insult.

Ryan fumed as Thadius addressed the sergeant.

"The boy is the son of the Magistrate of Aldwyn. He's a harsh man and the lad will take a beating for this trouble."

"I see he's taken the rod to you recently," the man observed.

"I'm responsible for the boy," Thadius stated.

The sergeant nodded.

"A boy who runs away needs firm discipline," the hard-looking soldier offered. "Where'd you find him, the sewers?"

"In an alley, covered in refuse." Thadius gave Ryan a sideways glance. Most of the men chuckled.

"You'll learn not to run away again, boy," the sergeant reproved. "Be off with you." He released Thadius' horse and stepped aside.

At the sound of other riders, all turned to see a squad of eight mounted men approaching. The warriors bore the colors of Lord Varis. "Close the gates!" one of them called out.

The sergeant reached for Thadius' reins. "Hold here, until we—"

Thadius kicked the sergeant away with a boot to the chest. "Ride!"

Ryan kicked his horse and launched into a gallop, matching Thadius' speed. Hoof beats pounded from behind as the warriors charged after them. Pushing their mounts, Ryan and Thadius raced down the dirt road. While they managed to put some distance between themselves and their pursuers, Varis' men remained on the chase. Ryan drew up alongside of Thadius.

"I think they'd follow us all the way to Aldwyn," he shouted.

"You're right," Thadius agreed. "Stay close."

Thadius veered from the road at the next bend and led them into the countryside. The pair circled a stand of tall trees and halted in the darkness. The sounds of pursuit passed by and faded into the distance.

"We lost them," Ryan let out a breath.

"They'll realize we've given them the slip and turn around. But now, we ride to the northwest."

The two brought their steeds to an ambling gait, making their way through a landscape of scattered trees and brush. When the animals showed signs of tiring, they dismounted and walked.

"We've plenty of provisions and carry our weapons and traveling gear," Ryan reported. "All we need is a safe place to hide until we figure out what to do next."

"I have something in mind. And it's not too late for you to go home."

"Home?"

"Yes. You'll claim to have been there the whole time. I'm sure Darien and Elias will swear so. Like you said, your disguise will have fooled the guards at the manor. And no offense, but I don't think Varis will suspect you of masterminding such a flawless escape from his dungeons."

"Wait a minute, I am not going back. Where you go, I go."

"I'm riding beyond the borders of Galanthor."

"Beyond the borders? Whatever for?"

"To locate the camp of some goblin outcasts. They have something that doesn't belong to them."

"*You* are going after the gemstone?"

"Who else will fetch it? The king and his new earl want war. If I can recover the Stone of Orinn, they'll have no support."

"I'm going with you. You'll need me!" Ryan pleaded. He caught himself, thinking he sounded too much like Darien, begging to be brought along. "We'll search for it together," he continued with more control. "And we can start by tracking the foul goblins who took the gemstone in the first place."

"The trail at the bandit camp will be cold."

"I guess that's true. What now?"

"You'll head home and I'll go north," Thadius said firmly.

"If you insist. But don't be surprised if I somehow get lost. My sense of direction isn't always good, and I might end up riding north by mistake."

"You're as hard-headed as your horse."

"That's why we get along so well."

"Fine," Thadius relented with a grunt.

"So, where to?"

"We're skirting the Darkwood Forest. On the northern fringes is a Huntsman's outpost. If anyone is there, they'll know best where to look for these goblins. Perhaps along the way, we can get you to take a bath."

Ryan's horse snorted as if in agreement.

*    *    *

The arms merchant drained his goblet and the serving lass promptly delivered another bottle of dark wine to the table. He thanked the young girl and turned back to the beautiful woman in his company. He refilled her goblet and gazed into her bright green eyes. The expensive drink came all the way from Tyresia, an island kingdom almost four hundred miles off the coast. The meal was one of the finest the Dragon's Tooth Inn offered and he spared no expense in his attempt to impress the lady she pretended to be.

Wrella sipped her wine and feigned interest in his dull conversation. It had been no great effort to attain the merchant's interest. She had specifically picked this man out. The flattering dress she wore was stolen, and the gems that sparkled in her jewelry were each as false as her motives. It was an uncomfortable disguise for a woman more accustomed to leather and steel.

From the booths around them, patrons called for song and drink, a stark contrast to the merchant's melancholy mood.

"Sure, everyone's breathing a sigh of relief. War might be averted, blah, blah blah. What about me? Do you know how many karas I would have made arming just one garrison?"

"There will be other opportunities," she consoled. "Wait, *would* have made?"

He drank deeply, wiping his goatee on the sleeve of his embroidered shirt, ignoring the fancy napkin. "Word's been spreading all day. Where've you been, woman? Ilsgaard's not to blame. Goblin renegades have stolen the Stone of Orinn. A whole band of 'em."

"Renegades? Are you sure about this? Sounds like more gossip."

"Oh, I have it on good authority — straight from Varis' manor."

Wrella had assumed the gemstone was lost, well on the way to Ilsgaard, and completely out of reach. She was certainly not about to chase after it. But this was the most unexpected news! The Stone of Orinn was not so unattainable, especially if this latest caper was successful.

He stroked his goatee. "Let's continue this conversation in private. Perhaps in my chambers?"

With a playful smile, Wrella responded with a nod.

Though his men-at-arms stationed themselves outside of the door, it did not worry her. She had anticipated and planned for this. Wrella spent several evenings in the inn's upper lounge, observing the lay out and those gathered there. She had chosen her victim with care and expected to be handsomely rewarded for her nights of expensive drinks. Inside, he turned to close the door and draw the bolt.

"Oh, this one's too easy," she murmured to herself.

He faced her with a broad grin and a look of half-drunken lust in his eyes. She led him across the opulently furnished sitting room to a wide couch. He reached out for her, only to have her lean away. His face expressed confusion until he saw her retrieve a flask from her belt pouch. She undid the top and handed him the silver container.

"Are you up for something stronger than Tyresian grape juice?" Wrella teased.

He stared as she slipped off her earrings and necklace. "I'll match you in whatever poison you choose," he boasted.

"It's Karganthian and may be a bit strong for your taste," she offered him the first swig. He drank deeply as she unpinned a brooch of green glass and placed it with the other worthless jewelry. These trinkets she no longer needed and did not want to be caught with them in her possession when she was done.

"Let's see what else we can take off you . . ." Abruptly, the arms merchant passed out.

"I'm glad I mixed that batch a little strong," she whispered. "Now, time to pay up."

Wrella removed his gold jewelry and went through his belt pouches. She relieved him of his bronze dyras and silver karas but was sure he had hidden funds. A hasty search of the bedroom produced a locked box, hidden underneath the dresser.

"Where might you be hiding the key?"

She labored to pull off his boots and was rewarded when a small key was shaken out of one. She rushed to the box, almost forgetting to check for a trap in her excitement. Rows of silver karas gleamed and her eyes brightened. The box held enough coins to fill her pouch. As they spilled out, she caught a flash of gold.

"A royal. You're the first I've seen in months." She admired its shine in the lamplight. "You should be more careful about the women you pursue," she counseled the unconscious merchant.

Wrella shed the tight dress and strode to the wardrobe. She tried on a long-sleeved shirt and a pair of oversized pants, cinching the belt tight. She traded her fancy sandals for more sensible walking shoes and stuffed an embroidered handkerchief into each toe to help them fit. With a whirl, she wrapped herself in a heavier cloak and admired herself in the mirror. It was good enough to get her out of here.

She eased open the shutters to see a group of men talking outside of the inn below. She moved back to the window in the sitting room. It overlooked the stables. If she was stealthy, she could walk along the top of the stable and past the watchman on duty. Wrella stepped up onto the window ledge. It was a short leap onto the roof, and she was thankful the pitch was not steep.

She froze in place and strained for any indication she had been heard. After a moment of silence, she continued. The weathered roof held loose shingles and she was forced to tread carefully. At the other end, she glanced about the deserted street. Wrella lowered herself from the corner of the eaves, dangling a second before releasing her grip on the rough wooden shingles. She dropped the remaining ten feet and landed with a roll.

"Who's out there?" a voice called from within the stables. She was gone before the watchman opened the door.

She had half the city to cover before she reached her inn room. It lay on the seedier side of Drynas and was a third the size of the bedchamber she left behind. Wrella walked swiftly, avoiding the main avenues and patrolling guardsmen out of habit. As she passed a row of shops, she made a mental note of all the equipment she needed. Now that she could afford it, she would also purchase new leather armor and a fast horse. The gods willing, she could be away from Drynas by midday.

Wrella had in mind where to start her search. Hale had mentioned goblins — outcasts living somewhere north of the Darkwood. Surely that meant the Lost Hills. While these hills were wild lands, they were less dangerous than trying to enter Ilsgaard itself.

The pealing of a bell interrupted her thoughts. Something was going on. The knell came from Varis' fortress. Wrella quickened her pace. She needed to get off the streets before they filled with constables and soldiers.

Once within her cold, cramped room, she lit a squat candle. It was all she had for light. Without shedding the cloak, Wrella lay down on the dirty straw mat and drew her thick blanket up about her. Her breath formed clouds in the air, for it was nearly as frigid indoors as out.

"This is the last time I pay to lie shivering on the floor with the bugs!"

# ❧ Chapter 10 ❧

By noon, Ryan and Thadius passed the trail that the men of Llerwyth rode when they tracked the company of brigands. Thadius declared them far ahead of any pursuit and they settled to rest within a grove of trees. Ryan readied a meal and brewed a strong tea of chamomile to speed healing. He handed Thadius a steaming cup.

"Why must *we* retrieve the gemstone? Won't Malikar send soldiers to hunt these outcasts?"

"From what I learned during my pleasant stay as his guest, an expeditionary force is being prepared to cross the Cimrinn. I think it's been the new king's plan all along to wage war on whatever goblins he finds. Installing an earl from the House of Rhuddlun was a means of assuring he had Galanthor in his pocket. Rhuddlun has close ties to the royal family, and also lost a son to Ilsgaard just before the Battle of Drynas."

"So the Stone of Orinn provides a convenient excuse," Ryan supposed.

"Many already question the need for war. The fact that Ilsgaard doesn't have the gemstone is spreading and its return will thwart their plans. The king could command the other earls to raise him an army, but his efforts will be seriously hampered without their full support."

"And he'll have no support should we recapture it."

"Exactly. However, I don't think we'll be riding into Drynas holding it high."

"We won't?" Ryan was sure recapturing the Stone of Orinn would make them heroes.

"I'm still an outlaw, and I'll lose my head should I fall into Malikar's hands. And we need to keep you out of any further trouble."

"I guess you're right. But since this falls on us, I'm joining you on this adventure, so that's settled."

Thadius finished the bitter tea in silence and applied a powerful ointment of lavender, comfrey and other ingredients to his bruises. The two stole a brief nap, then were back on the trail. They traveled deep into the night, riding by the light of a bright moon. Ryan dozed in the saddle at times. Thadius allowed them little rest, in case they were tracked. It was no more than a few hours before sunrise when they set up camp at the edge of the Darkwood Forest. Ryan spread out his bedroll close to the fire. The temperature was near freezing and they often added dead wood to maintain the blaze.

Ryan woke with the sun high overhead and the smell of breakfast cooking. He was glad to see Thadius in better shape. Thanks to their healing concoctions, his lip was improved and the bruises had already begun to lighten.

"Maybe our goblins will be found by a patrol," Ryan remarked.

"Not likely, I'm afraid. They'll keep to the woods, especially while on this side of the Cimrinn," Thadius explained. "Besides, one of them is wounded. They won't risk being caught out in the open."

"And once they cross the river? Could goblins from the Red Moon Clan find them?"

"Ilsgaard's border lies south of Ardan, where the Ravenwild River branches off the Cimrinn. But the woods north of the clans aren't much safer. Many outcasts find refuge there."

"I know war with Ilsgaard isn't justified in this case, but what about the goblin raids that occurred in Angwyn?" Ryan remembered the events that had led to the former Huntsman's sentence. "Weren't those goblins of Ilsgaard?"

"Yes, from the Clan of the Black Wolf. Those raids weren't severe enough in King Trevin's eyes to warrant a full-blown war. Anyway, that's all in the past."

Ryan changed the subject as they ate. "What do you know of the Lost Hills? The stories I've heard tell of horrid creatures and hidden evils."

"I've never been into those hills," Thadius admitted. "Few men have, but I won't be deterred by wild rumors and campfire stories."

"Then neither shall I," Ryan affirmed.

Thadius paused before his next bite. "Those stories . . . What kind of horrid creatures?"


Ryan and Thadius followed the boundary of the Darkwood Forest, which Ryan found appropriately named. Black alders and twisted oaks dominated the wood, with a fair amount of maple and black walnut. Tangled vines, brown and leafless, snaked upward to cling to the trunks and branches of tall and barren trees. However, scattered about the wood were patches of green, as several varieties of evergreens could be seen.

In the skies above, gray clouds clustered and Ryan expected snow. He thought of Darien and was thankful the larder back home was well-stocked. Ryan felt sorry for leaving him again, with hardly any explanation. He vowed to make all of this up to him when he returned.

As the afternoon waned, snowflakes swirled on the breeze. From somewhere in the woods, a wolf howled. Startled, Ryan's hand went to his sword. The occasional cry sounded over the next hour, never far off. Thadius seemed unbothered by the wolves' proximity. Yet when they halted, he helped Ryan light a fire and collect enough fallen branches to keep it burning bright. Afterward, he strung his bow.

"Trouble?" Ryan strung his as well.

"Perhaps they've moved on. Perhaps not," he answered.

Ryan knew he referred to the wolves. "Do you think we're being hunted? I haven't heard them in a while."

"Wolves go silent as they close on their prey. Be on guard."

As twilight gave way to darkness, the horses grew skittish. Ryan nocked an arrow to his bowstring. They camped on level terrain, some distance from the wood line, and had an excellent field of view all about them to the edge of the firelight. A pair of golden eyes materialized to stare out at them from the woods. Another soon joined them.

"Do you think they'll attack?" Ryan asked nervously. "We could mount up and ride."

"Then the chase would begin. No, we'll stand a better chance on foot."

More eyes appeared in the woods. Ryan estimated from between six to eight wolves. It was hard to make an exact count, as they shifted about. Thadius threw more wood onto the flames and embers whirled skyward.

"I have a feeling we're in for a long—" Ryan spun about at the sound of padded footfalls.

Thadius' bow sang and he sent an arrow into the beast's chest. With a thump, wolf collided with human and Ryan was knocked to the ground. He scrambled to his feet and drew his sword. As the gray wolf lay dying, Thadius loosed another arrow into a second charging wolf. His missile pierced flesh to lodge in the creature's rib cage. The animal ran off with a high-pitched cry. Thadius drew a third arrow, but no other wolf approached.

"I didn't hear them until they were practically on top of us!" Ryan exclaimed in a voice higher than he intended. Breathing heavily, he brushed grass and fur from the cuirass, the hardened leather scratched by the impact. He was about to sheathe his blade, when he saw that the first wolf still clung to life. Though it had tried to kill him, Ryan did not want to see it suffer. He brought his sword down in a quick blow that saved it a lingering death.

The eyes in the woods continued to watch them. Thadius studied the wolves in turn. He shouldered his bow and gathered the dead wolf in his arms.

Bow in hand, Ryan joined him. "What are you doing?"

"Cover me, I could be wrong," he shrugged.

Thadius strode to the edge of the woods, despite Ryan's protests. The wolves retreated as Thadius left the body before the trees and backed away. Cautiously, the animals came forward to sniff their dead companion. Howls and cries erupted from the pack.

"We killed the lead male," he shared the credit with Ryan. "I wasn't sure until I saw their hesitation. They know we're dangerous, and without a strong leader, they'll leave us and seek for easier prey."

Sure enough, the wolves did not linger. In another moment, they disappeared, slipping away like ghosts into the night. Their yelps and cries faded away. Thadius returned to the fire.

"Come and warm yourself, Ryan. The danger has passed."

Even after they ate and settled in, Ryan could not fully relax. He kept one eye on the woods until sleep claimed him.

Ryan and Thadius rode due north, Ryan a bit sore from the collision the night before. Their course remained steady, until Thadius veered them to the east.

"There's a fort at the edge of the Darkwood, built on the river. We'll need to give it a wide berth and avoid any patrols if possible."

"What if we can't?"

"We're merely a couple of bounty hunters, on the lookout for a renegade goblin. It's not far from the truth."

Thadius led them several miles out of their way before they swung about and headed for the river. When they reached the Cimrinn, Ryan washed up as best he could and rinsed the black dye from his hair. The two followed the unhurried waters to a weathered wooden bridge.

"It was built during the first years of the Goblin Campaign," Thadius pointed out. "Hastily constructed and forgotten once its purpose was served."

Ryan was wary as they traversed the structure. After all, the last dilapidated bridge he crossed had collapsed into a ravine. He patted his horse on the neck. "It was the day we first met, old boy . . . and nearly died together."

"Did you say something?" Thadius asked over his shoulder.

"Just a little reminiscing." He nudged his mount with a gentle heel to hurry him along. "You need a proper name. And I promise, it will be one you deserve."

By the next afternoon, their path had taken them around the nearby fort and back to a westerly direction, rounding the northeastern fringes of the Darkwood. To the north, the Lost Hills rose against an ashen sky, much higher than the gentle hills that surrounded Drynas and Llerwyth. An expanse of tall amber grass, dotted with trees and brush, lay between the hills and the forest.

"How far are we from this Huntsman's outpost?" Ryan was curious as to what they might find. He imagined a concealed hideout with secret spy holes or an underground bunker with a hollowed-out tree for an entrance.

"A few days' ride. Less, if we push ourselves."

"How will you be received?" Ryan was almost afraid to ask.

"We will see."

It was a long, cold night. The wind picked up, and at times, thick flakes fell sporadically. The chill kept them from a restful sleep and the fire was reduced to coals by dawn. The horses stood together, affected by the temperature as well. Ryan shivered as they broke camp.

"If we ever get ourselves out of this predicament, I think I may return to the southern Elderwood."

"You *are* getting out of this predicament," Thadius told him.

"Of course, we both will," Ryan tried to sound as confident.

He appreciated the effort Thadius would go to in an attempt to keep his name from any wrongdoing. However, Ryan could not allow him to accept all of the blame, nor the burden of their actions. Even if it meant living as an outlaw, he was determined to stand by his friend and his conscience.

Darien was another matter. If that was how things turned out for him and Thadius, he could always dig up some of the gold buried in the stables and hire a governess of some sort for his younger brother. Of course, things could also end very badly. Ryan suddenly regretted not leaving some kind of note or message for Darien.

Ahead, snow dusted the upper reaches of the Lost Hills, enough to obscure any features at this distance. Ryan eyed the landscape about them.

"What are the chances of coming across goblins?"

"The river marked the border of the kingdom and the limits of normal patrol routes," Thadius informed him. "The chances improve with every mile."

"Comforting. So we're beyond any help."

"Only a full war band would venture past the Cimrinn, or fools such as us."

"Or a Huntsman. Is there a lonelier or more dangerous place for a soldier to pull duty?"

"Lonelier? No. More dangerous? I'd say so," Thadius responded.

"Where?"

"The Tangled Wood, where Angwyn meets the Superstition Mountains."

"You've mentioned those mountains," Ryan recalled. "You also promised to tell me about them sometime."

"If you're sure you won't have nightmares . . ."

Ryan balled up a fist and twisted his face in exaggerated indignation. Thadius dodged his half-hearted jab and kicked his horse into a gallop. The chase was on and it broke the somber mood.

Darkness came early, and the hills loomed before them, sinister and foreboding. Ryan was glad Thadius had told his stories during the daylight. A full moon hung in the sky, circled by a halo of light that foretold of snow. He passed another night with little sleep. Huddled in his heavy blanket, Ryan kept close to the flames and his eyes on the nearby hills. He was tired and sore in the morning.

The day unfolded much like the last few — the sky shaded gray with overcast and each breeze brought with it scattered snowflakes. Ryan rode cold and weary in the saddle. He longed for just another hour of sleep. At noon, they halted for a rest and a meager portion of their dwindling rations before resuming their trek.

"At this pace, we'll make the outpost by evening," Thadius stated. "If all goes well, we might be able to pick up some provisions."

"That's encouraging. What about—"

"Wait," Thadius signaled for silence. They brought their mounts to a stop.

Then Ryan heard it too. The distant clash of steel upon steel.

"Someone fights for their life," Ryan declared.

Their eyes met and the decision was made. With a kick, the two sped across the frozen grassland, toward the Lost Hills.

# ᧒Chapter 11᧒

The din grew louder and Ryan could hear shouts and cries. He and Thadius rounded an outcropping of rock to see a figure dressed in buckskins engaged in a running battle. More than a score of goblins attempted to encircle him, but he was swift, taking them first one way, then another. The tactic kept the majority of them off balance and his sword flashed as he struck down those who closed in.

Thadius' horse shot forward. "Wait here," he tried to wave Ryan off.

"Not a chance!"

Adrenaline pumped as Ryan drew his sword and charged after him. Thadius led them into the right flank of the mob, scattering goblins. The maneuver gave the man an opening and he dashed for a tall, solitary boulder less than a hundred or so feet away.

"Stay close!" Thadius instructed Ryan.

Most of the goblins fled before the thundering horses. Others rallied to meet the new threat. Ryan lashed out at a green-skinned warrior as he streaked by. The goblin returned the swing, but both missed by a wide margin. His blade a silver blur, Thadius cut his way through a pair of axe-wielding goblins and steered his horse for the lone boulder.

Atop it, the man fought off the goblins attempting to reach him. The wounded and dying lay sprawled about the base. However, the goblins would eventually overpower him and Ryan caught sight of some readying bows. Thadius made for the far side of the boulder, where they would have some cover. He reined in his steed and brought his blade down, cleaving the skull of a goblin scrambling up the side of the rock.

"Get on!" Thadius cried.

The man shoved a warrior onto its comrades and made the short leap from the rock, sword in hand. Thadius allowed his horse a few tentative steps under the additional weight, then with a kick, they raced away from the boulder as barbed arrows flew past. Ryan drew alongside him, and once out of bowshot, he turned in the saddle to see some of the goblins already scavenging from the dead.

They rode across the grassland at a gallop, back the way they had come. Satisfied there were no goblins in pursuit, Thadius slowed and swung them toward the woods. At the fringes of the Darkwood, they dismounted.

"I owe you both my thanks," the man extended his hand. His long black hair was tied in a ponytail and a week's worth of beard framed his lean face. A broadsword and a dagger hung on his belt, and over his shoulders hung a light pack, a bow and an empty quiver. "The name's Jona."

"I'm Thadius," the woodsman accepted his hand. Inwardly, Ryan cringed. News of Thadius' escape should not have traveled this fast, but why use his real name?

"Thadius . . ." Jona held his gaze.

"So, what did you do to upset those goblins?" Ryan sought to divert his attention.

Jona pulled a rag from a pocket to clean the black blood from his blade. "You know goblins. The slightest thing gets their dander up."

"This far from help, it pays to be skilled with a sword," Thadius complimented.

"I'm better with a bow," Jona shrugged. "Unfortunately, I ran out of arrows before I ran out of goblins. As far as skill with the sword, I can't complain about the pay."

"No Huntsman does."

Jona grinned. "I recognized your name. Your story is a legend among the Legion."

"Is that good or bad?" Ryan interjected.

"Many of us would have taken the same action given the same circumstances," Jona empathized. "It's an honor to be in your company."

Thadius' cheeks reddened with the unexpected praise. "Yes, well, it's all in the past."

"Of course." Jona changed the subject. "I don't mean to sound ungrateful, but what in the world are you two doing out here?"

"It's a long tale," Thadius let out with a breath. "We can share it on the way to the outpost."

They walked into the Darkwood, leading the horses along a winding path, as Ryan and Thadius brought Jona up to date on the whole gemstone affair. In return, the Huntsman related what he could of the goblins living in the Lost Hills.

"A goblin named Torr leads the band you seek," Jona informed them. "He's ruthless and cunning, and aspires to be the chieftain of his own clan."

"Have you word on this Torr's whereabouts?" Thadius questioned.

"His camp lies in the western hills. Torr has united most of the goblins north of Ilsgaard under his banner. Rumor has it they're over five hundred strong."

"Five hundred strong?" The number shocked Ryan.

"And the more warriors he gathers, the more are drawn to him," Jona replied.

"What about the gemstone?" Thadius asked. "Any sign that it's in Torr's possession?"

"Not exactly," Jona admitted. "Torr has sent parties out, as if they're searching for someone, or something. I'll tell you another thing that's odd. While I've heard of the gemstone's loss, I've received no instructions to find it."

"That is odd," Thadius agreed. "The recovery of such an important religious artifact should be a priority for the Huntsman Legion."

"The Legion has been given other priorities. Half of the Huntsmen in northern Angard will soon assemble for new orders."

Thadius stopped Jona. "The king plans to invade Ilsgaard."

"That's our consensus as well. These are troubling days for the Legion." Jona lowered his voice, though they were far from the nearest pair of ears who could have heard. "There's no cause for war with Ilsgaard. We haven't had a raid or a skirmish with the clans for two years now. Furthermore, there's no evidence that the goblins are preparing for war against Angard. If anything, the situation appears to be the opposite."

"Opposite?" Thadius wrinkled his brow.

"We think the increasing number of outcasts is due to conflict within Ilsgaard."

"You mean a war?" Skirmishes were common among the tribes, but any serious fighting was a revelation to Ryan.

"Maybe not an all-out conflict, but some kind of feuding is going on. Some of the exiles have attempted to buy or steal human-forged weapons."

"Why does a clan exile a warrior?" Ryan was curious.

"We're not exactly sure," Jona answered. "Failure in battle is a likely possibility. Many of the outcasts I've encountered bear nasty scars. Whatever the reason, their numbers have increased. This is good for those like Torr, who take them in and swell their ranks."

The Darkwood seemed less intimidating to Ryan as they walked. Perhaps because it was still daylight, or perhaps it was the company he found himself in. Although there was nowhere near the level of noise and activity he had experienced in the Elderwood, it was winter after all. Not all of the rumors about this forest could be true.

Half an hour into the woods, they arrived at the Huntsman's outpost. Ryan was a bit disappointed to find it merely a small log cabin. But with the sun dipping on the horizon, he looked forward to the warmth of a fire and the possibility of a hot meal. The roughly constructed cabin was tight quarters for three. The single room was simply furnished, containing a plainly fashioned chair, a sleeping mat and a squat table. A fireplace was built at one end and rows of shelves lined the adjacent walls. Gear stored in one corner was in a tidy pile and the floor was swept clean.

Jona held the door for them. "I'll collect some wood. We can start a fire once darkness falls."

"What a lonely place to spend months at a stretch," Ryan sympathized. "I can see why Huntsmen are well-paid for their service."

"That's one reason they're among the highest paid of the king's soldiers," Thadius told him. "The men assigned here will spend little time in these quarters. Most of it's spent out in the wilds. Jona will soon be back to his patrols."

With a fire lit, Jona prepared a meal of cured deer meat, baked potatoes and heated some flaky biscuits he had made the day before. Ryan was starved but forced himself to eat slowly and enjoy every bite.

"The dinner is greatly appreciated," Thadius thanked Jona. "What else can you tell me about the hills?"

"There are things besides goblins prowling those hills. Truthfully, I've never been very deep into them. A trail lies not much further west from where we left that goblin band. It leads to an old goblin shrine. I think it's the limit of Torr's territory. Or it was. After today, I need to rethink those boundaries."

"What about this goblin shrine?" Ryan managed with a mouth full of potatoes.

"Leftover from the days when the clans of Ilsgaard could claim everything south of the Cimrinn, all the way to the hills of Drynas. I've seen it once. It rises at a crossroads of sorts."

"And one of those paths leads to Torr's camp?" Thadius tore a bite from his biscuit.

Jona nodded. "Judging from the condition of the trails, I'd say Torr's camp lies somewhere down the western path."

"The gemstone may not be in his possession now, but you can be sure it's on the way," Thadius surmised.

The three ate for the next few moments, each within their own thoughts. Ryan savored his last piece of meat and contemplated reaching for another potato.

"So you alone will enter the hills and retrieve the gemstone?" Jona addressed Thadius.

"Was I that transparent?"

"While I don't doubt your skills, I believe it's a task no man could accomplish alone. Even if you were to locate Torr's camp, and the gemstone is there, it'll be heavily guarded."

"He won't be alone," Ryan spoke up. He read Thadius' smile as acceptance. He certainly had not come this far to be left behind.

Thadius and Jona swapped stories of their adventures on the kingdom's frontiers into the night. Fascinated as he was by their recounts, sleep gradually overtook him. Despite his best efforts to stay awake, he drifted off as he lay before the flames.

He woke in the morning to find Thadius gone.

# ❧ Chapter 12 ❧

"How could he do this?" Ryan fumed.

"He thought it for the best," Jona attempted to console him. "You're safer here."

"Safe? Who cares about being safe? The best thing to do was to take me with him. What was he thinking?"

"Of you, apparently."

Ryan stormed from the cabin. Thadius' horse was still tethered outside. "He's on foot, so he can't have gotten far. I can . . ."

Jona followed after him and Ryan could read his face.

"Don't tell me he asked you to keep me here."

"If it's any consolation, he refused my help too."

Ryan returned to the cabin and slammed the door. He paced the floor as Jona went about his morning chores.

"Every minute I spend here, Thadius is getting farther and farther away," he complained to himself.

Eventually, Ryan's anger subsided. He packed his gear, storing everything in a corner, and joined Jona outside as the Huntsman rubbed down Thadius' steed. Ryan picked up a brush and set to work on his own horse.

"My apologies, Jona. It's not your fault he left me behind."

"I'm glad you bear me no ill will. Thadius will be back soon enough."

"What are his chances of recovering the gem and making it out of the hills?" Ryan scrutinized his face.

"His are better than most. If any man in the kingdom can do it, I'm sure it will be him."

Though Jona attempted to guard his response, Ryan read a different answer in his eyes.

As the day progressed, Ryan passed the hours practicing with his bow. Jona offered his tutelage, and the two fired practice arrows until hoof beats interrupted the lesson. A roundabout path wound about the isolated cabin, designed to alert those on duty to the approach of riders.

"You'd best wait inside, Ryan," Jona cautioned.

Ryan withdrew indoors and kept the door ajar to observe the unexpected company. A line of horsemen appeared, and as Ryan feared, all bore the griffin of Angard on their surcoats.

"Don't tell me you've come all this way for us," Ryan whispered aloud. To his dismay, the band dismounted and began to unpack.

Jona was handed a rolled parchment by the officer in charge. He unsealed and read the paper as he walked back into the cabin.

"It seems the outpost is to be turned over to the earl's forces. I'm to report to Ardan . . ."

Jona found the cabin empty.


Ryan had prepared for an opportunity to steal away, and the arrival of the war band granted him one. He tossed his gear out of the window and slipped out. He kept the cabin between himself and the soldiers, careful to avoid any stretches of soft soil or patches of mud, where he might leave a trace.

The previous day, Jona had mentioned a mysterious structure to the northwest, not far into the hills. The Huntsman believed it to be an ancient goblin shrine. From there, the trail split. One path led westward and the other wound higher into the hills. While Jona did not know what lay to the north, he was certain Torr's camp lay to the west. And that was surely Thadius' destination. As the sun set, Ryan reached the edge of the Darkwood. Across an expanse of tall amber grass, the Lost Hills rose before him.

Nightfall plunged the land into near total blackness. Fearing a torch would be easily spotted from a great distance, Ryan waited for the moon to clear the trees before continuing. Assuming Thadius would waste no time, he set as fast a pace as he dared, to generate warmth, as well as the fear that Jona might pursue him. He was sure that Huntsmen took their word to each other seriously. He kept to the fringes of the woods, where he could seek cover if necessary.

Throughout the long night, Ryan moved whenever the moonlight allowed. He halted at every rustle, crouching motionless with his sword ready. Once he was sure it was nothing more than some woodland animal foraging, and not wolves, goblins or something worse, he resumed his journey. Sometime near dawn, an exhausted Ryan crawled into a large patch of evergreen bushes. He curled up in his heavy blanket, intending to take just a short nap.

He woke suddenly, his mind racing. The sky was already bright. How long had he slept? It felt like hours. Ryan started to crawl from the foliage and froze. Nearby voices spoke in a strange tongue.

Goblins.

Ryan could not catch a glimpse of the creatures through the thick tufts of greenery. He listened for a moment and guessed there were at least three of them, less than a dozen feet away. He lay still as a stone as he listened to their harsh, guttural language. Although he did not understand a single word, it was obvious an argument was underway.

Ryan took advantage of the boisterous conversation to shift into a more comfortable position. Startled, a sparrow flew from its perch with a trilling chirp. The goblins went silent and Ryan's heart pounded. A fourth goblin spoke, its scratchy tone was commanding — quick and to the point. Ryan's hand went to his sword. Sweat beaded on his forehead and ran freely down the sides of his face. If he understood the goblin language, his panic would have dissipated. The leader of the band merely scolded the others for being noisy enough to scare off lunch.

To Ryan's relief, the goblins collected their gear and departed. Cautiously, he crept from his hiding place and followed the sound of their conversation through the trees. It grew louder, and he risked a peek from around the trunk of a wide oak. Five goblin warriors crouched in a semi-circle and poked about the ground at the forest's edge. One motioned to the north, and after a short discussion, the band was off again. Ryan let them clear the area before he investigated the spot that had so interested them. At first, matted grass and goblin prints were all he found. Then he discovered what had captured the goblins' attention. In the damp earth was the smudged impression of a boot. It was enough to tell Ryan it was a human boot.

Thadius. And the goblins were on his trail.

Ryan set off, determined not to let them out of his sight. He spotted them in the open grassland, making their way northward, toward the Lost Hills. The goblins were swift, pausing only to inspect the ground in one spot or another. Ryan was often forced to run to keep up. He dashed from bush to bush, using the sparse brush or solitary tree as concealment, lessening the chance of being noticed by a backward glance.

By midday, the goblins arrived at the lower slopes and hiked the first in a series of grassy hills. Tall grass gave way to a shorter variety and trees grew fewer and farther between. Ryan waited for the goblins to crest the next hill before pursuing. He peered over the rise to see them at rest.

The goblins sat beneath the bare branches of a gnarled tree. They ate from their rations and rested for the better part of an hour. During their respite, a worn-out Ryan ate a meager lunch and rubbed his aching legs. When the goblins resumed their trek, they led him onto a footpath. It snaked its way into a valley littered with boulders and loose stones. He wondered if they still pursued Thadius, for he had seen no further signs of him.

Ryan stopped abruptly. Two sets of footprints veered off from the others. Perhaps they had lost Thadius' trail and spread out in an effort to pick it up again. He proceeded after the main group and soon came across three of the goblins. He spied on them from a stony outcropping with a curious fascination. The goblins seemed at ease, sitting on the ground and casting stones in some kind of game.

He started at a creak from behind.

Ryan recognized the sound of a bow stretched taut and his heart leapt into his throat. He spun to face the other goblins, both with arrows pointed at him. He was at their mercy, and with a feeling of dread, recalled something Thadius had once said.

Goblins take no prisoners.

\*　　　\*　　　\*

Wrella had ridden hard since leaving Drynas, pushing herself and her newly purchased horse to their limits. She did not skirt the Darkwood on the northward leg of her journey but kept to the east until well beyond the Cimrinn River. Then swinging onto a westerly course, she finally reached the southern edges of the Lost Hills. Not long after, she spotted vultures circling in the sky ahead.

Wrella slowed her steed to survey the remains of a battlefield. More than a dozen goblins lay dead, most sprawled at the base of a tall boulder. The rest were strewn about a field of amber grass. Crows took flight as she led her horse through the aftermath of a fight. The bigger vultures ruffled their wings and carried on with their grizzly feast, giving her little notice. Her steed snorted as Wrella paused at the ring of bodies about the boulder. Any items of value had already been stripped from the dead. She saw no symbols or devices of Ilsgaard among the slain. Encouraged, she kicked her horse into a gallop. The crows returned to feed in her wake.

Daylight faded into dusk as Wrella made her way up into the Lost Hills. The landscape was more gloomy and foreboding by night, and she could not help but reflect on her decision. Was this all a mistake? Was the gemstone worth the risk? Even if she could somehow lay her hands on it, what then? She certainly could never sell it in Angard. Perhaps far to the south, in Vyrena . . .

Wrella was torn from her thoughts by a nervous whicker. The horse picked up its gait and its head swiveled from one direction to the other. Her hand dropped to the short bow riding in its sheath. A nearly full moon cast a pale glow, illuminating the open spaces and adding to the contrast of the deep shadows.

"Don't go getting skittish on me," she soothed the horse. Nevertheless, she trusted the animal's instincts. She slid the bow from its sheath and drew an arrow from her quiver. The danger she anticipated was not long in coming.

In a dale between sloping hills, sinister shapes sprang from cover to surround her. Wrella took aim at a figure before her and let an arrow fly. The man-sized form grunted and grasped the shaft in its chest. Kicking her mount, she loosed a second arrow and another enemy fell. A barbed arrow darted past, narrowly missing her. The goblins tightened their circle about her.

With a sharp pull on the reins, Wrella brought her steed about and scattered the goblins around her. She shoved the bow into its sheath and drew her blade. The goblins regrouped and she parried a series of strikes before she could counter-attack. All the while, Wrella kept her horse on the move, lest they come at her at once. She knew these tactics could not last.

"Come on, you savages!" she shouted. "Your quarry escapes you!"

Wrella broke free of the ring of warriors and continued up into the hills until she located a more easily defended spot. She concealed the horse behind a rock formation and waited. The night deepened as clouds drifted across the moon. Footfalls sounded and she readied an arrow. However, Wrella had not considered that goblins see much better in the darkness than humans.

Wrella jumped as an arrow struck the rock beside her. She could not see a target to shoot at. She rolled to the right as another arrow whistled by, then risked a peek to see the goblins break cover. Before the goblin archer could draw another arrow, Wrella rose and sighted in on him. Her missile flew true, piercing the goblin's armor of skins and leather and lodging in flesh and bone. The goblin fell with a gurgling cry.

Wrella dropped the bow and drew her sword as she rushed the nearest pair. She deflected a curved blade and delivered a wicked slash across an abdomen. The goblin stumbled, and blood flowed from the gaping wound. She dodged a swipe from her other opponent and ran the goblin through. She planted her boot on its chest and kicked its body into yet another arriving goblin, freeing her weapon. The creature shoved its dead comrade aside, giving Wrella the opening she needed. Steel flashed in the moonlight. Wounded, the determined fighter lashed out. Wrella fended off another blow before her foe collapsed.

She whirled to face two last goblins. Both looked at each other, apparently hesitant to engage the warrior who had slain the rest of their company. What Wrella did not know, was that these were the last survivors of the war band that had attacked Jona. The goblins exchanged a few short words with each other, and to her surprise, fled back down the slope.

A brief search of the slain revealed no clues as to where the gemstone might be. Wrella cursed herself for not taking a prisoner. Though she did not speak their rough tongue, she carried with her a sketch of the gemstone. She had drawn it on a piece of parchment and even shaded it with green ink. Wrella mounted and kept to the heights, riding a fair distance before allowing herself a rest.

She woke with the dawn and guided her mount upward through barren hills and around rocky crags. Try as she might, Wrella could not maintain the same bearing for any length of time. At these higher elevations, shaded passages blanketed in snow led her first one way, then another. Often, she was turned completely around and relied on the sun to navigate.

She encountered no other being as she trekked westward and sighted only the occasional bird. Perhaps it was the icy bite of winter, or the storm that the darkening clouds promised, that kept the animals in their dens. Goblin footprints soon explained the scarcity of wildlife. They crossed her path and headed south, toward the Darkwood. She estimated it was a band of at least a score and it had not been long since they passed. Further signs indicated multiple units, varying in size and direction.

"Why the reason for so many heavy patrols?" she asked herself.

Did it have to do with the gemstone? Or maybe the goblins had heard whispers of war from the human lands. Whatever the explanation, their number was greater than she expected.

Later in the evening, Wrella sat in solitude on the leeward side of a lofty ridge as she ate from her rations. The night was bitterly cold and snowflakes danced on the breeze. An odd noise drifted from somewhere nearby. Wrella wrapped her woolen blanket tighter around her and followed the sound. She climbed to the summit and peered between the hardy scrubs that clung to the rock.

In a dale below, a square tower rose at least half a dozen stories, topped with a tall, conical roof. A fire burned in the courtyard and washed the area with an eerie, flickering light. A throng of goblins danced and beat sticks together in rhythm. The din grew louder as strips of meat were set on spits. Wrella settled in to spy on them.

"What are you savages eating? Something rotten, no doubt. No banners of Ilsgaard in sight. These are definitely outcasts. Now, will this mob lead me back to their camp?"

# ⁓Chapter 13 ⁓

With a whistle, the other goblins were beckoned. The three ceased their ruse and rushed over. A stunned Ryan was roughly disarmed. He grimaced as his arms were jerked forward and his wrists bound tightly with a frayed leather cord. In spite of his fright, he held out a glimmer of hope. He was captured, not dead.

Ryan was thrown to the ground and watched, helpless, as the goblins rummaged through his belongings. The warriors cast stones to divide his property. The biggest, and presumably their leader, snatched up Ryan's sword for itself and did not participate in dividing the other spoils.

Ryan's items distributed, the goblin in charge shouted orders at the others and hauled Ryan to his feet. Ryan tried to hide his fear as he stood eye to eye with the snarling humanoid but twisted away from the stench of its rank breath. The goblin gave a guttural laugh and shoved Ryan into line. The patrol moved out, and he was forced to follow along.

Fear and panic eventually ebbed and allowed for more rational thought. Why was he taken prisoner and not slain? He risked a backward glance at the ill-tempered leader and was rewarded with a slap to the side of his head. The blow was worth it. The goblin wore the emblem of Torr's band branded on its leather jerkin.

As the troop marched on, the day grew from bad to worse. Thunderclouds gathered above and frigid drops began to fall. The goblin leader halted the troop and barked commands. Ryan was relieved when his hands were untied. However, relief gave way to uneasiness, as a length of rope was placed in a loop around his neck. A wiry goblin sneered at him and wrapped the other end about its wrist. Without another word, the squad of goblins launched into a run.

Although they adjusted the pace for their human prisoner, the long-footed goblins ran steadily. At the end of the crudely woven rope, Ryan labored to keep up. He estimated it was somewhere between two and three miles before the troop slowed to a brisk walk. Ryan's chest heaved and he tried to stop to catch his breath. A violent tug made him stumble and march on.

"If only I could answer you with steel!" he gasped. His retort brought a swift kick from behind.

Frozen raindrops turned to sporadic flakes as the small troop wound its way higher into the hills. Nearly spent, Ryan shivered and struggled to put one foot in front of the other. Each deep inhalation brought with it a rush of cold air that filled his lungs with a stab of icy pain. At last, the goblins entered a dale surrounded by bleak ridges. To Ryan's amazement, a tower stood at the center.

The square building was ancient and rose over six stories. There were four sides to the high-pitched roof, culminating in a slender spear of stonework, long ago broken near the peak. Though missing tiles and of a construction style unfamiliar to Ryan, he envisioned its appearance as once graceful. The remnants of a courtyard lay half-buried by the passage of unknown years. A path ran from the tower to the west. In the fading light, Ryan could detect the faint trace of another trailing off to the north.

This was the goblin shrine Jona had spoken of!

The courtyard contained a shallow cooking pit, encircled with boulders of various sizes. Discarded bones littered the ground and the odor of cooked meat and burnt wood hung in the air. Ryan concluded that the goblins used this place, maybe as a shelter for hunting parties or patrols. A charcoal sketching of a boar's head next to the entrance confirmed it.

There was little time to study his surroundings. He was shoved into the arched entry of the tower. Two goblins pushed him up a flight of stairs, down a short hallway, and up another set of steps. At the end of a rubble-strewn corridor, the rope was removed and Ryan was thrown through an open doorway and into a chamber. Outside of the room, he overheard a brief exchange before one of his captors departed.

Ryan pulled the collar of his cloak tighter about him. The indoors felt as cold as the outside. He rubbed his aching legs and fought the urge to collapse and give in to the need to rest. He cast about for something that could prove useful. The chamber contained nothing but splintered pieces of wood and loose stones. Even as his mind worked on a plan of escape, he puzzled at their reasons for taking him prisoner. What could they want with him?

Activity outside drew Ryan to the narrow window on the opposite side of the room. In the courtyard below, the goblins had filled the cooking pit with dry brush and dead branches. One used a rod of flint to start the fire, and as the flames blazed forth, the courtyard was bathed in a yellow-orange glow. The sun had set, and the intermittent snowflake wafted by, twinkling in the reflected light. Another of the green-skinned creatures sat on a crumbled section of wall and sharpened a large skinning knife. It looked up and spotted Ryan in the window. The goblin grinned wickedly and made a gesture with the knife across its throat.

Ryan saw no game to clean, nor any vegetables on hand. What were they going to cook for dinner? A sickening realization washed over him and with it came a wave of terror. These preparations were for him. This was why he had been spared.

Ryan turned from the window and considered rushing the guard out in the corridor. He discarded the idea of attacking the armed goblin with only a broken stick or a loose brick. Then again, he held no doubt that the goblins intended to do away with him. With nothing to lose, he groped about the unlit chamber until his hand closed on a sturdy piece of aged wood. Ryan crept toward the doorway.

His heart beat wildly as he peered out into the short corridor. He could not see in the near pitch-blackness and expected to be challenged. He readied his impromptu club. Seconds passed and the anticipated confrontation did not come. A nasally snore echoed softly. The sentry slept, somewhere just ahead.

Ryan set out, blindly feeling along the wall to his right. He winced and repressing the urge to moan. His legs burned with each measured step. Ryan could smell the stink of the goblin's unwashed body. With the noise of its slumber to direct him, Ryan held his breath and inched along the wall. Despite his best efforts, bits of fallen mortar crumbled beneath his feet. At a snort from the sentry, Ryan raised the stick. After a tense minute, the snoring resumed.

Fearful the goblin could wake at any second, Ryan pressed on. He found the steps, but as he reached the second floor landing, he could hear a commotion out in the courtyard. The sentry's footfalls suddenly padded on the stairs behind him. Too late to move out of the way, the collision sent both sprawling down the stairs. He and the goblin guard tumbled limb over limb to spill out onto the ground floor. In the dim light from the fire outside, Ryan leapt to his feet and faced the bewildered warrior.

Though he had come out of the tumble with a few new bumps, Ryan still held onto his stick. The goblin had lost its sword on the stairs. Before the creature could react, Ryan brought the makeshift cudgel down on its head. A loud crack resounded and splinters flew. The goblin fell with a groan.

Ryan collected the goblin's sword and limped for the arched entryway. He was shocked to find the curved blade so heavy. The large goblin appeared to block his escape. At the sight of the human, it raised Ryan's sword . . . and froze. The goblin pitched forward, an arrow embedded in its back. Ryan recognized the fletching.

"Thadius!"

All had gone quiet, and Ryan risked a peek outside. Thadius approached with an arrow at the ready.

"Any more about?"

"There's one in here," Ryan responded, "knocked flat out. How did you—"

"Quickly, gather your things," Thadius instructed.

As Ryan reclaimed his scattered weapons and gear, he counted the goblin dead. "Thadius, one of them is not here. And a larger company must have stopped here not too long ago."

"Then we should hurry."

Ryan's legs burned anew as they set off to the north. Thadius led them up a steep ridge and they kept a careful watch as they climbed among gigantic boulders and rocky crags. The goblin shrine disappeared from view once they crested the top. When they found a place to rest, Ryan expected harsh words from Thadius for his disobedience. Thus far, none had come. Relieved and grateful for his rescue, he ventured to speak.

"Thadius—"

"Do you have any idea the danger you've put yourself in?"

"Yes, I realize it wasn't the smartest thing—"

"No, it wasn't. In fact, this may have been the most ill-conceived scheme you've ever concocted," he reproved with a jabbing finger.

"I'm truly sorry," Ryan managed, "I just wanted—"

"To make my life harder."

Ryan said nothing while Thadius fumed in silence.

"Are you hungry?" Thadius asked at last.

"Starved!" Ryan let out.

They shared a rationed meal as the moon broke through the cloud cover to illuminate the rocky overlook. Snow and ice clung to nooks and crevices sheltered from the sun. Ryan wished to escape further chastisement and kept quiet. He occupied his mind with thoughts of home while he massaged his throbbing legs. Darien . . . what was he doing right now? Would he ever see his brother again?

The shrill notes of a horn sounded in the distance.

"The goblins at the shrine have been discovered," Thadius announced. "We'll stay on the ridge and head north. Once we're in the clear, we'll make new plans."

Ryan knew this likely meant his return to the Huntsman's outpost. As he picked his way among the boulders, he mentally prepared his case. He must be allowed to stay. Diverting to the outpost was too risky and time consuming. He added these to a list of reasons why he should continue as they progressed between the wind-hewn crags. It was late in the night before Thadius called a halt.

"We'll stop here and get some rest. There's no sense stumbling about in the dark."

"I won't argue with you," Ryan replied. "My legs are ready to give out."

Ryan was beyond tired, and his legs were sore from running with the goblins, as well as their rapid ascent up the steep ridge. As they nibbled on hard rolls, Thadius requested the details of his escape from the outpost. His mood softened as Ryan related his adventures.

"I suppose I should commend you on your courage and resourcefulness," Thadius complimented when Ryan concluded. "Reluctantly commend," he stressed with a raised finger.

Ryan beamed with the unexpected praise.

Thadius stretched his legs out. "We should sleep while we can, even if it's just for a little while."

Ryan settled on a flat stone and leaned back into a rocky nook. Exhausted and wrapped in his thick blanket, he allowed his heavy eyelids to close.

Ryan was wrenched from his slumber. He shed his blanket and freed his sword from its scabbard. A piercing screech lingered, much too close for comfort. As the cry died away, he tried to get a sense of its direction. The horrible shriek echoed off ridges and about the valleys, giving him no definite answer. Thadius was a shadow against the rocks.

"What in the name of the gods was that?" Ryan ventured.

"I've never heard such a cry," Thadius confessed. "I don't want to meet up with whatever produced it."

Both remained motionless in the silence that followed.

"Maybe it eats goblins," Ryan whispered.

Though they did not hear the eerie cry again, neither slept more than a wink. The dawn was long in coming, and with it returned Thadius' foul mood. Thadius did not say a word, yet Ryan could read his face. His stern expression told of another lecture brewing.

If it were possible, Ryan's legs were worse off than the day before. He moved stiffly, his limbs experiencing a new level of sore. He secured his pack and removed all evidence of their passing while he waited for Thadius to speak.

"Truly, this is an impossible situation," Thadius threw up his hands. "I can't pursue the gemstone with you along."

Ryan wanted to protest but also wrestled with the guilt of being more of a burden than a help. He decided to hear him out. Thadius continued as they resumed their trek.

"Frankly, it'll take a lot of skill, and some luck, if I'm to locate and somehow steal the gem away from this goblin band. I can't do this effectively and protect you as well."

Ryan realized the circumstances called for more than merely growing up. To accompany Thadius, he needed the skills of a trained fighter and woodsman. Anything less would put them both in greater danger than they already faced. He resolved to abide by his friend's decision.

"On the other hand, I can't waste the days it will take to get you to relatively safe territory. Apparently, you can't return to the Huntsman's outpost, and I certainly can't let you strike out on your own."

Each walked in silence and Ryan knew he wrestled with a difficult decision. There was only the wait before the other shoe dropped. Ahead, the ridge line dipped into an uneven slope. Ryan spotted an unusual mound of stones, devoid of any snowy covering.

"It's a cairn, isn't it?"

Curious, Thadius led them closer. The cairn was hastily constructed and incomplete. Bits of fur and skin showed in places.

"Whoever they are, someone has gone to the trouble of concealing them up here. It's pure chance we happened by." Thadius knelt and shifted a few of the stones. "As I suspected — a goblin."

"I need to see its face."

Thadius brushed away the loose dirt from the creature's face. The corpse of a crooked-nosed goblin stared up at them. They held their breath and replaced the stones.

"This is one of the goblins that were at the bandits' camp," Ryan declared after the grisly work was done. "But how did it end up in this isolated place? And where is the one I wounded? Could they be the reason there are so many goblins afoot?"

"Perhaps," Thadius shrugged. "This pair was definitely not heading to Torr's camp."

"They did avoid the western trail," Ryan agreed. "Torr has no clue which direction to look, but we aren't far behind, are we?"

"No, we aren't. And this goblin hasn't been dead long. Let's catch the other one before its friends do."

Ryan and Thadius followed the ridgeline as it narrowed and wound about, eventually intersecting with the inclining slope of the northern trail. Thadius pointed to the occasional print of a single goblin, telling them they were on the right track. The trail might have once been a proper road, Ryan mused. Time and the elements had all but erased any evidence of its existence. Nevertheless, the goblin kept to its faint lines and into the ever-rising hills.

A mile further along, the trail ended at the sheer stone base of a ridge higher than the last. A symmetrical crevice granted passage, arching at the top as if carved by hand instead of by wind and rain. Beyond the opening, a steep and uneven path led upward, nestled between rock walls. At the foot of the path stood a strange sight.

Canine skulls sat above crossed rib bones, affixed one atop another to a sturdy wooden post. The sun bleached bones were likely wolf and black feathers adorned the remains, creating macabre headdresses.

"Goblins erected this as a warning to other goblins," Thadius stated. "Danger lies ahead. The more skulls, the greater the threat."

"How do you know?"

"It's part of the Huntsman lore."

Ryan counted five skulls. "Have you ever seen one of these?"

"Yes, near the Tangled Wood."

Ryan knew little of the Tangled Wood. Thick with twisted trees and fetid bogs, the area lay in the shadow of the Superstition Mountains. Tales told of evil creatures and hidden dangers. It was a place no man should venture alone.

"How many skulls did that one have?"

"Three," he answered. "Just three."

The ascent through the passage grew difficult, with loose stones and larger boulders slowing their pace. They crested a sharp rise to find themselves at the edge of an expansive plateau, covered with a thin blanket of snow. A cold wind buffeted them, biting Ryan's face. On the horizon ahead, high walls and stone towers spread across the landscape.

"Am I seeing things?" Ryan shook his head. "Could that be . . . a city?"

"It *is* a city," Thadius confirmed. "Look at those fortifications."

"Surely not a goblin city. It's huge!"

Thadius motioned to the footprints in the snow. "Whoever or whatever built it, that is our goblin's destination."

# ❧ Chapter 14 ❧

Distant ramparts, dotted with immense square towers, stretched across a dreary horizon of gray clouds. Disregarding the ache in his legs, Ryan matched Thadius' strides, feeling vulnerable on the open plain and unnerved by the cryptic warning the goblins had erected.

"It certainly appears formidable," Thadius observed as they neared the stone walls. Great blocks in a multitude of earthen hues rose to a height almost twice that of Drynas.

"I see no sentries, or anyone else." Ryan kept a wary eye on the ancient battlements. "Abandoned?"

"Perhaps, and probably not built by goblins, either. They aren't known for their architectural achievements."

"There's a breach in the base of the wall," Ryan pointed out, "but I don't see a proper gate."

"The outline is faint," Thadius was the first to pick up the slight discoloration in the surrounding stonework. "The city gates were walled in for some reason."

Then Ryan saw it as well. The newer construction consisted of blocks of a slightly different size and had sealed an entrance wide enough for double gates.

"Maybe there was a siege?" Ryan theorized. "Someone eventually got in. There's a lot of stone scattered about."

"Mostly outside of the wall. Probably nothing more than a collapse."

As they drew closer, it became plain to see that not all of the stones lying about were the same. "Thadius, some of those aren't pieces of the wall."

What they first thought to be part of the debris, were life-sized figures carved of an alabaster stone. The mysterious effigies numbered in the dozens, all curiously posed, as if each had broken free of the city. However, a closer inspection revealed frightening features. The beings depicted were not human.

While many of these had lost varying degrees of detail to the years and the elements, others reminded Ryan of ghouls from the old tales, with their twisted faces and bared teeth. Some reached out with long claws, perhaps for a victim, he imagined with a shudder.

"What are these? More goblin warnings?" Ryan speculated.

Thadius eyed the darkened arrow slits of the high towers to either side of them. "They're a curiosity," he agreed, "like this city."

Beyond the breach in the newer section of wall, buildings of diverse shapes and sizes spread out as far as the eye could see. Snow accumulated in the sheltered spaces and the wind wailed hauntingly as it blew through empty windows and door frames. Numerous roofs had collapsed and the buildup of sediment within the shells of empty buildings ranged from ankle to knee level in depth.

Tracking the goblin was no difficult feat. It had followed neatly laid out streets deeper into the city, leaving traces whenever it passed over stretches of softer soil or disturbed the drifts of snow between buildings. Ryan found their situation unsettling — a seemingly deserted metropolis was the last thing he would have guessed they might come upon in the Lost Hills. He half-expected goblins to leap out at every turn. Thadius bent to examine a piece of discarded cloth. The strip was stained with black blood.

"It recently changed bandages or might have lost this wrap in its haste. Be on guard. Though I've seen no evidence of other goblins, I've no doubt this one knows exactly where it's going."

"Do you think it's hiding from Torr in here?"

"Not likely. Its path is purposeful, no wandering about."

"How close do you think we are?" Ryan's excitement grew. The Stone of Orinn could be within their grasp.

"Not far at all."

With his bow at the ready, Thadius led the way up an avenue and into a district of what Ryan guessed could have been more upscale shops, smithies and other businesses. Built of finer stone, those he could glimpse into were gutted, with little woodwork visible. Although weathered, most buildings were in remarkable condition despite the passage of unknown years. Ryan was amazed to see so many intact. Then he noticed something familiar.

"Do you see those roofs?" As they topped the rise of a hill, Ryan pointed to some of the structures about them, all with the same type of conical roof as the goblin shrine.

"I see. That goblin shrine may not be so very goblin after all."

The trail led them from orderly avenues onto an overgrown street. They wove between thick shrubs and trees stripped of their leaves by the winter. The footprints continued and Thadius halted them at the next street.

"What is it?" Ryan asked.

Thadius knelt beside a track left in the frozen mud on the leeward side of a tall building. The print was human shaped but with the impressions of clawed toes.

"Not completely deserted . . ." he said in a low tone.

Ryan peered over his shoulder. "Whatever has claws like that can't be friendly. At least it isn't heading in our goblin's direction."

"The print is old," Thadius stated. "No telling what or where the thing is now — or if it's alone."

With no time to ponder the odd print, Thadius resumed the chase. The goblin's path wound higher into the heart of the city, ending at the broad steps of a three-story building. What had once been a regal entry of double doors flanked by fluted columns was now an ingress partially obstructed by tangled shrubbery and littered with dead leaves. Above them, lichen-covered bricks held carved characters. Ryan could see they were divided into words but was at a loss as to their meaning.

Thadius motioned for Ryan to take a position behind one of the pillars. "Stay here. I'll scout the perimeter to make sure our goblin hasn't gone out a back door."

Ryan unshouldered his bow and nocked an arrow. He kept watch as Thadius disappeared around the corner. It was a moment before he reappeared on the opposite side.

"There are two other doorways," he reported. "Both are barricaded with stone blocks and earth."

"The goblin has reached its destination," Ryan concluded.

"Yes, and I have a feeling it's not alone."

With Thadius in the lead, they approached the entrance. Ryan was relieved to be included and not sent to hide away somewhere. He kept his eyes peeled for trouble as they entered a leaf-strewn atrium illuminated by a row of high windows. A semi-circular balcony overlooked the space. Before them was a crudely fashioned but stout door, clearly a recent addition. Ryan and Thadius quietly stepped toward it.

A single word echoed loudly about the atrium. A hooded figure emerged from a shadowy alcove above, a twisted wand outstretched and pointed at them. Ryan could not move. He strained to raise his bow but could not budge an inch. Beside him, Thadius let out a growl of frustration. He was in the same predicament.

The hooded stranger spoke another foreign word, punctuated by a gesture of the wand. Ryan and Thadius were thrown backwards by an unseen force. Their arrows launched harmlessly away as they struck the cold, hard floor. Both struggled in vain to rise.

"We can't have you running about brandishing weapons, can we?" the man's gruff voice rang out. "Let's come to a more comfortable arrangement. Then we can speak together like civilized men."

"A sorcerer for sure," Ryan whispered. He was as powerless as when Gadrin had held him by magic on that fateful night outside of Othgard. However, this spell felt much stronger.

"Garr!" the dark-robed man called out. "Come along and properly prepare our guests."

As the man withdrew from sight, the door opened with a loud creak. Before them stood the goblin they had so doggedly pursued. Battered, bandaged and bleeding, it limped toward them bearing coils of rope in its filthy hands. With the mage out of sight and the goblin closing, Ryan struggled anew. He reasoned that because the sorcerer no longer fully concentrated on the spell, and he might somehow escape. Yet, he was still held by powerful magic and could not move by his own will.

The goblin disarmed them and bound their wrists while Ryan issued a variety of curses upon it. Thadius was unusually subdued. Before Ryan could ask him what they should do next, the robed man strode through the door and surveyed the goblin's work.

"Come, Garr, let's retreat to warmer quarters."

With a word of magic, Ryan and Thadius were free of the spell and rose awkwardly, their wrists tied behind them. Meanwhile, the goblin collected their bows, quivers and sword belts.

"Keep in mind what I can do to trespassers," the hooded man warned.

With the goblin in the lead, they were marched into an airy chamber. Their captor closed and barred the door behind them before prodding them across the dimly illuminated room. Ryan's eyes adjusted to the low light, to see plaster peeling from the walls and crumbled stacks of insect-eaten boards lying about.

They were directed up a set of stairs, onto a second floor that was divided into several large rooms. These contained the remnants of shelves, cases and other leisure furnishings. As they passed through each room, their captor dropped a heavy bar to secure the door.

The hooded man ushered them up a spiral staircase. At the top of the stairs was a chamber where a fire burned brightly and oil lamps provided a bright glow. A crowded table and a pair of chairs sat near a wall, where hung an inexpensive tapestry. Ryan had seen its simple design in the markets of Drynas. Before he could give it another thought, he was shoved into a corner along with Thadius. The goblin piled their weapons in the opposite corner and seated itself. Fatigued and feverish, it maintained an eye on the captives and a hand on its dagger.

"My good wizard," Thadius broke his silence, "we certainly intended no trespass."

Ryan noted how he addressed the sorcerer using a title meant for those who practiced magic for the benefit of others and for self defense. He had no doubt as to what side this spellcaster really placed himself on. Surely no wizard would have dealings with goblins.

Thadius continued, "We're bounty hunters by trade and have tracked this creature on the authority of the Magistrate of Drynas."

The sorcerer eyed them. "Bounty hunters, you say?" He brushed back the loose hood and Ryan guessed his age at about fifty, judging by the lines on his face and the color of his uncombed hair. "Not many make it out here, this far from civilized lands."

"I'm afraid we got lost, and frankly, I've no idea where we are," Thadius bluffed. "It would be most kind of you to tell us the way back to Galanthor. It's obvious this goblin serves you, and is therefore not the criminal we seek."

"You've come this far only to give up your bounty?" the mage inquired with a hint of sarcasm.

Ryan sought to help their situation. "Sir, we're honestly not sure how far we've come. Tell us, do you live in these wild lands?"

"Live here? Not exactly. But it has been . . . at least a year," he recalled, rubbing his gray-stubbled chin.

"Have you not heard?" Thadius feigned concern. "There's a new earl in Galanthor. He's set a bounty on any goblin found within his borders."

"I'm already aware of this Malikar. In fact, I'm sure I'm up on the latest gossip. You see, I pop out of here for supplies now and again." He picked up an apple from a basket on the table and tossed it to the goblin.

"What is it you do here?" Ryan asked as innocently as he could muster.

"You must be an apprentice. I once had one, years ago," the robed man sighed. "These days, research and study are my focus."

"And we're keeping you from your books and scrolls," Thadius apologized. "We dare not trouble you any further. If you could have your goblin friend lead us out of this forsaken city, we'll disturb you no more."

"Friend?" The sorcerer snickered and cast a glance at Garr. The road-weary goblin devoured the apple, core and all.

"How long has it been in your service?" Although Ryan was a bit curious, he was not at all comfortable speaking with a sorcerer — especially one who had captured and bound them, and seemed in no hurry to release them.

"Old Garr here has been in my employ almost since my arrival," the mage explained. "He was an outcast, living in the hills near here. Quite brave to do so, being their people shun this place. After a rocky start, we came to a comfortable enough arrangement. I've learned a fair bit of their tongue, as he has ours. Yes, Garr has become invaluable in dealing with that self-styled chieftain."

"Do you mean Torr?" Thadius ventured.

"The same. So, you do know something of these lands."

"I've heard that name mentioned here and there. I've also heard Torr's goblins have fanned out all over these hills. Looking for what, I don't have a clue."

"Yes, everybody's out searching these days," the mage mumbled.

"Sir, what may we call you?" Ryan sought to uncover more about him.

"My name is Askelon, young man."

"Garr is gravely wounded. We can lend some aid. Our packs downstairs contain healing herbs and fresh dressings," Ryan proposed. Perhaps it could be their opportunity to overpower the sorcerer, or at least make an escape.

"His purpose has been fulfilled," Askelon replied darkly.

"A sad ending for one who has served so loyally," Thadius returned.

"Loyalty?" Askelon cackled. "Not loyalty, bounty hunter. The goblin obeys me because of magic."

"You've ensorcelled it," Ryan broke in.

"It was rather easy," Askelon boasted. He motioned the goblin forward and produced the twisted wand from his sleeve before Ryan could blink.

"Now, shall we see what you two are really about?"

# ✂Chapter 15✍

With the reappearance of the wand, Ryan feared that the false pleasantries had reached an end. What he at first had taken to be twists in the hazel wood, was a dragon carved to wrap itself around the length of wood. The wand ended with the beast's head and set within its mouth sparkled a sky blue gem.

"We'll share our part in this drama, if you'll share yours in return," Thadius suggested, changing tactics.

Askelon considered the proposal for a moment and nodded. "Why not, bounty hunter? Though, I think you're no great puzzle to work out."

"Maybe," Thadius countered. "I'll begin by asking if it was you who used magic to escape from the bandits' camp."

Askelon shrugged. "Granted, it was I. My business with those gentlemen was rudely interrupted. Did you have something to do with that?"

"One of us did. Torr's men sought weapons. What brought you to such a meeting?"

"An intelligent question for sure. I came to collect something," Askelon grinned. "There may indeed be a bit of a mystery to you, but I will root it all out in the end."

Ryan did not like the sound of that. What good was all this information if they were not around to use it?

"Why pursue these particular goblins? What was so interesting about them?" It was Askelon's turn.

"In all the confusion, the goblins collected something too. The curious thing is that instead of returning to their camp, they set out for an abandoned city. How did you convince them to come here?"

"I convinced both with magic. I couldn't wait around to be captured with those rogues. I'm too old to see the inside of the dungeons. A spell cast over both goblins bound them to bring me what I desired."

"But why did Garr kill the other goblin?" Ryan asked out of turn.

"They met up with another of their band while still in the Darkwood. Poor Garr was wounded and forced to rest often. Somehow, the other goblin discovered that they had no intention of returning to camp. It ran straight to notify Torr."

"So Torr sent out search parties," Ryan concluded.

"Garr and his companion avoided them by taking a roundabout route. In the end, only Garr survived. He's safe now. Torr won't expect to find him here, in Hazen," the sorcerer seemed confident.

"They won't look for him here?" Ryan wanted to do his part to gather information.

"There's a legend among the Red Moon Clan that tells of a horrible event. Whatever occurred, it left the city abandoned . . . for the most part. It was all ages ago, but that's another tale."

"Garr slew the other spellbound goblin," Thadius stated. "The task you assigned it must be very important. To avoid its fellow goblins and come here, to a place of such danger . . ."

"While powerful, that particular enchantment does have its duration. The spell wore off on the one first, and it had the notion to take matters into its own hands. Garr did not let that happen, as you've apparently determined.

He stumbled into the city scarcely ahead of you. And I have pieced together enough of this story to tell me you are no ordinary bounty hunter." Askelon waved the wand menacingly. "Perhaps you seek more than goblins?"

Thadius met his gaze. "Have I found more than goblins?"

With a thrust of the twisted wand and a word of magic, Thadius was hurled into the wall behind them. He slid to the floor and Askelon issued orders in the goblin tongue. Garr grabbed hold of Ryan and shoved him into the next chamber. The goblin bound him to a large chair and tied his hands behind him.

Surely Thadius was waiting for the right moment to spring his own trap, Ryan hoped. He worked subtly on the rope around his wrists as the goblin stood guard at the door. Garr's wound seeped black ooze and the creature was drenched in perspiration.

One small lamp lit the chamber, casting a dim glow on the sorcerer's bed and a low table, piled with tablets of stone and various other odds and ends. Were these artifacts scavenged from the city? A pair of squat trunks sat in a corner, and a shelf near the bed held half a dozen rings of differing designs. Some held precious stones that winked with reflected light. It was not long before the door was thrown open again.

"I can tell your friend will be a stubborn one," Askelon said impatiently. With a motion, he dismissed Garr and retrieved a leather-bound book from atop the table. "I'll warm up with you."

Ryan glared at Askelon in defiance. "What have you done with Thadius?"

"Don't be afraid, boy," Askelon soothed. "We're simply going to have a chat."

"I've nothing to say to the likes of you."

Askelon smiled. "I beg to differ. In fact, I think you'll have much to say. The spell I will cast compels you to speak the truth, for a short time anyway." He flipped through several pages before he found what he searched for. "Shall we begin?"

Askelon read aloud from the book of worn and dog-eared pages. Words of magic and power flowed. Then with a slam, the book was closed.

Ryan's head reeled. He had to resist and lend this foul sorcerer no aid. But try as he might, he could not focus. His mind wandered aimlessly. He was lost. Ryan turned at the sound of Askelon's voice. When he met the sorcerer's gray eyes, the questions began.

"Who are you, boy?"

"I am Ryan of Llerwyth," he answered without pause.

"Why have you come here?"

"We seek the Stone of Orinn."

Askelon nodded. "Of course you do. Who is your companion?"

"Thadius of Corin."

Askelon shrugged. "Your names mean nothing to me. Nevertheless, the fact that you're on the trail of the gemstone is cause for concern. What do you want with the stone?"

Ryan felt as if he saw the first glimmer of light after a long and grueling night. He had a direction to go, a path to follow back to himself and to control. Still, he responded to the question truthfully.

"We will return the Stone of Orinn to the temple and prevent a war with Ilsgaard."

Askelon's bushy eyebrows shot up. "What do you know of the Stone of Orinn? From the beginning now, all of it!"

"Karsten had the gem . . . when we freed him from Hathren." Ryan hesitated, his first real effort to regain his own will. "I never actually got to see it then, and didn't know it for what it was. The first time I saw it, was that morning at the bandits' camp. The stone was in the goblin's hand."

"So, you were part of those mercenaries we hired to steal it from the temple?"

"No, no," Ryan struggled to slip from the spell's fading grip.

"If not, then what brought you into their company?"

"Gad-Gadrin's death."

"Gadrin?" Askelon was visibly taken back. "That old fool! What do you know of his death, boy?" the sorcerer demanded with the shake of a crooked finger.

The veil of confusion was lifted. Ryan shook his head to clear away the spell. Once again in control of his senses, he recalled all he revealed.

Askelon grabbed him by the shoulders and shook him. "Tell me!"

Thinking clearly again, Ryan turned the tables. "I'll tell you that he received his just due!"

Askelon stared. Slowly, the sorcerer stood and regained his composure. "I expected the spell to last a bit longer," he mumbled more to himself than to Ryan, "but it tends to wear off quickly on the pig-headed. The others must know of this immediately. We will continue this later." Askelon stormed from the room.

Ryan expected the goblin to return any minute. Taking advantage of what might be his only opportunity for escape, he cast about for something sharp to free his wrists. Amidst the items stacked on the table, he spied a small knife, and rocked the chair forward until he had the leverage to stand. Ryan shuffled the few feet he needed. He scooted the back of the chair against the table and felt for the knife behind him. The tips of his fingers found the handle and he inched it closer until he could get a firm grip.

Setting the sharp blade against the ropes at his wrist, Ryan set to work. His hands were soon free and he wriggled out of the remaining coils. He cast about for a better weapon than the undersized piece of cutlery. The paring knife was all there was to be seen. Though not meant for combat, it would have to do. He pressed an ear to the door but heard nothing. Ryan grasped the iron handle and gently opened the heavy door. To his relief it made little noise and he thanked the gods that Askelon oiled the hinges.

Ryan was surprised to see Thadius already free of his bonds, and quietly joined him beside the tapestry. There was no sign of Garr.

"I managed to keep one eye on Askelon," Thadius whispered. "He slipped through a concealed door."

"How—"

"Later."

Thadius pulled aside the wall hanging and motioned to the outline of a hidden door. Askelon's voice reached them from within, and he eased the door inward. All they could see from their vantage point was a portion of a furnished chamber. Thadius dared not push on the door any further, lest it announce their presence with a creak. Shadows danced across the wall in their view and Ryan could make out the silhouette of the sorcerer.

". . . I tell you, they played a role in Gadrin's death," Askelon spoke with an urgent tone. "I believe they know of both the citadel and the gemstones."

Thadius placed a hand on Ryan's shoulder and with a nod, told him they would stay and hear more.

"We need time to investigate this further. Are both secure?" came another voice. At first, Ryan thought someone else was in the room. Yet the voice sounded somehow distant. He realized Askelon communicated through a spell.

"Both are tightly bound and guarded."

"We expect you with the Stone of Orinn shortly. As for the flies in your web, question them further. I agree, we must learn more, even if it means destroying their minds. When they're no longer of use, dispose of them."

"It will be done," Askelon promised.

Carefully, Thadius edged the door closed. As Ryan turned to retrieve their weapons, the goblin sprang. With a hoarse cry, the creature flung itself from atop the table and onto Thadius, slamming him against the wall. Ryan grabbed the goblin and yanked it off his friend. But the tables were turned as it latched onto Ryan's arm and flipped him over its hip. Briefly vulnerable, the goblin had no chance when Thadius struck. His kick sent the goblin sprawling and its head struck the stone floor. Garr lay there, unmoving.

"Our swords!" Thadius gestured.

The hidden door swung open. Askelon burst into the room, wand at the ready. As Ryan dove for their weapons, the sorcerer began the word of command. Thadius was already in motion. At the first glimpse of the wand he flung a slender throwing knife.

With a yelp of pain, Askelon grasped his hand and cradled it to his chest. The clatter of the ornate wand striking the stony floor echoed about the room, overpowering all other noise. While Ryan snatched up their swords, Thadius launched himself at the sorcerer. Askelon moved surprisingly fast, and it was the wide table full of clutter between them that allowed him to cover the short distance needed. The sorcerer reached the room where Ryan had been taken earlier, with barely a second to spare. The door slammed and the latch dropped.

Thadius put his shoulder into what he assumed was ancient wood, only to discover that the wood was not so aged. Ryan joined him on the next attempt and the door gave in as a peal of thunder boomed. Both stumbled into the chamber, where dust and mortar fell from the ceiling. Ears ringing, they cast about the empty room. Askelon had escaped.

*       *       *

For the better part of two days, Wrella tracked the goblin patrol from the ancient shrine, westward through the Lost Hills. Her quarry was easy to follow. They made no effort to hide their passage and traveled with haste. She was thankful to be on a horse, as she never could have paced the goblins on foot. Then came the worst kind of luck.

Her horse stumbled as she guided him up the rocky slope of a steep hill. A misplaced hoof slid on an icy slab of stone and the animal reared, making his predicament worse. Though far from an expert in the saddle, Wrella was an accomplished enough rider to know she could not save the horse from going down. Judging from the terrain and slope of the hill, the fall could kill her. She slid from the saddle to land feet first amid the loose stones and weathered rock. As she had feared, her mount tumbled, legs kicking wildly in an attempt to gain purchase among the sharp rocks. But it was to no avail. The steed toppled and rolled, all the way to the base of the hill.

She did not need to examine the animal to discern he was mortally wounded. Wrella descended to where he lay. His labored breath issued misty clouds into the cold air and it was plain to see at least one leg was broken. With a sinking feeling, she realized that she was now on foot and deep within goblin territory.

However, her practical side took charge and would not allow her to wallow in defeat. She drew her sword and put an end to the animal's misery. Wrella methodically stripped any gear and supplies she could carry and climbed back up the hill.

The goblins' trail continued, with the discarded bones of a meal lying amid long footprints. As the day wore on, she gained ground on the patrol. Their exact number she could not accurately gauge, as they often tread in each other's footsteps. Then atop a grassy rise, she spotted the band.

Wrella ducked into the tall grass and inched her head up. There was more than a score of goblins at rest and each bore sword and spear. She followed them over the next set of ridges, where wisps of smoke could be seen.

"Fires," she whispered to herself. "Campfires . . . and a lot of them. I've come to the right place."

Wrella spent the remainder of the day seeking a suitable place to hide. She needed to scout the goblin's outer defenses and determine if the gemstone was even among them. She did not look forward to hours of creeping about. Still, this was all very promising. Surely such an extensive camp was the base of these outcasts.

By morning, she had worked her way closer and was astonished to find the goblin camp was more like a village. Hundreds of goblins went about their lives, much as any other race of beings did, she supposed. While squad-sized elements patrolled the surrounding ridges, larger troops of heavily armed warriors departed whenever another arrived. Could these be search parties? Perhaps these exiles were not in possession of the gemstone after all.

Later in the day, she hid near a worn path in the surrounding hills as she considered her next move. The sound of footfalls tore her from her deliberations and she peered from her position to see a lone goblin running toward the village. As it approached, Wrella sprang from behind the cluster of boulders. She slammed into the goblin, tackling it to the ground. Her dagger was soon pressed against its throat.

Wrella wasted no time. She thrust a piece of parchment before the bewildered creature. Despite its fright, the goblin did not take its black eyes from the colored sketch.

"You recognize this, don't you," Wrella coaxed. She was not sure what response she expected to get, yet its expression told her all she needed to know. It marveled at her artwork as though it were the Stone of Orinn itself.

"Where is it?" She pointed in the direction of the village and nudged the dagger as if it could make the goblin understand better.

The goblin raised a nervous hand to the east and motioned.

"The gemstone is on the way," she guessed. "Well, it won't be staying long. Now, what to do about you?"

# ❧ *Chapter 16* ☙

"He's fled," Ryan groaned, "and probably with the gem!"

"We'll look for it anyway, in case he didn't have it on him," Thadius said optimistically. "He did leave in a hurry."

A faint metallic ringing lingered and a flash in the lamplight caught Ryan's eye. He rushed to investigate, hopeful for a second it was the gemstone. The small item turned out to be one of the rings that had sat on the shelf above the chests. Apparently, Askelon had snatched them up in haste and dropped this one as he whisked himself away.

Ryan pocketed the ring and threw open one of the chests on impulse. Inside, he found stacks of neatly folded clothes. Tossing them onto the floor revealed nothing more. "I guess you cut yourself free. I forgot about the throwing knife in your boot."

"I moved it from my boot to my sleeve before Garr tied my legs. Luckily, the goblin didn't check me very well."

As Thadius searched the rest of the room, Ryan opened the second chest. Within, lay carvings and trinkets fashioned of semi-precious stone. He sifted through these to make an unexpected discovery. A pile of shiny metal links filled the bottom of the square chest. Ryan lifted a mail shirt of intricately fashioned links.

"Looks cumbersome," Thadius commented.

"It hardly weighs a thing." Ryan held it up for him to examine.

Thadius bent closer. "If this is some kind of relic from bygone days, it should have rusted away long ago."

"Askelon kept it here, with these other items that are surely from the city."

"Good point. There may be some kind of magic at work here. Definitely take it." Thadius headed for the door. Ryan hoisted the armor over his shoulder, and they returned to the main chamber.

Both were surprised to find the goblin was gone.

"That goblin must be part magician, the way it keeps disappearing. I should have tied it up," Ryan chastised himself.

"There wasn't a chance. Grab whatever might be useful," Thadius requested. "I'll search the secret chamber."

Ryan grabbed a shoulder pack and stuffed it with what rations were on hand. This included apples, a loaf of bread, a round of cheese and a bulky pouch of dried beef. He scooped up Askelon's dropped wand and an additional water skin, before joining Thadius in the secret room. He found the woodsman carefully rolling up a large map. This he slid into a cylindrical case, along with several loose sheets of parchment. On a table sat a clay bowl, filled with murky water, and adorned with archaic symbols.

"A scrying bowl," Thadius said. "He saw us coming. And it may have been how he communicated with his unknown ally."

"Using water in his spell, like Trenn uses fire?"

Thadius threw the bowl, water and all, into the fireplace. "From what I've learned, some mages communicate through flame, others prefer water."

"No gemstone? How in the world are we going to find it now?"

Thadius tossed him an empty pouch, crudely sewn and smelling of unwashed goblin. "This was on the floor and I'm reasonably sure it doesn't belong to Askelon."

"So, Garr wasn't out cold after all. Could it have stolen the gem back?"

Thadius grinned. "At least the sorcerer didn't escape with it."

As they turned to leave, Thadius halted. A single rune was painted on the wall opposite the fireplace. "I wish I'd seen this earlier," he grunted. "We've got to hurry." The two collected their weapons on the way out of Askelon's chambers and raced for the rest of their gear downstairs.

"That rune was bad, wasn't it?" Ryan asked.

"Remember the sigil Trenn created beneath the citadel?" Thadius reminded him.

"Yes. The rune enables him to open a kind of gateway through the netherways."

"Let's get our gear and be swift about it. Askelon will be back, and with more help than we can handle."

Once outside, Ryan blinked and shielded his eyes. As he became accustomed to the light, he saw a line of staggered footprints in the dusting of snow, trailing off to the north.

"It won't get far," he reasoned. "The creature's half-dead as it is."

"Wounded and feverish, perhaps only Askelon's spell gave it the will to make it this far," Thadius speculated.

Garr's tracks led them down buried streets and past stately buildings, with tall columns wrapped with dormant ivy. Characters chiseled upon many of the structures seemed familiar to Ryan.

"I've seen some of these letters before," he realized.

"On coins," Thadius declared. "Coins from Arakronis' treasure trove. It's the Old Tongue."

"Can you make sense of any of it?"

By the end of the block, Thadius had an answer. "We're in the city of Hazen, as Askelon said."

"I've never heard of it," Ryan admitted. "You?"

"I remember some lore about an ancient city-state in the far north, sometime in the distant past."

"I wish you'd paid more attention in class. Especially when it came to this Old Tongue."

Thadius growled in response.

"Why would the Huntsmen be concerned with an outdated language anyway?" Ryan continued.

"It's spoken in the isolated villages of Avan-Rhun, and every once in a while, the odd relic is uncovered, or some remnant of the past surfaces. Such as today."

"I see." Ryan shifted the chainmail shirt from one shoulder to the other. Though very light for metal armor, there was still some weight to it. Slung over his shoulder, along with a backpack, water skins, weapons, and his bow, it had become uncomfortable to carry. Thadius noticed his growing discomfort.

"Perhaps we should leave it — at least until we've recovered the stone," he added hastily. "I know you're eager to try it on, but we don't have time."

It was the truth. Ryan could tell the mail was a bit oversized for him, even with the leather cuirass underneath. It would take some effort to cinch down the armor for a snug enough fit. Besides, they had come too far to lose the goblin now.

Ryan stopped at a building that may have once been a grand inn and ducked into the doorway. After a brief look around, he settled on a spot and used flat stones to conceal the suit of armor.

"We'll return for it," Thadius promised.

They picked up the pace and turned onto a broad avenue. The north gate came into sight, framed by high watchtowers. These gates had been sealed off as well. However, the tower to the right had partially collapsed into the more recent stonework, creating a gaping opening in the shape of a jagged arch. Garr rested on a fallen pile of blocks ahead. The goblin limped away at the sight of them.

"We have it now!" Ryan exclaimed.

They were shocked to see a band of goblins come into view, just beyond the breach. The warriors sighted Garr, and though they immediately drew weapons upon seeing Ryan and Thadius, none advanced toward the opening in the city gates. Garr was an equal distance between the two but drew closer to its fellow goblins with each step. And more goblins gathered.

"Will they enter the city?" Ryan's heart quickened. The band was at least thirty strong.

Thadius drew an arrow and fired. His shot struck Garr behind the right knee and brought the creature down in a tumbling heap. Both sprinted for the fallen goblin.

A warrior much larger than the rest, wearing armor of overlapping metal bands, pointed a long scimitar at Garr. The big goblin barked orders as it shoved and kicked the others forward. Archers reached for arrows. Overwhelmingly outnumbered, Thadius directed Ryan to the nearest cover.

"Into the tower!"

Barbed arrows chipped at the stone about them as they dove into the entryway of the tower to the left. Thadius led them up a spiral flight of steps to the second level. With the floors rotted out, the stone steps and walkways between were the only structure left within the tower. They skidded to a halt and trained arrows on the entryway below. Seconds later, goblins rushed in, swords waving.

"Steady, Ryan." Thadius let fly and his arrow found one. Ryan's hand trembled and he missed his mark. Before he could draw another arrow, Thadius fired again. The shaft sunk deep into another goblin as it ran for the stairs. It tumbled to the ground and Ryan's next arrow wounded the goblin behind it.

"Keep them bottled up!" Thadius' arm moved with a smooth rhythm Ryan could not match. The woodsman sent arrow after arrow into the doorway, his aim at this distance flawless. Goblin wounded scrambled to retreat over the dead or dying.

The sharp note of a horn sounded and the goblins broke off their assault. Thadius kept his bow taut. "See what's going on. I'll cover the entry."

Ryan circled upward to an arrow slit. The goblins gathered around what had to be their leader. The big goblin stood over Garr's still form and raised its curved blade high. In the other clawed hand, it held aloft the Stone of Orinn. Cheers erupted.

"It has the gemstone!" Ryan cried in disbelief. In haste, he aimed an arrow and released. The shot went wide but drew the goblin's attention. With a howl and a wave of the curved sword, the goblin leader directed a renewed assault on the tower.

Ryan ran up the steps, praying that Thadius would not run out of arrows. If he could gain the ramparts, he would have a better shot as their attackers crowded about the base of the tower. The stone steps wound twice more before he reached an open hatchway to the roof.

Ryan emerged into the overcast afternoon, high atop the tower. He dashed across a roof littered with loose stones and gazed down from above the entry. Mortar crumbled and a block shifted under his weight. Setting his bow aside, he pushed on the parapet wall with all his strength. He hoped to dislodge a few blocks with his effort, and was surprised when an entire section toppled and fell onto the goblins below.

He retrieved his bow and ventured a look to see goblins sprawled out amidst scattered stone and mortar. The survivors retreated beyond the breach in the city wall and seemed to be reconsidering their plan of attack. Ryan noticed how small their number was. Then he spied the rest of the band. Half of the goblins had sped off to the west, following their leader. Thadius joined him on the ramparts.

"These warriors were left to finish us off, or at least keep us busy. They'll wait until night before the next attack, when their eyesight is best," he announced solemnly.

"We'll get a little rest at least." Ryan tried to smile.

"That was good, the avalanche."

"Thanks. I was trying to make up for my marksmanship."

"You did fine. We did what we had to do. We'll do it again and we'll get out of here."

"But the stone . . ."

"It's a setback, that's for sure," Thadius shrugged.

"Do you think their leader was Torr?"

"Possibly . . ."

Their attention was diverted from the distant goblins to the grassy plain beyond the city. Mounted figures streaked their way. A dozen in all, they rode steeds Ryan could not quite make out. They were definitely not goblins. In fact, the remaining goblins drew together and held a hasty council, their siege of the tower momentarily forgotten.

"Quickly, we'll cut off their retreat," Thadius slapped him on the shoulder. "The right actions might gain us an ally."

Ryan and Thadius sped down the tower steps. The two emerged to fire on the nearest goblins. Faced with enemies to the front and rear, the goblins scattered. Once beyond the breach, Ryan got his first good look at those who rode against the goblins.

Centaurs!

Ryan could scarcely believe his eyes as the beings of myth and legend swept across the plain. Arrows flew, and other centaurs leveled heavy spears as they rode down the fleeing goblins. Ryan called out a warning to Thadius as a goblin archer fit a black-fletched arrow to its bowstring.

Its target was a dark-coated centaur, whose spear would not reach the archer in time. Thadius aimed, drew and loosed with a fluid motion that sent an arrow deep into the goblin's rib cage. The warrior slumped and the barbed arrow fell harmlessly to the ground. The centaur slowed and turned their way, coming to a halt before them. His long hair matched the color of his coat, and he stamped as he eyed Ryan and Thadius warily. He was soon joined by the other centaurs, who formed a semi-circle about them.

"Sheathe your sword," Thadius said to Ryan. He slid his bow onto his shoulder. "Make no threatening moves. I think this one is the leader."

"They haven't attacked us yet, so that's encouraging." Ryan was awed by them despite his uneasiness. True to his childhood book, *Tales of Ancient Lore*, the beings were a strange mix of man and horse.

Most stood about Thadius' height, slightly over six feet. The centaurs appeared human from the torsos up, and while the equestrian part of their anatomy was smaller and slimmer than that of a true horse, the variations in color and pattern were similar. All were male, and wore their hair long, with thick beards of varying length. Each bore either a longbow or wide-bladed spear. The centaurs wore jerkins of leather, lined with fur but seemed otherwise unbothered by the chill in the air.

The dark-coated leader addressed Thadius in a thick accent. Although Thadius attempted to communicate, it was clear to Ryan that neither fully understood each other.

"They don't speak the common tongue. Still, some of their words are familiar," Thadius explained.

"Could it be the Old Tongue?"

"I believe so, though I'm a bit out of practice. Maybe their language shares common root words. I'm sure they realize we mean them no harm, but they're definitely upset about something."

"*We* mean *them* no harm? I hope the sentiment goes both ways!"

Some of the centaurs argued with their leader, pointing to the east. Others motioned in the direction of Galanthor. The lead centaur spoke to Thadius. He was short and to the point. From his gestures, Ryan guessed he wanted to know from where they came from.

"South," Thadius indicated.

The centaur's eyes blazed and his expression hardened. Orders were given and spears leveled at them. With deliberate caution, Thadius raised his hands in surrender.

# Chapter 17

"Stay calm and do as I do," Thadius warned.

"What do they want?"

"We're being disarmed and we're to go with them, that's all I know for sure."

"That doesn't sound good."

"It'll be okay. I'm sure we can resolve the situation."

Ryan allowed a centaur to take his bow and remove his sword belt. "It seems we have no choice."

The centaurs formed a double column and kept Ryan and Thadius separated. There was little conversation as they moved out in a northeasterly direction. The centaurs kept them at a swift march and Ryan soon drained his skin of water. As twilight approached, they reached the edge of the vast plateau. At last, Ryan and Thadius were permitted a rest. The centaur leader trotted on alone as the others passed around their own water. None offered to share with the humans. Thadius sipped from his skin and handed the rest to Ryan.

Ryan was fascinated by them, regardless of their unfriendly scowls. He tried to recall all that he had read about centaurs in stories from *Tales of Ancient Lore*. He was encouraged that they had always been portrayed as good and honorable. Yet he wondered if the writers had ever really met one.

"They don't trust us," Ryan observed.

Thadius nodded. "Maybe not, but I hope to convince them to aid us."

"I think it's a long shot."

A short time later, a distant whistle alerted the troop. Once again on the move, they descended into a sheltered valley. The smell of hot food wafted on the breeze. Centaurs gathered about campfires, and lean-tos of skins supported by wooden poles ran the length of the valley floor. Many of these screens were linked together, creating multisided shelters where small groups congregated.

"There must be a hundred of them," Ryan estimated.

They were led to the opening of a spacious glade ringed with trees, where the leader of the troop that brought them conferred with an assembly of other centaurs. While they held council, Ryan and Thadius sat on a flat boulder nearby. A pair of centaurs stood close, armed with heavy spears. Another brought them a folded skin. Thadius thanked him, though the centaur did not respond.

Ryan unwrapped his skin to reveal freshly cooked fish and some type of pale tubers. He picked one up and smelled it. "It's some kind of turnip," he guessed.

"Beggars can't be choosers."

"I'm not complaining," Ryan clarified. "I'm so hungry, I'd eat my sock if it was cooked just right."

Ryan wolfed down the baked turnips and was careful to pick the bones from the fish. As he ate, he watched the centaurs settle in for the night. Some tended racks of fish that smoked over coals. Others tightened or adjusted the skins that made up the series of lean-to shelters. He noted how the centaurs situated these to block the wind, as well as help conceal the light of their fires. Another detail that did not escape him — every centaur he saw was male. There were no women or children present.

After their meal, Ryan and Thadius were summoned. Under escort, they made their way through a growing crowd of curious onlookers. Everywhere Ryan turned, stern faces stared back at him. They were clearly trespassers in centaur territory.

Ryan and Thadius entered the glade, the crowd lingering outside the ring of trees. An assembly of nine solemn centaurs stood to form a half-circle, all with gray in their hair and braided beards. Each bore only a long-bladed dagger as a weapon. Their escort bowed to the nine, then withdrew several paces. One of the centaurs strode forward. Although he wore a simple fur-lined jerkin, and armbands of the same material, Ryan had the feeling that this centaur was the equivalent of their patriarch. The centaur's brow wrinkled and his thick lips pursed as he looked them over.

"I am Oenar," the centaur spoke the Old Tongue with a deep voice.

"Thane Oenar," the eldest of the nine interjected.

"He's their chief," Thadius told Ryan.

"You are not men of Avan-Rhun." Oenar stated. The centaur's thick accent, combined with his own lack of proficiency in the ancient dialect, left Ryan at a loss.

Thadius bowed before addressing the Thane. "We meant no trespass against your people," he tried his best to return in the ancient dialect. Thadius spoke awkwardly, often punctuating his words with hand gestures as he introduced them and tried to explain their story. Ryan could only pick out the occasional word. All the while, some of the centaurs grew agitated. Heated words were exchanged in their own language and some pointed at the human prisoners.

"Whatever you're saying, please change the subject," Ryan whispered.

"I'm trying to tell them that we are not trespassers, we were pursued by goblins," Thadius growled.

"Well, say it nicer. Maybe . . . smile or something."

Thadius glowered at Ryan before turning back to the thane. When he did, it was with a broad grin. "We are thankful for your aid," he conveyed to the council. "Without it, we might be dead."

"Our help was given because we assumed you men of Avan-Rhun," Oenar made clear.

"Not Avan-Rhun," Thadius confirmed. "We journeyed from the south. We are searching—"

Thadius was interrupted by the dark-coated centaur who had led them into camp. He stormed into the glade, looking more imposing than when he had battled his goblin foes. The centaur thrust an accusing finger in Thadius' face and directed his tirade toward the council. Ryan had no idea what his harsh words meant but recognized anger when he saw it. They were in a bad situation and it could easily grow worse.

The thane raised a hand and a hush fell over those assembled. "Angry words will get us nowhere. And being my son gives you no excuse to disrupt this council. Let us listen before we speak."

With a snort, Oenin withdrew, though he stood close by and glared at Ryan and Thadius.

"Forgive my son. But understand that he is protective of his people." Oenar motioned for Thadius to continue.

Through patient dialog and pantomime, Thadius was able to relate to the group the gist of their tale. He kept his narration focused on Torr and the goblin outcasts, and referred to the Stone of Orinn simply as a religious artifact. He omitted the sorcerer, Askelon, altogether.

"With the stolen artifact in their possession, Torr will gather more followers. Perhaps with your assistance, we can recover this artifact, before they become too strong. We're grateful for what help you've already given us, and whatever else you might provide," Thadius concluded with a bow.

The majority of the centaurs spoke little of the outdated language and Oenar translated for the others. Whenever he did, Thadius updated Ryan on what was being said.

"The men of the clan are on their last big hunt before winter sets in. It's traditionally led by the thane," he explained to Ryan. "Oenin and his hunting party happened to venture near Hazen. They spotted us atop the tower, cornered by the goblins Torr left behind."

"And they mistook us for simple villagers?"

"Luckily they did. It's the reason they rode to our aid."

"And now what do they think of us?"

"We're a big unknown. They've had no contact with anyone south of these hills. The only humans they trade with are men from the fishing villages of Avan-Rhun."

"So we're near the sea?" Ryan was surprised.

"About a day south of the Merrian, I believe. I wish Trenn were here, he's much more proficient in the Old Tongue."

With things more civilized, the call went out for refreshments. Other centaurs came and went from the glade, and Ryan had the feeling that most wanted a look at the strangers from the south. Bowls of dried fruits and various nuts were placed upon tripod stands of precut wood. He and Thadius stood as they ate, and a skin of wine was passed around. Ryan had tasted wine that previous summer, and had no liking for the taste. He waved it by in favor of the spring water the centaurs provided.

Later, they were led to a shelter, where they discovered a fire burning low and two pallets of thick furs. All of their gear was present, and even the water skins had been refilled. Ryan gazed about to find some of the centaurs already bedded down for the night, lying on their sides, the human portion of their anatomy wrapped in thick blankets. He had wondered how they managed to sleep.

Ryan laid some cut wood on the fire and looked up to see stars for the first time in days. "Do the centaurs live in the Lost Hills?"

"They're mostly nomadic, roaming the northern reaches between the hills and the sea." Thadius rummaged through his gear and produced the long scroll case. He drew forth the map taken from Askelon and unrolled it before the flames. He placed a finger on a red dot situated within the Lost Hills.

"Hazen," he pointed. "And here is centaur territory, from what I gather." His finger hovered between the Lost Hills and the Merrian Sea. "And there, north of the Sarlonns, lies Avan-Rhun."

Ryan noticed another red dot, within the Sarlonn Mountains, near where he thought the Dragon's Spire should be. "This map shows the location of the citadel. And there's a third mark, deep within the Darkwood Forest."

"Drynas has the same marking and that one is circled," Thadius observed.

"What does it mean?"

"It means we must get this map to Trenn. Askelon knows, or at least suspects, where the citadel is located. But what's the connection to Drynas or the Darkwood? "

"Askelon mentioned others, and I assumed that he meant sorcerers. And he knew Gadrin," Ryan recalled.

"He asked about Gadrin?"

"I didn't have the chance to tell you before. Askelon cast some sort of truth spell on me."

"Askelon also mentioned other gemstones to whoever he was speaking with."

Long into the night, Ryan and Thadius sat before the fire and spoke of sorcerers and citadels. Both sensed larger works afoot, and it all involved sinister elements. Ryan wished they could contact Trenn, but neither had the means to do so. Finally, exhaustion claimed them and they fell into a deep sleep. When they rose, Oenin was waiting for them. Ryan was relieved to see that he appeared less formidable today.

"You are to come," the centaur swept an outstretched hand toward the glade. Ryan and Thadius followed.

All about them, centaurs ate, lounged and went about camp chores. The mood was a far cry from what it had been the night before. Some of the centaurs practiced throwing their broad-bladed spears. Ryan did not have the chance to study one earlier. Stoutly shafted, with a tapered butt cap at the bottom, these were weapons crafted to inflict damage from either end.

Once again, they found themselves before Oenar and the centaur council. Thadius greeted them with a bow.

This time, it was the eldest of the centaurs who spoke. While he sometimes stumbled over the words, Thadius understood enough to relate his story to Ryan.

"Hundreds of years ago," Thadius translated, "their people dwelt within the Brightwood Forest. They even shared it with humans. After the downfall of Hazen, came the tribes of the monstrous races. Goblin, ogre and troll began a conquest of the land. The centaurs were forced from the forest. Humans eventually withdrew from these lands as well, and the centaurs were driven further north by the goblin tribes that came to dominate what would become Galanthor. During these years, Brightwood Forest was corrupted and twisted into the Darkwood."

There were a hundred questions Ryan wished he could ask, interested in how their history fit into Angard's past. But for now, his desire would have to wait. Thadius continued his rough translation.

"The centaurs felt abandoned by their former allies. It took years for the men of Avan-Rhun to rebuild their trust and develop trade with them."

"What about the goblins?"

"They warred, mainly with the Red Moon Clan for years, until the Goblin Campaign drove the goblins from the northern woods. The centaurs despise the outcasts who inhabit the Lost Hills and steer clear of them when possible. They're aware that Angard has laid claim to the land as far as the Cimrinn River. They're unsure what to do about it, so avoid contact."

After the elder centaur finished speaking, it was Oenar's turn.

"In spite of their mistrust of strangers, the clan elders have agreed to grant you arrows, provisions and additional herbs and dressings for wounds." Oenar sent some of the younger centaurs to collect these items before he continued.

"Our warriors will guide you to the goblin camp. They will wait nearby, no more than one day," he warned with a raised finger. "No centaur shall attack goblin on your behalf. Our people will not start a war for men of the south."

"It is best if the goblins see none of your people," Thadius concurred. "We can ask no more of you."

"You have spoken openly and conducted yourself with honor," Oenar complimented him. "May all men of the south be of such character."

"I thank you for those words, Thane. May we always know peace between our people."

Oenar nodded. "We understand that you do not speak for your people. Yet, you give us hope. Prepare yourselves. Our warriors will make ready."

Back at their shelter, Ryan and Thadius worked to re-pack their gear more efficiently. They needed to make room for additional supplies, as well as the sheets of parchment and map taken from Hazen. These would be packed for the ride west.

"Why take everything with us on this dangerous venture?" Ryan asked.

"There's no guarantee we'll return to the centaurs' camp," Thadius pointed out. "We'll leave our supplies with the warriors who wait for us, but we can't risk losing what we've recovered. There may be nothing of value here. On the other hand . . ." He drew Askelon's dragon-carved wand from his pack. The sky blue gem sparkled within the dragon's mouth.

"Too bad we can't use that against the goblins," Ryan said wistfully.

Thadius packed it away with care. "It might make Trenn a nice present."

Ryan wished the blond-haired wizard were with them now. His thoughts wandered to Arlena, apprenticed to Trenn, many miles away in the southern Elderwood. Memories of time spent with her warmed his heart, and he realized how much he missed her. He suddenly struck on the perfect gift for her. He thrust a hand into his pocket and pulled out the ring he had picked up from the floor of Askelon's bedchamber.

It was a rather plain band of silver, fashioned for either a man or woman. Ryan did not know if the ring would fit Arlena's slender fingers, but that was a matter easily remedied. The silver band turned out to be larger than he expected and fit snugly on a finger of his right hand. He decided to wear it so he would not lose it.

Centaurs soon arrived with ample provisions for them. Two horses, slighter of build and leaner than their own steeds, were also furnished for the journey.

"You might find the animals hard to control," Thadius advised Ryan. "They're accustomed to bearing loads for the centaurs. I'm not sure if they've ever borne a rider."

There were no saddles in the camp, so Thadius fashioned makeshift ones of thick blankets and wide leather straps. Ryan aided in the outfitting of his borrowed steed, although he doubted the comfort of the improvised saddles.

Oenin would lead the expedition and he greeted them with his usual stern expression. He handed Thadius a small clay jar.

"Our cleric offers this."

Thadius removed the lid and his eyebrows rose in question. Oenin searched for the right words.

"The powder will make a deep sleep. Very powerful," he added with a gesture.

"Thank you," Thadius returned.

Not one to stand on ceremony, Oenin called for the centaurs to assemble. A total of eight warriors made up the squad, including Oenin himself. By then, the entire camp had gathered about. Oenar drew near and exchanged words with his son. Each placed a hand on the other's shoulder and Ryan knew they had said their goodbyes. The centaur thane turned to Thadius.

"May your path bring you what has been lost."

"I am in your debt, Thane Oenar. Someday, I will repay your kindness," he replied.

With a nod from Oenar, the squad moved out.

Normally comfortable in the saddle, Ryan found the ride hard going at first. It took him several minutes to adapt to the temporary saddle. Their steeds were used to freely following the centaur or horse before them and not accustomed to being guided by hand. They often tried to drift out of formation. He looked to Thadius, to see how he fared with his own mount. He seemed to be experiencing the same difficulties, and Ryan felt they were in for a rough ride.

Once away from camp, the centaurs broke into a steady trot. It was not long before they left the sheltered valley behind and returned to the plains of Hazen. The band skirted the flatlands, riding along the edge of the plateau, which dropped away into rocky crags and deep ravines. At the pace the centaurs set, Ryan was grateful for the ambling gait of these light-footed steeds. It made for a more comfortable ride.

The centaurs ran throughout the afternoon. They stopped briefly to trade off equipment and rested in short intervals. Sharing the weight of their gear in this manner allowed the warriors to press on until nightfall. They crossed the flat plateau on which Hazen sat, climbing into the hills west of the city. Here, the land rose sharply and returned to a landscape of rock and bare-branched shrubs. On the leeward side of a slanted rock formation, the centaurs set up camp in an area of dead grass.

Ryan and Thadius lent a hand, raising and assembling their own shelter, linking it with the others to shield themselves from the wind. Though Thadius disapproved, a shallow pit was dug and a fire lit. Even after the meager pile of sticks was ablaze, little light escaped the shelters. In the end, Thadius was won over, as the flames provided enough warmth for comfort and could not be seen from a distance.

Crowded about the fire, the centaurs not on watch knelt and eventually sat, long legs folded neatly beneath them. Rations of dried fish, fruit and a grainy bread were passed about, and they spoke to one another in low voices. Thadius accepted a water skin from Oenin.

"How far away are the goblins?"

Oenin motioned with a hand to symbolize the sun moving from horizon to horizon. "One day."

"We're closer than I thought," Ryan admitted.

"We've covered a lot of ground today," Thadius stated. "Still, I had hoped to catch Torr before he made it back to their camp."

Ryan stared into the flames and gathered the heavy blanket about him. "Instead of a dozen goblins, we'll be facing the entire band." He knew Thadius must feel just as discouraged. How would they get anywhere near the Stone of Orinn, let alone snatch it up and escape from what could be a small army? Perhaps sensing the mood, Oenin's deep voice broke the silence.

"Sleep, men of the south."

Thadius nodded. "We can share the watch," he offered. A wave from Oenin told him it was not expected of them.

Ryan needed no encouragement to sleep. But while his body sought rest, his mind wandered restlessly, his thoughts on goblins. He was not sure exactly what they might face. What they needed was a clever plan.

# ᔥChapter 18᙭

It was still dark when Ryan woke. He helped dismantle the shelter and bury all evidence of food and fire. Gear and provisions were packed and once again, equipment was doled out to each centaur, save those designated as scouts. In quick order, it was as if their camp had never been.

The morning was crisp and clear as the band wound its way through the rise and fall of the Lost Hills. While spring would bring more green to the landscape, this area held none of the tall grass that covered the eastern portion of the hills. Ryan could easily envision how this nearly barren land earned its name. It was not hard to lose one's direction in the twisting valleys or among the irregular rock formations. At the noon hour, Oenin called a halt. His warriors had kept a faster pace than the day before, and after a short rest, the gear was redistributed.

"We turn south," Oenin announced.

Ryan could tell this leg of the journey would be different. Two scouts sped ahead and the centaurs adjusted their positions so that Ryan and Thadius rode in the middle of the squad.

"We must be drawing near," Thadius surmised.

"Should we string our bows?"

"Not until we reach the point where the centaurs will go no further. We must respect the thane's wishes. We won't do battle while in the centaurs' company."

Ryan resigned himself to stay alert and do his part to keep an eye out for goblins. The day passed without incident and the band of humans and centaurs traveled southward through a land that gradually showed more signs of life. The tall grasses returned and the hills here had a much gentler slope to them. Scrub and other twisted brush gave way to dormant foliage, evergreen bushes and scattered trees. At the height of a wooded ridge, the centaur scouts awaited them. After a brief conversation, Oenin turned to Thadius.

"There are many goblins to the south," he reported. His hand made an arc to indicate the next ridge.

"Are these the goblins we seek?" Ryan asked.

"They have to be," Thadius related.

"We will wait until dawn, and no longer," Oenin punctuated with a gesture.

Thadius surveyed the centaurs. "We are grateful," he thanked them. Each returned a nod, though few likely understood the words.

Ryan donned his pack, but Thadius waved it off.

"You won't need that."

"Now, if you think—"

"We won't need packs," Thadius interrupted. He shouldered his bow and quiver. "We're only going to take a look," he said with a raised finger.

Ryan followed him in silence as they hiked to the top of the ridge. He had not expected Thadius to allow him this far, so decided to hold his tongue. He would take things one step at a time and see what happened once they saw the camp for themselves. A sparsely wooded ridge rose on the opposite side of a grassy valley.

Thadius sat motionless as he studied the terrain. "I don't need to tell you to speak softly and keep low, I guess."

"Shouldn't we come across a sentry?"

"I expect to once we've made the ridge," Thadius confirmed. "I want to spy on them while the sun is up. Goblins don't see well in the sunlight. Besides, they're used to having the run of the hills. We might catch them unawares." With the breeze, came the smell of burning wood. And the sounds of drums.

Arrows at the ready, they crossed the valley and ascended the next rise. Creeping upward, they angled toward a stand of trees and evergreen bushes. Thadius eased his head up until he could see what lay beyond the ridgeline. After a minute, he signaled for Ryan to join him.

The smoke of many campfires created a misty haze that hung over a long valley. Goblin figures moved about a sprawling shanty town of animal hide tents and lean-tos, clustered about common fires. A well-defined line of trees and thicker growth meant a creek ran along the center. A cacophony of drums, pipes and horns blared and Ryan could detect an underlying beat.

"It's music," he declared. "A celebration."

Thadius nodded. "For the gemstone. It must be. And that's no camp."

"It's more like a village. There's way more goblins than we expected."

"A crowd is gathering at the center." Thadius pointed to a line of bushes that could allow a better view. "I'll go on from here."

But Ryan would have none of it. "Let me go with you, just a little further. They're raising such a commotion, we could practically walk down there," he pleaded.

Thadius pursed his lips and grunted. "Stay close, and for Orinn's sake, keep your belly to the ground."

Flat on his stomach, Ryan crawled through the high grass. In the effort to stay low, he could see only the heels of Thadius' boots as they worked back and forth. Fearing to raise his head even for a quick peek, he trusted the woodsman to steer them accurately. At last, they reached their destination. They were in a precarious position, for they might not make it back to Oenin and his centaurs should a sharp-eyed sentry spot them. Thadius brought them to a gap in the leafy coverage. Ryan could smell roasting meat.

"What are they cooking?"

"Goat." Thadius sniffed at the air. "Who knows what else they've been feasting on? And the goblin spirits are probably flowing in abundance."

From their vantage point, a building of logs and mud could be seen in the middle of the village. Above, a flag fluttered, adorned with the outline of a boar's head. Ryan had seen its long-tusked design before. Without a doubt, it was Torr's banner.

Near the log structure, rose the broken trunk of a massive tree. Jagged fingers of splintered bark shot upward, crowning the tall stump. A fire burned in the stone-lined hollow of the stump, and before it, knelt a goblin in black robes, a crooked staff held in one hand.

"What is it doing?" Ryan whispered.

"It's a shaman," Thadius said, "in the middle of some wicked ceremony."

"So that's an altar. It sure has attracted an audience."

More goblins gathered until it appeared as if the whole village had assembled. The robed goblin stood and raised a fist high. Ryan saw a brief glint of green.

"The Stone of Orinn!"

The mob cheered and the shaman placed the gem into a setting atop the twisted staff. Then at a signal, a dozen goblins rolled a large cage built of thick branches forward. The hulking form within thrashed against the wooden bars and let out a loud grunt. It was a wild boar, but to Ryan's amazement, it was easily the size of a horse. Thick tusks as long as sabers jutted from its lower jaw. Thadius nudged Ryan.

"A dire boar. Very dangerous. The goblins must have laid a trap for it. If it got free of that cage, it would do a good deal of damage."

The shaman flung something into the fire, creating a flash and a belch of smoke. When the shaman raised its arms, the crowd hushed. It thrust the staff toward the cage and barked a command. An aura of darkness surrounded the gemstone, an unnatural void absent of any light. In the next instant, lightning, as impossibly black as the emptiness from which it spawned, lashed forth. The goblins gasped as one and shrank back as multiple bolts arced, connecting with the great boar.

A thunderous squeal escaped the writhing animal. A leg burst from the wooden enclosure, digging into the ground, and gaining the beast enough leverage to roll the entire cart over. The boar convulsed and withered before their eyes. The goblins who had moved the cage did not escape the deadly spell. They, too, collapsed and shriveled, as if long dead. Standing furthest from the rest, one goblin managed to run a few steps before it stumbled and fell to a crawl, succumbing to the power of the gemstone. Its final shriek echoed about the valley.

"Can it be the same stone?" Thadius questioned.

Ryan stared, horrified by the spectacle. The afterimage left purple trails in his vision.

The shaman stepped to the altar and placed the staff into a niche among the upright segments of bark. The power of the gemstone left the goblin crowd silent. The shaman motioned a figure forward and Ryan recognized the big, armored goblin from their earlier battle at the gates of Hazen. It drew its curved sword and thrust the blade into the air. The goblins chanted with a roar.

Torr!

A pair of warriors strode forward, each bearing a banner. These were laid at Torr's feet and both knelt in fealty. The chant quickly became a unified shout. The goblins hooted, hollered and beat sticks as others dragged away the bodies.

"I think Torr was just named their chieftain. Let's get back to the ridge," Thadius said.

As darkness fell, they made their way back to the trees and bushes of the ridgeline. Below, bonfires sprang to life and the goblin celebration began anew.

"How did the goblins do this?" Ryan shook his head in disbelief. "I mean, how does this witch doctor know how to use the stone in this way?"

"Somehow, the goblins know more about the stone than we thought," Thadius responded. "There's a duality to its power, that's for sure. And you're right, their shaman knew this."

"All the more reason to take back the gem — and fast. Torr will use this power as a weapon."

Thadius grew quiet and Ryan sensed that he needed time to think. In the meantime, he began to form an idea of his own. Then at last, Thadius' long sigh broke the silence.

"Even if I can get to the gem, it could easily turn into a running battle to escape with it — against what amounts to a small army."

Ryan considered how to word his own plan. The more he did, the more excited he became, until he could hold it in no longer.

"I have an idea. It might be the best idea for sneaking into a goblin village I've ever had."

"At this point, I'm willing to listen to anything."

"The goblins will be drinking late into the night," Ryan pointed out. "When they're finally asleep or too drunk to care, we'll walk into the village and take the Stone of Orinn."

"Now wait, we're going to—"

"Walk into their midst, disguised as goblin warriors."

Thadius was silent.

"You have your doubts."

"Yes," Thadius admitted. "This sounds like a story right out of your old-timey tales."

"*Tales of Ancient Lore*," Ryan corrected. "And it worked like a charm. And speaking of charms, we also have the sleeping powder."

There was more silence.

"If this scheme stood *any* chance of success, I would need to do this alone," Thadius stressed.

"I realize that you're just looking out for me, but two swords are better than one, and you'll need a trusted friend at your back. Besides, all alone, you look suspicious . . ."

"Suspicious?"

"You're too tall to make a good goblin. Another goblin with you diverts enough attention so you'll be less conspicuous," he explained.

"You're grasping at straws," Thadius growled. "But . . . I suppose I have no better plan." He let out another sigh. "You will do as I say—"

"Yes!" Ryan practically shouted.

"You can begin by keeping your voice down!"

"Yes!" Ryan whispered in triumph.

Thadius fumed a bit more, mostly in mumbled curses, as he double-checked his weapons and gear.

Ryan did the same, gloating in victory, until he considered the danger. What if they were discovered before getting near the gemstone? What if the goblins could smell humans in their midst? A sense of foreboding crept over him and he wanted to share his apprehension with Thadius. Yet, voicing it might cause Thadius to leave him behind again. No, he was committed now, no matter what may happen.

"Rest here, and stay put," Thadius ordered. "I'm going to see where the nearest sentry is."

"What if a goblin spots me?"

"Hoot like an owl."

"Have you heard my owl? It's not very convincing."

"Then try to be . . . less noticeable."

It was an hour before Thadius returned. He reported several goblins further down the ridge, each bundled under heavy blankets against the cold. As the night wore on, the goblin festivities began to subside. Ryan and

Thadius kept watch in turns, while the other stole a few hours of sleep at a time. An hour before daybreak, Thadius shook Ryan's shoulder.

"I'm awake," Ryan replied.

"I'll be back." Thadius piled his gear besides one of the trees. "Remember to hoot if there's trouble."

"You're leaving your sword and bow?"

"Stealth is my strongest ally right now." Bearing only his long dagger, the former Huntsman melted into the darkness.

Ryan shivered and tried to lie motionless to conserve body heat. He longed for his warm blanket and would have gladly accepted a smelly goblin hide at this point. At least it wasn't snowing, he mused. The clamor of the goblin village had faded away. Fires burned low and he imagined warriors who had over-imbibed dozing off. Above the valley, the haze of smoke combined with fog and hung in a thick cloud.

Ryan gave up trying to count the minutes. He paced beneath the ridge line, rubbing his arms to generate heat. At the snap of a twig, he drew his sword.

"If I were a goblin, you'd be dead," Thadius said softly.

Ryan released his breath in a misty fog. "I've half-frozen waiting for you!"

Thadius tossed him an armful of material. "This should do," he offered with no explanation.

As Ryan sorted out the coarse material, he found it needed none. He held his breath and donned an ill-smelling cape of skins. Thadius already wore his goblin attire, but despite the lack of light, he really was too tall to pass for a goblin.

"You'll need to hunch a bit," Ryan instructed. Thadius tried a short walk, but it still would not do.

"More hunch," Ryan told him. "Try bending at the knees. Think smaller."

With a little practice, Thadius soon looked more goblin-like. He had also secured them blankets to wrap up in, to help with their disguise, as well as warm them up a bit. With the circulation returning to his extremities, Ryan was eager to be on their way.

"Won't the sentries be missed?" he asked.

"Not until dawn. This should be the last watch until then. Are you ready?"

Ryan raised the fur-lined hood over his head. "Let's go ruin Torr's plans."

# ❧ Chapter 19 ❧

Ryan and Thadius descended the ridge, reaching the line of bushes that concealed their approach. Some campfires still burned, where the last of the die-hard revelers gathered in small groups. Most of the fires had died to softly glowing embers, and figures lay about, sleeping and bundled against the cold.

"We'll avoid any contact if we can," Thadius warned, "but we're too close now to escape. If we're caught, I'll keep them busy. You get back to the centaurs."

Ryan nodded, wondering if he should have kept his plan to himself. He glanced at Thadius to evaluate his performance. Thadius' hunched shoulders and bent-kneed walk shortened his height and was a surprisingly convincing portrayal of a drunken warrior in search of another drink. Perhaps this could work.

Thadius led them through the scattered shelters as they avoided wandering goblins. Ryan could hear snorts and snores from all directions. The air reeked of stale alcohol and other odors he would rather not think about. The occasional stand of trees or clump of brush provided additional cover as they navigated their way into an area of taller tents, shored up with packed earth and long enough to house whole squads.

Thadius paused at one of the largest tents to peer inside. The front flaps were folded to the sides and Ryan recognized a smithy, by the sights and smells. At its center sat a stone-lined forge, complete with rudimentary bellows fashioned of stretched skins. Coals burned within, but thankfully, the tent was currently unoccupied. Ryan eyed a row of weapons racks. Each contained newly forged blades, curved in the typical goblin style. Thadius stepped inside to draw one from its rack.

"Poor quality," he declared after a quick examination. "Not much better than pig-iron. These won't hold up in battle very well."

"But they're making a lot of them," Ryan pointed out. "There are twin anvils in here, and look at this set-up."

On either side of the forge was stationed a stone anvil, crucible, and a line of quenching troughs. Hammers and tongs of various sizes hung from the beams above and a bin of iron ingots lay half-filled. Ryan looked into an open barrel to find it filled with spearheads. Another contained knife blades.

"Torr is gearing up for something," Ryan voiced his suspicion.

Thadius knelt near the glowing forge and scooped some soot from the ground into his hand. He rubbed some onto his face and wiped the charcoal ash onto Ryan's as well. "It's poor camouflage, but it's the best we can do under the circumstances."

They departed the smithy to make their way deeper into the village. As the number of goblins increased, it became harder to steer clear of them. They found themselves on a winding and erratic course, until at last, the inevitable occurred. Forced to choose one path or the other, they attempted to skirt by the fewer of two groups. Ryan's breath caught in his throat when some of the goblins called out and waved them over.

The goblins sat on rough-hewn log seats, several kegs overturned about them. Thadius did not hesitate. He nudged Ryan and strode toward the more dimly lit end of the group. The fire had not been fed and the darkness might hide them if they were careful. Ryan fell in behind him, his hands cupped to his face to exhale some warmth into them as if chilled to the bone, which was not a far stretch. He thought of playing a mute as one of the goblins rose to slosh a dark liquid into a pair of wooden cups. Before he knew it, one was shoved into his hand. He raised the cup and wrinkled his nose, looking to Thadius.

Their host hoisted a cup and spoke in a slurred, guttural tongue. Thadius mimicked the gesture and gulped down the brew. The goblins laughed in approval, until one fell from its seat. Not wanting to raise suspicion, Ryan tasted of his cup. He gagged and coughed on the bitter liquid and feared they would be discovered for sure. However, the drunken goblins simply laughed harder and one even got up to pat him on the back.

Thadius offered a gruff chuckle and slapped Ryan on the shoulder. He took Ryan's mug and set both on a keg. With a parting wave, he threw an arm over Ryan's shoulder and started them on their way. Ryan wiped nervous perspiration from his face and breathed a sigh of relief. But relief turned to alarm when one of the goblins called to them. Thadius ignored it and guided them into a collection of tents, where they could duck out of sight.

The goblin followed, its tone more challenging. Thadius picked up the pace and Ryan grasped the hilt of his sword. It caught up with them, and the goblin gave a hoarse command as it tugged on the blanket around Thadius' shoulders. Thadius whirled about. In a flash, his dagger was in the goblin's throat. He held the goblin firmly as a strangled gasp escaped the dying creature. It went limp and Thadius let it fall to the earth. Ryan stood motionless.

He had always felt sure that any foul goblin that got in their way deserved death, if not for the gemstone, then for his parents. But this was not a death in the heat of battle. This was somehow cold. It was a side of Thadius he had never seen. Though he knew his friend was no killer, and acknowledged that this had to be done, it was still unsettling. Ryan wondered if he could ever be capable of such an act.

"There is a stony place in the heart of every warrior that allows him to kill when needed," Thadius said quietly. "Take care that you keep this place as small as possible."

At that moment, Ryan vowed to use his sword only in defense if at all possible. He helped prop the goblin along the side of a tent, as if it slept off a night of drink.

They slipped through a line of pine trees and paused in the shadows as a pair of boisterous sentries passed. Before them, a perimeter of bigger tents and makeshift corrals surrounded a clearing. Ryan could smell goats.

"Torr's dwelling." Thadius pointed to a log structure.

"The altar is somewhere nearby," Ryan whispered.

They waited for another goblin to pass before stealing their way along a crudely railed fence. Across the village center sat the A-frame cabin of logs and packed earth, circled by large tents. Ryan spotted the broken tree that served as their altar. He was relieved to see the shaman's staff still in place. Unfortunately, the altar was not unattended.

Seated at a table next to the cabin was a squad of guards. They drank freely, weapons close at hand. Occasionally, one dipped its mug into a barrel. A shorter figure arrived to deliver a tray of food and Ryan realized that not all of the goblins were warriors. Some were servants.

"Let's follow it," Thadius suggested.

They trailed along as the goblin made its way into a wide tent, where other servants came and went. Those who entered often left with a barrel, presumably of drink. When Thadius felt the tent might be empty, he risked a peek inside.

"Distilling equipment and lots of casks," he reported. "I have an idea."

They ducked into the tent and opened one of the small barrels to find a murky-colored spirit. They hurried from the tent with it. On the way, Ryan picked up two wooden ladles. Once out of sight, he handed one to Thadius, who raised his brow in curiosity.

"The servers hung these from their belts," Ryan explained.

"Good eye. Every little detail will help us get out of here with the stone."

From inside his shirt, Thadius withdrew the jar of sleeping powder Oenin had given them. He poured the entire contents into the cask as Ryan stirred. They resumed their watch of the guards and it was not long before Thadius deemed them low on drink. He pulled a fold of cloak across his face and instructed Ryan to remain concealed.

"If anything should go amiss," he added, "get yourself out of here. Walk, don't rush, until you're over the ridge. Then flee with all haste to Oenin and his centaurs." He was gone before Ryan could argue.

Thadius assumed his goblin-walk and ambled in the direction of the guards. Sure enough, they called out to him. Ryan tensed and slid his sword from its scabbard. He did not think them drunk enough to fall for the ruse. To his astonishment, Thadius ladled out his tainted goblin spirits without interruption. He refilled their cups and set the keg at the end of the table before taking his leave. His pace quickened as he strode away.

"This won't take long," Thadius promised as he rejoined Ryan. "They've been drinking for hours and didn't even look twice at me. All they saw was a servant with more alcohol."

Thadius stood tall and stretched, stiff from his hunched portrayal of a shorter goblin. As he did, Ryan could hear laughter. They turned at the unexpected sound to see half a dozen goblins — all female. Afraid to move, they froze as the group strode by. Most paid no attention to them and Ryan breathed a bit easier. But before he could count his blessings, one of them paused to eye Thadius.

The goblin sauntered toward them. She wore a long skirt and a goatskin coat. Her black hair was tied back into a twisted braid and jewelry of polished bone pierced her green ears. She smiled at Thadius and spoke in a raspy voice. Thadius bowed and tried to hide his face as he eased back into his goblin persona. Ryan had no clue what she had said and avoided eye contact as he pretended to wipe his ladle.

She lay a slender, clawed hand on Thadius' arm and felt his muscles under the goblin cape. With an "ooh" and an "aah" universal in any language, she squeezed his bicep. Interrupted by a shout from her friends, she dismissed them with curt comment and wave. With a chorus of snickers, they left her and walked off into the night.

The intoxicated goblin flung her arm around Thadius. He gently removed it and attempted to send her off with a gentle push. She persisted, ignoring his rejection, and threw both arms about him. He looked to Ryan, who could offer no assistance. She stood on her tiptoes to steal a kiss and uncovered the fur-lined hood to reveal his face. Shock played across her broad face. For a second, Ryan feared she might cry out in warning. However, their luck held. The goblin woman fainted, dead drunk.

Ryan eased her to the ground and let out a sigh of relief. "You sure took long enough to do nothing!"

"What could I do? I had to wait until her friends were gone. Who knows how loud a goblin woman can scream?"

"Things almost got out of hand, that's all I'm saying," Ryan shot back. "I expected we might have to fight, even be captured and tortured or what not. I didn't expect you to go around kissing any goblin girls you happened to meet."

Thadius wiped his mouth with the back of his hand. "Let's put this behind us and speak no more of it." He shuddered. "Ever."

"I'll try to," Ryan half-promised. He remembered the day on the road to Drynas when he had tried to talk to

Thadius about girls. The woodsman's taunts came back to him. "Was that the girl your parents didn't approve of?"

With only a scowl for an answer, Thadius returned to his watch of the guards. All slept soundly and the fires at the center of the village burned low. The servants were elsewhere at the moment. Thadius turned to Ryan, who knew his expression all too well.

"There's just as much chance I'll get caught waiting here than going with you," Ryan argued. "You know I'm right."

"I know I should have sent you home right after leaving Drynas." Thadius set out and Ryan hastened after him.

They skirted the edge of the clearing and made their way around to the goblin altar. Ryan was relieved to see the Stone of Orinn had not been removed from the twisted staff. One of the guards mumbled and twitched in its sleep. In the dim light, other figures walked about, silhouetted against the backdrop of animal hide shelters. Ryan darted ahead impulsively.

"I'll fetch our prize while you keep an eye out." With no time to protest, Thadius grunted as Ryan leapt onto the stump.

From atop the goblin altar, Ryan could see into a gated pen beyond. Thick branches, intertwined and lashed, formed a nearly impenetrable barrier. Within, a black mass stirred and a deep snort sounded. The goblins held captive a second dire boar.

"Hurry," Thadius urged.

Ryan grabbed hold of the staff and froze. He felt a powerful presence and goose bumps rose on his arms. A strange jolt shot through his right hand, but he shook off what he assumed was a case of the nerves and seized the gemstone with the other hand.

Instantly, he was alone, engulfed in a void of utter darkness. Not a star hung in the sky, nor did any fires glow around him. The oppressive presence grew stronger, a malevolent power that smothered him.

"The stone is mine," a booming voice rumbled.

Gripped by terror, Ryan's strength ebbed. Sweat ran freely down his brow and his stomach churned. "W-who are you? What are you?" he managed to squeak.

One word thundered in his head.

"Jaull!"

The shaman had called out that word during the ceremony. No, it had evoked that name. This was the evil god of the goblins — and likely his end. He could feel his very life draining away.

With a jerk, Thadius pulled Ryan down from the altar, the Stone of Orinn along with him. Ryan was torn from the void, and though contact was broken, he was dazed. He could not hear Thadius' voice or feel himself being shaken. Thadius slapped him hard on the cheek. At last, he recognized his friend.

"The stone . . . it can summon the power of the goblin god."

"Are you hurt? Can you walk?" Thadius shook him again.

Ryan steadied himself on shaky legs. The stars had returned to the sky and campfires burned low once again. "I'm all right now."

"Let's go. You can tell me all about it later."

They turned to see a goblin standing there, mouth agape. The short creature dropped a tray of cups and let out a high-pitched shriek.

"Every goblin in the valley heard that!" Ryan exclaimed.

Thadius hefted his dagger and prepared to throw.

"Wait!" Ryan interceded. With an effort, he forced his legs to take him to the pen beyond the altar. He lifted the cross bar and it swung open with a creak. "Come on, you oversized mountain of bacon!" He stumbled back to find Thadius holding onto the smaller goblin by the hood of its cloak. Other servants gathered, drawn by the commotion.

"What have you done?" Thadius asked.

"We need a distraction."

Cloven hoofs beat the ground behind them, and all three spun to see the dire boar charge. The goblin screamed again, a piercing cry answered by a mighty squeal from the boar. Thadius released the goblin, who immediately fled, the wild boar in pursuit. While the drugged guards continued their unnatural slumber, goblin warriors emerged from Torr's cabin and stumbled from tents all about. His legs working again, Ryan and Thadius dashed the opposite way and shot between a row of shelters.

"Calm and unhurried," Thadius cautioned as he resumed his goblin gait.

In the heart of the village, goblins cried out and a signal horn blew in alarm. Ryan kept his head lowered and his feet moving as warriors all around them threw on coats or snatched up weapons and headed for the center of the settlement. As they neared the smelting forge, a trio of goblins stared at them from within. A gnarled-looking one stepped out to confront them, perhaps wondering why they hustled in the opposite direction as everybody else.

Thadius did not hesitate to cut the goblin down. The others rushed from the forge, curved blades in hand. Thadius sidestepped and struck again, eliminating a second opponent. Ryan drew his weapon and was ready when the remaining goblin swung its iron sword at him. He met the blow with a sturdy parry. Then Thadius' blade flashed and ended the goblin's life.

"Now we run!"

They ran for the ridge, goblins shouting behind them. The sky above began to lighten and Ryan turned to see half a dozen warriors closing in. One blew an off-key whistle and others raised bows. Black-fletched arrows shot past, narrowly missing them as they reached the line of bushes. Though the stretch of foliage provided a measure of cover, some of the goblins flanked them from the other direction and raced to intercept them. Then to Ryan's surprise, one of the goblins pitched forward, a feathered shaft in its side.

Ryan and Thadius started up the slope with a warrior on their heels. From atop the ridge came another well-placed arrow, and the unseen bowman brought this goblin down as well. As they crested the ridge, a figure stepped into view.

"Move it, I'm low on arrows!" came a female voice.

Ryan was shocked to see a woman standing there, bow in one hand and the other planted impatiently on her hip.

Wrella!

# ❧ Chapter 20 ❧

Wrella fired past them, wounding another goblin archer. "Who in the—"

"Introductions later — let's move!" Thadius ordered.

The remaining goblins halted below the ridgeline, reluctant to advance. One blew an alert on a curved horn, but the goblin settlement was in an uproar. The clamor created by the loose dire boar drowned out the shrill note.

"Their alarm won't be heard with all that racket. It looks like reinforcements will be delayed," Wrella pointed out.

"They won't stay distracted long," Thadius panted. Both shed their goblin attire. Dumbfounded, Ryan ran in silence. They descended the opposite side of the ridge and crossed the valley on the other side.

Wrella.

What in the name of the gods was she doing here? Of all the places to see her again . . . Then he pieced it all together. The gemstone. It could only be the gemstone. Why else would she be out here, in the middle of nowhere? And why had she not recognized him? Of course, his face was marred with ash and soot. He was curious as to how Thadius would react when he found out who she was.

Oenin and his centaurs met them on the next ridge. The humans were ushered down the other side, out of sight. The appearance of Wrella was a surprise and an animated conversation broke out among them. Oenin gestured at the newcomer and aimed angry words at Thadius.

"The goblins won't be far behind," Thadius countered. "This is no time for centaur stubbornness. Get us out of here, before you're seen!"

His outburst silenced the bickering centaurs. A sour-faced Oenin reached out and thrust open Thadius' cloak. Ryan feared a fight, until he saw the bright red patch on Thadius' shirt. Thadius snapped the cloak closed.

"It's just a graze. Both of you, mount," he directed Ryan and Wrella.

"Thadius . . ." Ryan started

"Later. We ride now."

Oenin grunted his disapproval but gave the command to move out. In the hustle of activity that followed, Ryan could ask no more, only worry. It was not a small amount of blood staining his shirt.

The centaurs raced northward, riding in a single file line and retracing their route through the hills. Ryan doubled-up and rode behind Wrella. Whatever else he thought of her, she was no coward. She had come after the gemstone and tracked it to Torr's camp — alone. His mind flashed back to his time spent with Adran's company. He wasn't sure if she should be admired or arrested. He had not forgotten how beautiful she was. Neither had he forgotten how they had used him as a decoy for the king's men.

When Oenin deemed it safe enough for a short rest break, Ryan rushed to Thadius' side. Together, he and the centaur leader examined the wound. A barbed arrow had grazed his flesh, leaving an open and painful gash.

"We have salves, and I can wrap this, but we need to make a fire and prepare something more powerful," Ryan assessed.

"We need to get much further away first," Thadius said.

While Ryan retrieved the salve and a wrapping from his pack, Oenin spoke with Thadius in the Old Tongue.

"It doesn't look life-threatening, but it will need stitched. Did you find what you sought?"

"We did," Thadius nodded.

Ryan worked quickly to infuse a bandage with an oily mixture of bistort, agrimony and other healing herbs. He placed the bandage over the wound and wrapped a long strip of cloth tightly around Thadius' waist. He knew Oenin had asked about the stone, and suddenly remembered that he was the one who carried it. As he felt for it in his shirt pocket, Wrella's voice came from behind.

"Not even a hello for an old friend, Ryan?"

Ryan hesitated before answering. "Maybe for a friend. Not for you, Wrella."

"Is that so?" she smirked. Wrella walked away but turned to add, "And by the way, you're welcome for saving your lives."

Ryan opened his mouth to respond as Wrella stormed off, but a snort from Thadius stopped him.

"Say as little as possible," he advised. "I have only one guess as to why she's here."

Ryan reached into his pocket. Thadius shook his head. "Keep it for now."

*     *     *

Wrella had watched closely the exchange between the tall warrior and the centaur leader. Although she did not understand the language, she was sure by their faces it was about the Stone of Orinn. Why else would they have risked sneaking into what amounted to a goblin army camp? And to stir them up like a nest of hornets . . . Of course it was the gem. Stumbling upon the lad out here was equally astounding.

She recognized Ryan after he had shed his goblin cape and blanket, even with the soot that remained on his face. She had not expected anyone to go to such lengths to recover the Stone of Orinn, let alone know where to look. To discover that one of these would-be heroes was the boy who could barely keep up with them on the road to Hathren last summer, left her speechless.

Wrella did not care for being speechless. In fact, the more she thought about this unexpected turn of events, the angrier she grew. She had gone to a great deal of trouble to track the goblins to their so-called village. She had risked life and limb and lost a good steed in the endeavor. To think that her efforts might have been in vain was intolerable.

On the other hand, perhaps her timing was not so unlucky after all. They had saved her hours of risky skulking about. If she played the situation just right . . .

*     *     *

The centaurs' path cut to the east sooner than the route that had taken them to the goblin village. Stealth was no longer a concern, and there was another reason

Oenin had chosen this way. The many areas of flat rock and hard soil better hid their hoofprints. Every so often, he sent the unburdened centaurs out to lay false trails, a tactic that might delay any pursuers. While Thadius hoped the goblin search would concentrate to the south, which was the quickest route from the hills and back toward Galanthor, it was safer to assume that Torr's goblins were probably no more than a few hours behind them.

An irritable Ryan rode behind Wrella. Already uncomfortable with the makeshift saddle, he was positively miserable with their close proximity. To make matters worse, Wrella insisted he hold onto her tightly, admonishing him whenever he loosened his grip.

At the next rest stop, rations were passed out and Ryan checked on Thadius' wound. The flesh around the gash was red and swollen. Ryan was aware that goblin weapons were sometimes poisoned. However, Thadius would not yet allow a fire or the time needed for making more potent medicines.

Afterward, Ryan and Wrella sat on the opposite sides of a huge rock to eat. Dried fruit and baked turnips were all that remained of their rations, which Wrella wrinkled her nose at. Neither spoke a word to the other and exchanged only icy glares. Feeling as though if anyone should be angry, it was him, Ryan broke the tense silence.

"Why are you in the Lost Hills anyway?"

"Hunting goblins for bounty," she shot back. "Why are you here?"

"The same."

"You? A goblin hunter? Ha!"

Ryan fumed and held his tongue.

As the waning afternoon faded to dusk, the band turned north. Their progress slowed, and they walked to rest the horses as they followed a dry creek bed. At least it should be more difficult for the goblins to track them, Ryan reasoned. He was more relieved that he didn't have to ride with Wrella. At this pace, the centaurs did not need much rest, and it became increasingly difficult to stay awake as the frigid night dragged on. Just after midnight, Oenin called a halt. Thadius' protest was overruled, and they settled on a grassy hillside.

"We will rest here and you will sleep," the centaur stood firm.

Thadius gave in, which Ryan found uncharacteristic of him. With no light, he was unable to tend to Thadius' injury and prayed that they would reach a safe place to properly treat it. Despite his worry, Ryan fell asleep as soon as he stretched out.

When at last dawn broke, Ryan was awakened by the sound of approaching centaurs. Thadius had already risen, and after speaking with Oenin, he reported to Ryan that there were no signs of goblin pursuit.

Goblins were not Ryan's main concern. "What about your wound?"

"I've already taken care of it. I can make it back to the centaurs' camp."

"Your color doesn't look good." Ryan grabbed his hand. "You're cold and clammy—"

"It *is* winter, and it's nearly freezing," Thadius scowled.

"Your scowl is even off."

"What?"

"Your infamous scowl. It's all . . . less infamous. Let me see—"

"It'll need to be stitched," he admitted, "but not here."

"I can do it for you," Wrella broke in. "I've done a bit of needlework in my day."

"It may come to that. I'll keep you in mind." Thadius walked off to join Oenin.

"He's not very social," she commented. "How about you, Ryan? Can we ever be friends again?"

"I've got gear to re-pack," he replied sourly.

The little sleep he had been granted had gone a long way to refresh his body. Yet, Ryan's mood was no better. The sooner they were away from these hills and Wrella, the better. He wondered if Thadius might send her packing, for he knew all about Ryan's adventures with Adran's company. Thadius was aware of her part in all of this. Why did he wait? However, Ryan was not looking forward to stitching up Thadius' side. Perhaps Wrella could be helpful after all, though he would keep a sharp eye on her.

Back in the saddle, Ryan resumed his place and tried to make the best of the situation. Yet each shift of the wind brought with it a face full of dark red hair. At times, he was sure Wrella tossed her head on purpose to whip him with her long, thick tresses. Fed up, Ryan spit out an errant strand of hair for the last time. He was about to shout in her ear, when the centaurs ahead slowed to a stop. Oenin circled back as Thadius slid from the saddle. Something was wrong.

"We still have much ground to cover," Oenin declared. His expression softened when he saw Thadius favor his side.

Ryan dismounted and helped unwrap the bandage. A yellowish ichor beaded within the gash.

"You need care and rest. You cannot ride much further," Oenin counseled.

Ryan did not understand all of Oenin's words, but he got the point. He liberally reapplied the salve and rewrapped his side tighter this time. Despite the chilly temperature, Thadius dripped with sweat.

"If Oenin insists we stop, you should listen," Ryan voiced his opinion.

Thadius remained quiet for a moment. "We've only one choice," he spoke to Oenin. "Take us to Hazen."

Oenin's eyes widened. "It is a city cursed by the gods. No one enters."

"Then the goblins might think twice," Thadius countered. "At least for a while. Better than being caught out here in the open. And better than having centaurs seen with us. The goblins will see you as equally guilty and will cause trouble for your people."

"Did they not enter the city once?" Oenin argued.

"The goblins scarcely made it past the gate, and that was under threat from Torr himself. We might be able to treat this wound, rest and leave before they enter the city, if they do. There's no good choice. Besides, whether it's Hazen or not, we'll be playing hide and seek all the way out of these hills and back to Galanthor. Take us to Hazen."

Oenin grumbled his consent and passed the word to his men. They would lead the humans to Hazen, and there, part ways. He turned back to Thadius.

"I have judged you harshly. You have courage and honor." Oenin took his place in the lead, and they were off.

They resumed the trek and traveled due east with increased speed. Ryan understood enough to know that Hazen was their destination. He prayed they would reach the city with some daylight to spare. His prayers were answered when Hazen came into view earlier than he anticipated. Wrella gasped at the expanse of its mighty walls. As they approached the ancient city, Oenin pointed out a weathered stone marker, perhaps where the side of the road may once have been. The characters carved into the stone were a mystery to Ryan.

"It's in the Old Tongue. *This city and its people be cursed*," Thadius read.

"Should we go on?" Wrella asked with concern.

"There's a chance the goblins won't enter the city, at least until they've gathered in numbers," Ryan presumed. "They have some sort of superstition about it."

"If we must stop, this is better than out in the open," Thadius stated, for Wrella looked unconvinced. "But if you wish to continue on, I'm sure the centaurs will welcome you."

"Lovely, ancient curses or horse-men turnips," she smirked.

Thadius urged his horse onward. As they made their way to the north gate, crows took to the air. The goblins slain days earlier lay scattered about. Ryan turned his gaze away from the grisly mounds. Oenin's centaurs halted before the rubble of the great gates.

"Take this," Oenin handed Ryan a deerskin pouch. "Crush the roots and tear the leaves," he mimed. "Do this soon." He shot Thadius a sideways glance.

"I promise, Oenin. Even if we have to knock him out."

"This is where we part, men of the south." Oenin laid a hand on Thadius' shoulder and gave Ryan a nod. "May our paths cross again."

"May they cross many times, my friend," Thadius responded. Ryan added his farewell, and with a final chorus of goodbyes, Oenin and the centaurs departed.

"Let's hurry," Ryan suggested. "Nightfall is coming."

"What is this place and what's this curse?" Wrella trailed behind. "What's this city doing in the middle of nowhere?"

"Hazen is a city long abandoned," Thadius told her.

"Mostly abandoned," Ryan murmured.

"Even if Askelon returned with help, he found us long gone," Thadius lowered his voice.

"What if he can somehow scry us out, like Lohkar did?"

"We'll avoid the area," Thadius promised. He looked worn and pale.

With Thadius in the lead, the three entered the city. Their destination lay halfway between the north gate and Askelon's abode. It was one of the governmental buildings they had seen while tracking Garr. Thadius felt it held the best hope for defense, for what little time they planned to spend in the city.

They had not walked long before Ryan requested they wait for him, disappearing into the doorway of what once might have been a luxurious inn. Thadius leaned against a stone column, arms crossed. He and Wrella eyed each other.

"Goblin hunter, huh?" she asked casually.

"For years."

"Very bold, sneaking into that ramshackle village. Lucky you weren't skewered and put on the spit."

"Lucky for us you happened by."

"Don't goblins prefer the dank of cave or the cover of dark woods?" she ignored the remark. The deflection did not go unnoticed, but there was no more time to banter. Ryan emerged from the doorway with the mail shirt he had hidden days before.

"Treasure hunting?" Wrella accused.

"Picking up my belongings," he defended.

In silence, they resumed their course through the deserted streets. With sunset just over an hour away, Thadius picked up their pace. Further along, the avenue opened up into a wide field. Overgrown with tall, brown grass and dormant weeds, the area may once have held the central marketplace of Hazen. Leafless trees dotted the field, and Ryan could imagine colorful tents and vendors' stalls selling goods from all over the northern lands.

They soon arrived at the building Thadius had in mind. Though the grand door of the main entrance was long gone, the structure was in remarkable condition considering the passage of unknown years. Situated atop a hill, its rooftop would allow them a clear view of much of the city. With limited access points and no windows on the ground floor, it provided them a formidable defensive position.

"We'll take a quick look around, then settle in," Thadius ordered.

They entered a spacious chamber, illuminated by a row of high windows. Benches of polished stone, now layered in dust, lined the walls. An immense horseshoe shaped counter sat centrally located and doorways led off in different directions. Time and weather covered the floor with a thick layer of dirt, and the beautifully carved reliefs and columns were marred by lichens and other mossy growths.

Their search did not take long. They discovered what may have been other waiting areas and several rooms, which could have served as officials' chambers. Most of what they found was rotted away, with the only intact wood planks upstairs. Satisfied there were no hidden dangers, they returned to the main floor.

Thadius cleared an area of the counter, wiping away dirt and debris with a pass of his cloak. "We'll move some of these benches across the entryway later, and barricade the back door as well. We can sleep upstairs, and leave the city before first light." He let out a long breath. It was past time to tend to his wound.

As Ryan unpacked their herbs and bandages, Wrella helped Thadius out of his gear and onto the granite counter. Carefully, she peeled away his shirt and the bloodstained bandage. He grimaced as the cloth tugged away from the sticky wound. Ryan did not like the looks of it.

"I'm making a fire." He headed out the door to gather fuel. Bushes stripped of their leaves by the winter surrounded the building and lined the street. Wrella emptied a water skin onto the gash and soaked a piece of clean cloth.

"This is going to hurt a bit," she warned. As she cleaned the wound, Ryan returned with an armload of broken branches, sticks and handfuls of dried grass. In a short time, he had a fire lit and a poultice ready, made from the roots and leaves Oenin had given them. He handed Wrella their field kit, which contained instruments and equipment needed to treat more serious injuries. Her eyebrows rose when she unfolded the leather flaps.

"You're certainly well-stocked for a couple of bounty hunters. If it weren't for your weapons, I'd swear you were a healer of some kind."

"It's always smart to be prepared," Thadius shrugged.

"You are that," she acknowledged. "This kit was costly." She chose an appropriate needle and sterilized it with the burning end of a stick from the fire. With a steady hand, she threaded the eye from a spool of strong thread. "This will hurt a bit more." Without delay, Wrella began to sew.

Thadius said nothing as she completed her task. Ryan had to admit, the woman knew what she was about. She did not hesitate, nor drive the needle too deep. Although the process was far from painless, she had done her stitching well. When she finished, he applied the poultice. Together, they tightly bandaged Thadius' side.

"I've got a tea of agrimony and bistort on the boil," Ryan informed him. Thadius nodded and lay back.

"So what's the plan?" Wrella asked as she re-packed the leather satchel.

"Barricade the rear doorway, if you will, Ryan," Thadius requested. After Ryan was gone, he answered her.

"We will leave Hazen and these hills behind." He winced as he rose on his elbows to face her. "Then you will have two choices. Leave us and never look back, or accompany us to Drynas and face the magistrate's justice."

# ❧ Chapter 21 ❧

Wrella's cheeks flushed red and her green eyes burned holes into Thadius. So, Ryan had filled him in on their previous adventures. She bit her tongue and stormed from the chamber. Wrella flew up the stairs two at a time, and seethed as she paced the main hallway.

This Thadius — who dared speak to her this way — was not going to stand between her and the riches she had worked so hard for. She did not know who he really was, but the man had infiltrated a goblin village and recaptured the Stone of Orinn. She doubted the boy had been of much help. The tall man was obviously a seasoned fighter, and there was something about him that left her hesitant to try force.

Wrella's anger subsided as she explored the upper rooms. The pointless activity occupied her mind and let her mood calm. At the rear of the building, she could hear Ryan as he labored below to barricade the only other way in. Not eager to lend a hand, Wrella retreated to a quieter spot. She had plans to make.

\*       \*       \*

Ryan stacked another layer of large stones on the pile. While he did not have time to completely seal the entry, he made it difficult for something to get inside, especially if he used his sword to persuade whatever it was to stay outside.

After filling in most of the entryway, Ryan stuffed branches into the empty spaces. He placed loose stones and bricks on the inside of the barrier. If disturbed, the clatter of falling material should alert them. Proud of his efforts, he collected his weapons and returned to the main chamber.

Thadius lay stretched out on the counter. The tea Ryan had left for him was finished and he added more twigs to the fire. Not wishing to wake him, Ryan dug into his pack and located an extra pair of thick bootlaces. He scooped up his shirt of chain mail and slipped away to don the loose-fitting armor before setting off to find Wrella.

Ryan checked the ground floor and the upstairs with no luck. Had the woman with the dark red hair abandoned them? Then in a room they had barely glanced into earlier, he came across a stairway hidden in an alcove. Judging from the cool breeze and the amount of dirt deposits at the bottom of the steps, Ryan guessed it led to the roof. That was where he found Wrella.

She sat upon the parapets as she took in the sunset over the deserted city. The suit of chainmail made a metallic rustle as Ryan approached.

"I can hear that antique pile of chains clinking from halfway across these ruins," she remarked without turning.

"I have some straps, if you'll help me cinch it down," he said, swallowing his pride.

"Anything, so long as it stops the racket." She slid from the stonework and snatched one of the laces from him. "These need to be thicker, so replace them when you can," she schooled. Wrella worked quickly as she wove the lace through one sleeve and then the other. With a practiced hand, she trimmed and tied knots until both sleeves were cinched and the girth tightened. Ryan stretched and tried some practice moves, pleased with the fit.

"If you're going to wear this much, ditch the cuirass and invest in a gambeson to wear underneath. It will be a lot more comfortable. What did you do, rob a tomb?" she needled.

Ryan scowled at her. "We are not grave robbers."

"Yes, I forgot. You're goblin hunters. Where is my patient anyway?"

"He's asleep, and I wouldn't wake him."

"You've changed a lot since last we met, Ryan. Perhaps I have too," she softened her voice. Ryan said nothing as he adjusted his sword belt. "At least tell me when you met Thadius."

"We met right after you abandoned me to the king's men." Ryan could not mask his bitterness. Their eyes locked briefly, before Ryan's were drawn away. Tiny flickers of light danced in the darkening night.

"Goblins!"

"Fetch your friend." She shoved him toward the stairs. Ryan sprinted to the ground floor. Thadius stirred as he entered the room.

"Trouble?"

"There are lights at the north gate," Ryan reported.

"Show me."

They made their way to the roof, where Wrella remained on watch. Distant flames winked in and out of view.

"I counted at least twenty torches," Wrella informed them.

"That's not the worst of it," Ryan groaned. Torchlights also appeared to the south. "I thought goblins see best in the dark?"

Thadius grunted. "They do, but this is a search party. Their trackers are scouring the streets for any trace. Count on many more goblins for every torch you can see."

"They're fanning out," Wrella observed.

"I was hoping we'd have more time," Thadius admitted.

"And less goblins," Ryan sighed. "That looks like half of Torr's warriors."

"We can't hold up here," Thadius expressed the opinion of all.

The three sped down the stairs and scrambled to collect their gear. They reasoned the eastern gate was their shortest route of escape and hurried from the district of columned buildings into a neighborhood of stately homes, most of them intact. These soon gave way to the crumbled shells of smaller houses. Built close together, partial walls and piles of brick lay scattered among the tall grass, creating a giant maze. Moving in a straight line became impossible. Forced to dogleg one way or the other, Thadius tried to keep them on course.

At last, they broke free of the ruined homes and crossed a buried street to find themselves in a field of dormant wheat. Ahead, the eastern wall of the city loomed. Ryan could make out high towers, spaced evenly and intact. As they drew nearer, it became clear that these gates had also been bricked in, like the others.

"This is disappointing," Wrella mumbled.

"We'll circle around and slip past the goblins to the south," Thadius decided.

Through the field they fled, the mighty walls of Hazen to their left. To the right, they skirted the ruins of the city's poorer quarters, where torches floated like will-o-wisps. With a gesture, Thadius brought them to a halt and they knelt amid the dry stalks.

"The goblins are moving fast." Thadius' voice was strained.

"Are we trapped?" Ryan whispered.

"Maybe not, but ready your bows."

"Now you're talking my language," Wrella smiled. Whatever else Ryan felt about her, he admired her bravery.

Working their way between the wavering lights, the trio began up a series of hills as they made their way toward the south gate. Nearing the summit, stands of fir and pine trees grew thick. They found themselves in an area crisscrossed with bushy hedges and vine-covered obelisks. In the darkness, each took on a misshapen dimension. To Ryan, every deep shadow held a goblin waiting to spring at them.

A bank of clouds passed overhead, blotting out the moon, and forcing them to slow their flight. A yellowish light flickered ahead, followed by a shriek that froze them in their tracks. Feet pounded on the other side of a hedgerow. Bows taut, they waited in ambush as the flame bounced their way.

Torch in hand, a goblin burst from behind the screen of foliage. It was not alone. On the heels of the terrified warrior was a hideous figure. Long limbs stretched forward and clawed fingers caught hold of the goblin's cloak. It brought down its prey in a tumble. The goblin screamed as the humanoid leapt on it, biting into its neck, and washing the creature's mouth and throat in black blood. Stunned by the spectacle, none moved.

The goblin went limp and the gray-skinned being took another hungry bite as if famished. It paused to sniff the air. Ryan's heart skipped a beat as it slowly turned and spied them. By the glow of the fallen torch, beady eyes as white as snow locked onto them. It froze, like a beast in the wild upon seeing another animal, or perhaps another meal.

"I don't know what that is, but if it takes one step in our direction, fire," Thadius ordered.

The thing stood. Nostrils flared in the bump that was its nose, and white eyes widened. It reminded Ryan of the statues they had seen at the city gates, it was about the same size. When it stepped closer, there was no need for a further command. All three let arrows fly, and at this range, all hit their mark, sinking deep into its chest. The ghoulish thing staggered backward and fell over the goblin's body.

To Ryan's horror, it rolled onto all fours and regained its feet. His hand shook as they loosed another round. Again, all struck their mark and caused wounds critical to any man. Yet the nightmare creature staggered forward.

"Swords!" Wrella drew her blade. Before Ryan could drop his bow, she was on it.

Slashing left and right, Wrella laid the ghoul out on the ground in pieces. At last, the creature ceased to move, but the warrior-woman stopped swinging only after Thadius called out.

"Whoa! You've finished it off."

"And nice job leaving us room to attack." Ryan expected a harsh retort or an insulting comeback. But Wrella was strangely quiet.

Though mindful that goblins hunted them, none could resist a closer look at the unnatural predator. Naked and bony, elongated arms ended in clawed fingers. Sunken eyes and a mouth full of sharp and misshapen teeth left Ryan at a loss.

"What is it, some type of ghoul?"

"That description will suffice." Thadius nudged a bare foot with his boot. "It's a match for the footprint we saw earlier."

Ryan cast a glance about. "Could there be more?"

Thadius shrugged. As they collected their bows, a goblin whistle blew — too close for Ryan's comfort.

"Let's go." Thadius set out.

"I'll not!" Wrella stood fast.

"We've no time for this," Thadius growled.

"You knew about these things and haven't said a word," she accused. "You've been here before, apparently taken the grand tour, and told me nothing!" Ryan feared her raised voice might give them away.

"We need to get out of this overgrown park," Thadius urged through clenched teeth. "I do think there are more of those things, and apparently, they feed on living flesh!"

"Then let's hurry," Ryan broke in. "If we can find a safe place to hide, maybe we can think of a way out of here."

The silence that followed was broken by a goblin horn.

"That seems reasonable," Wrella relinquished. She snatched up the goblin's torch.

"They'll see us for sure," Ryan pointed out.

"We need the light," Thadius agreed with Wrella, "and from a distance, we might look like we're part of the search."

That settled, they moved on with a renewed sense of urgency. Goblin warriors were near, and besides these ghouls, Ryan wondered what other dangers the city held after dark. Beyond the hedges, the silhouette of tall walls and peaked rooflines loomed. As they approached, the moon broke through the clouds to reveal slender towers and ancient battlements rising above them.

"This place is huge," Ryan said in awe. "It must be a palace!"

"The lad's right, and probably as good a place as any to hide out," Wrella recommended.

They crept along the stone wall and slipped into the first doorway they came upon. Drooping vines covered most of what may have been a servant's entrance, for it led them into what were obviously the kitchens.

"Some more light would be appreciated," Wrella suggested.

Ryan stopped to pull a torch from his pack. Thadius produced the oil flask and Wrella readied flint and steel. In short order, bright flames blazed, and they passed from the extensive kitchens into a great hall whose splendor far surpassed that of Lord Varis. Faded mosaics and skillfully carved frescoes were illuminated, and despite the passage of many years, the past elegance of the palace was evident.

Ryan caught his breath and tensed. At the far end of the hall, an immense dragon-like figure loomed. Wrella raised her bow.

"Statue," Thadius quickly determined.

Multiple heads adorned long scaly necks, some reared back, ready to strike. Others snaked lower to scrutinize any who approached its flanks. Frilled crests topped each head, tapering as they faded into the neckline. Most of the jaws were agape and lined with teeth as long as daggers. Raised forelegs ended in wicked claws, poised to deliver deadly swipes. The impressive creature cast flickering shadows against the far wall and a balcony above as they drew near.

"Five heads and no wings? It's a hydra!" Ryan exclaimed.

"The Mycean hydra. Straight from your *Tales of Ancient Lore*," Thadius mused.

The hydra overlooked a dry basin, sloping to several feet deep and bordered with stacked river stones. A long tail circled along its semi-circular edge, designed to stabilize and help bear the weight of the structure, but it had broken and separated long ago. From the crusted mineral deposits cascading down the cracked stone, Ryan deduced that the towering sculpture had once been a fountain. Then he noticed piping set within the open mouths. He could trace the trajectory of their streams, and the angles could well have converged at the base of the statue, the deepest part of the basin.

Beyond the great beast, a wide doorway was centered beneath the lengthy balcony, which spanned the entire wall. Majestic pillars rose at precise intervals as supports and arched niches held the dusty sculptures of now nondescript figures. Deep, square holes riddled the opposite walls, and rectangular mounds of debris on the floor left evidence of the wide stairs that had once reached the upper level.

"That's just a common hydra," Wrella corrected. "See, no webbing between the talons and only five heads, not seven."

"Common hydra? Hydras don't exist. They're a myth," Thadius insisted.

"Hmph. Like centaurs and lost cities?" Wrella cut narrowed eyes at him. "You don't know where I've been or what I've seen."

Thadius let out a sigh. "Really? Please, tell me the last time—"

With a cry, goblins sprang from the doorway beneath the balcony, swords drawn. Ryan dropped his torch. Adrenaline surged through him as he drew an arrow. Both Thadius and Wrella had already loosed theirs. One of the goblins staggered and fell and the others retreated the way they had come. From the kitchens behind them, whistles blew.

"They won't rush in blindly." Thadius shouldered his bow. "They'll surround us and await reinforcements."

Wrella trained an arrow on one doorway, then the other. "I won't be trapped like a rat!"

Thadius stepped into the basin and struck a stout leg with the flat of his blade. Bits of a stonework facade cracked and fell away. It was not made of solid stone after all. "We're going up. Ryan, help me push."

Ryan joined him and put his shoulder into the statue's hollow base. Although the hydra teetered, it did not topple. If it did, Ryan could see that the edge of the balcony above would catch the craning necks. They could climb up the leaning structure and have a means of escape. Thadius called for another attempt and Ryan repositioned himself to get better leverage.

"Here we go!" Wrella shouted. A squad of goblins poured into the hall from both doorways, some with bows.

Thadius and Wrella targeted their archers, each taking one down before Ryan let loose his first shot. Their arrows lessened the enemy's number by two more, before the goblins closed in. Bows were cast aside and swords unsheathed. Thadius shouted for Ryan to keep hold of his bow and target any other archers.

With a clash of steel, Thadius and Wrella met the goblins' charge. Though the pair was outnumbered, the goblins were no match for their combined skill. Ryan did his best to keep their archers at bay, firing as fast as he could in their direction. However, his arrows were soon better directed as he fought to control his breathing and steady his aim.

Wrella's blade flashed, slicing into goblin flesh in a silvery whirl. Thadius, hindered by his wound, struck more conservatively. Together, they slew half of the goblin attackers before the remaining warriors retreated. With a cry, Wrella chased them halfway to the kitchens before breaking off her pursuit.

The short battle had carried Thadius back into the basin, where he disarmed a lingering goblin. The desperate creature grabbed his sword arm at the wrist and pulled a curved knife from its belt. Thadius grasped it by the throat with his free hand and slammed it into one of the hydra's massive legs. The goblin slumped.

With a loud crack, fractures shot up the side of the once regal statue and a rumble reverberated underneath their feet. Thadius turned, eyes wide. For a split second, his gaze locked with Ryan's. A jagged fissure opened and the floor beneath the old basin gave way. Ryan was forced to leap back as stone tiles, rusted pipes and the entire fountain dropped away.

Thadius disappeared along with it, into the darkness below.

# ❧ *Chapter 22* ❧

"Thadius!" Ryan rushed to the gaping hole.

Just below the rim, Thadius clung to the more stable stones of the subfloor. Ryan braced himself and extended a hand. Thadius seized it and struggled to climb. An adjacent block of stone dislodged and fell away, taking with it his next handhold. Then a second hand shot down. Wrella grabbed hold of him by the sword belt and pulled with all her might. Thadius' face contorted in pain as he swung a leg up and over the ledge. With a final heave, Ryan and Wrella hauled Thadius to safety. His momentum carried Wrella with him as the pair rolled away from the edge. They came to a stop with her atop him. His eyes held hers.

"Thanks," Thadius managed, "but I don't want the goblins to catch us like this."

With a scowl, Wrella scampered to her feet and Ryan helped him stand. Sweat dampened Thadius' hair and blood stained his shirt anew. But there was no time for re-dressing the wound. A horn blew outside of the palace. The signal had gone out and the goblins would rally for another attack.

Thadius breathed heavily. "I'm afraid the chance of an easier escape is gone." As they picked up their gear and prepared for the next assault, Ryan peered into the chasm left by the collapse.

"Maybe not!"

Below them, shattered pieces of hydra, twisted pipes and loose stones lay scattered across a flat surface of dark sediment. By the light of the fallen torch, they could make out walls of uniform brick. With a drop of about a dozen feet, it seemed a plausible escape route.

"Can you see a way out?" Wrella asked.

Before Thadius could object, Ryan dropped to all fours and edged closer. "There's a big tunnel," he reported.

"It could be part of the storm drains." Thadius knelt beside him. "They should be big enough to lead us out of the city."

"If we're going, it better be now," Wrella warned.

Ryan swung his legs over the ledge. He lowered himself as far as he could and dropped to the ground in a spot clear of debris. His boots sank into the soft soil. Next to him lay the goblin's body, eyes staring vacantly.

"It's not a bad landing," he called up. "Your sword is down here too!"

Thadius and Wrella tossed Ryan their bows and joined him. Thadius recovered his fallen sword and torch and they set off to the south. It was not far before the tunnel ended in a large pipe filled with stone and silt. Reversing their course, they hurried back under the great hall. Goblins could be heard gathering above. Further along, they came to an intersecting tunnel and faced the choice of proceeding to the left or the right.

"To the left," Thadius decided.

"The right should be the shortest way to the eastern walls," Wrella argued.

"The goblins might expect us to take the shortest route and send warriors to await us. Besides, we've seen one collapse already. There's no guarantee we can even get out of the city using these tunnels."

From behind, a shout echoed. The goblins were in the storm drains.

"Left sounds good," Wrella agreed.

Moving swiftly through the cold and rubble-strewn tunnels, Ryan was soon disoriented. He lost track of how many turns they had taken and in what direction they were going. The size of the storm drains often dictated their path. Some narrowed into culverts of intersecting pipes. At times, they were forced to backtrack and choose another way.

Then somewhere beneath the deserted streets of Hazen, they came across a short flight of steps that led to an unusual door, reinforced with an iron framework. With Wrella on guard, Ryan and Thadius muscled it open. A square chamber with a low ceiling lay on the other side. Rusted racks made of iron leaned precariously amidst the rubble. Across the room was another door. This one was in much better shape and Wrella pulled it open.

"A long passage and better engineered," she peered beyond.

Ryan and Thadius shoved the iron-framed door closed and used what was left of the storage racks to wedge it shut. They joined Wrella and proceeded into the new passage. After a short time, they came to a split in the corridor.

"These aren't drainage tunnels." Thadius cast his dimming light about. "These passages serve another purpose."

"And where do you think they lead?" Wrella questioned.

"Stay here and light us fresh torches. I'll lay a false trail to our right, then we'll continue along this one."

Ryan set to work. To his surprise, Wrella knelt beside him and helped unpack more torches.

"Let's wait to light these. We should conserve our resources. No telling how long we'll be down here," Wrella shrugged.

Ryan acquiesced, more because he did not want to argue with her. While he blamed her less than Adran and the others, he could not forget how willing she had been to sacrifice him for their escape. Neither could he see trusting her anytime in the near future.

"Do you think we're heading the right way?" She leaned against the wall opposite him.

"I have no idea which way we're going. Your guess is as good as mine."

"What about once we're out of here? What will you do when you get back to civilization?"

"I'll take a hot bath and sleep for a week," Ryan's tone lightened.

"In Drynas, I suppose."

"Perhaps," he answered absently.

"Tell me, Ryan, what were the two of you really doing in that goblin village?"

Her voice was pleasant and it was nice to have someone to talk to under the current circumstances. However, he would not be deceived. She was after nothing more than information, he reminded himself.

"I mean, you haven't collected a single goblin bounty, have you?" she continued.

"Have you? What have you been up to since last summer?"

It was Wrella's turn to be silent.

"What about the rest of the old gang? I can tell you where Derric ended up."

"Where's that?" she finally asked.

"Arrested in Cambryn for thieving and probably still rotting in a cell."

"Hmph. Why should I care?"

"Because it might do you some good to think about things. Maybe even choose a different path."

"I'm not doing so bad," she defended.

Ryan hesitated before responding. "I'm sure Karsten didn't think so either."

"So you know . . . How?"

"Does it matter? The point was that he never changed."

With a snort, Wrella moved away to sit alone. They said nothing else to each other until Thadius returned.

"I've left a trail which should waste some of their time," he announced in a winded voice. With new torches lit, he flung the used ones behind them.

The corridor they followed was in surprisingly good condition. Few bricks had shifted or fallen, and there was no thick layer of silt as in the previous tunnels. Ahead, they spied another door. This one was solid in construction, with runes carved on the surface.

"Any clue?" Wrella was at a loss.

Thadius looked over the archaic characters. "None, except that they're related to magic."

"Sealed by a spell?" Ryan speculated.

Wrella pushed on the handle and the door opened. Ryan held his breath, expecting some magical ward to activate, tripped by her carelessness. When nothing occurred, Thadius stepped through.

The spherical chamber was some eighty feet in diameter and floored with a smooth white marble, reflecting with the iridescent sheen of a pearl. Inlaid within the polished surface, concentric circles of silver lines surrounded a pedestal of the same stone as the floor. About four feet in height, the square pedestal was flanked by twin braziers and topped with a small slab of green crystal. Ryan was sure the hue was a match for the gemstone. In its center was a pear-shaped depression.

Surrounding the strange room, curved benches of smoky granite ran in intervals, following the contours of the walls. A blanket draped a man-shaped form, lying atop one of the low benches near them.

"What is this place?" Ryan whispered, not really expecting an answer. Behind them, the door swung shut and fit snugly into the curve of the wall. Both the hinges and a slide bolt were cleverly recessed.

Thadius and Wrella approached the stained blanket. Each grasped a corner, and at his nod, they pulled back the material.

"What do you make of this?" Wrella marveled.

Short, white hair surrounded a human skull like a halo. Once fine clothing had nearly rotted away, leaving behind fragmented swaths outlined with gold embroidering. But these were not the long-dried bones Ryan expected to see.

"I'm not sure," Thadius confessed. "Judging by the stains surrounding the bench, this is where this person died and decomposed. The smell has faded, so these remains may be old but not ancient."

"Is it possible he wandered down here?" Wrella tried to reason.

"He?" Ryan studied the body anew. "How do you know?"

"The cut of his tunic. And look at that band," Wrella pointed. "That's a man's ring, and there's no other jewelry — earrings or necklace. This was a guy, all right. But it makes no sense."

"Perhaps he was an explorer," Ryan suggested, though what was left of the dead man's garments reminded him more of a priest.

"Someone placed the blanket over the body," Thadius presumed. He respectfully replaced the blanket and examined one of the braziers. It contained the remnants of a thick tome, charred beyond any use or recognition.

Meanwhile, Ryan walked the circumference of the remarkably clean chamber and saw no other exits. Shining his torch about, he discovered a glimmering fresco of the night sky set in the domed ceiling high above. Reflected gems twinkled, mimicking the stars. "There's no other way out."

Thadius gazed up at the ceiling. "It's the constellation of Orinn."

Wrella drew her dagger and inspected the edge of the altar. "This block of crystal must be worth something."

"Treasure hunting?" Ryan accused.

"If I could get this chunk of rock loose," she shot back. "Maybe one of these braziers would fetch a fair price."

Thadius shook his head. "We aren't lugging around—"

"Look inside it," Wrella cut him off.

Thadius checked the other brazier. Within the bowl was a small measure of oil and fresh wicks. Ryan poked at the ashes of the opposite brazier. "Could Askelon have burned this book and left the oil?"

"If he did, he found another way into these tunnels," Thadius commented.

"He needed Garr to return here, to Hazen," Ryan reminded him. He did not want to say anymore in front of Wrella, but there were too many coincidences not to think of the gemstone. There was the constellation of Orinn above and the empty setting in the altar was about the right size and shape . . .

With a nod, Thadius said he agreed. He dipped his torch and lit the wicks. The circles of inlaid silver radiated a soft, shimmering light. Mysterious symbols appeared on the floor, evenly spaced between the circular lines.

"Bolt the door," he ordered.

As Wrella moved to secure the door, Ryan reached for the pouch in his shirt pocket. "We've come this far . . ."

Thadius motioned to the altar.

Ryan withdrew the Stone of Orinn. The gem was warm to the touch and sparkled with an inner glow. Ryan placed the gem within the hollow depression on the altar. Its radiance spread to the crystal about it, bathing the chamber with an emerald light.

"I see your visit to the goblin village was a success after all," Wrella remarked sarcastically. Standing outside of the circles, she fingered the hilt of her sword.

Ryan never voiced his words of retort. At Wrella's gasp, he turned to see the blanket slowly rise.

The covering fell away to reveal a middle-aged man, white hair now gray and flesh fully restored. His priestly attire was as brand new and piercing blue eyes swept over them. The man was no ghost. He was as solid as any of them. All stared, and even Wrella was too stunned to draw her sword. The man who had returned to life appeared calm and unthreatening. Ryan had the impression that he sat there, waiting patiently for them to speak first.

"Say something," Ryan urged, his fear ebbing.

Wrella eased over to nudge Thadius. "It seems the polite thing to do."

Thadius cleared his throat and addressed the extraordinary man in the Old Tongue. "Who are you?"

The man stood and gave them a slight bow. "I am Gathion," he introduced himself. "High Priest and Grand Magi of Hazen . . . and cursed creature of the gods."

Ryan was astonished. "Y-you speak our tongue?"

"He spoke in the Old Tongue," Thadius corrected.

"I understood every word he said," Wrella confirmed.

"Forgive me. I have not heard my native tongue in so long, I thought you preferred it," Gathion explained to Thadius.

"What are you doing here?" Thadius switched to the common language. "Does it have to do with the curse on the city?"

"Cursed we were, for seeking to equal ourselves with the gods. Immortality is what we sought. Bypassing all prayer and logic, caught up in our faith in magic alone, we sought to circumvent the gods. Casting them aside, we attempted to draw from the raw powers of the universe ourselves. With the Council's blessing, we assembled every mage and priest in the city to perform a ritual of unimaginable power. A spell to fulfill the foolish desires of an arrogant people . . ." Gathion's hands squeezed into fists.

"Eternal youth," Thadius concluded. His gaze turned to the altar. "You used the Stone of Orinn. How did it come to be in Hazen?"

Gathion's face reflected his pain. "It was the time of Felmoore, the Dragon King . . . and the warlock, Arakronis. The gemstone was lost in the final battle that broke the warlock's armies. Seized by goblin shamans, it was carried off to Ilsgaard. The stone was later used in a failed attempt to invade the Brightwood. Hazen's army defended our allies, and during the fighting, the gem was recovered from goblin hands. The Stone of Orinn was ours."

"However, we selfishly misused its power," Gathion continued. "Our magic was flawed and our faith misguided. Most of our people withered away, consumed by the raw power unleashed."

Ryan was horrified. "An entire city of people . . ."

Gathion's eyes glistened, and while these events took place what must have been hundreds of years ago, Ryan had the feeling it was like yesterday to him. Gathion's voice grew strained.

"In time, I realized that these were the lucky ones. The priests and mages who called down this disaster received their immortality — reduced to an inhuman, ghoulish existence. Bound to the city, they shunned the light and retreated beneath the streets. Thereafter, any unlucky souls who ventured into Hazen after dark were set upon. The city gates were later sealed, and men abandoned these hills. Eventually, there was a collapse at the southern gate, and some of these tortured souls ventured out. However, any who left these walls turned to stone."

"We've seen them," Thadius told him.

"How many remain?" Wrella questioned.

"I do not know how many survive."

"What of you, Gathion? Somehow, I don't believe that you escaped the suffering," Thadius sympathized.

Though regal in his priestly vestments, and once a man of proud bearing, Ryan now saw a tired and aging man. He felt sorrow for Gathion.

"I had not aged since the great calamity fell upon us. I remained here, at the scene of my transgression, to ponder my arrogance, and ignorance. I was linked to the focal point of the ceremony."

"The Stone of Orinn," Ryan stated.

"Correct," he confirmed. "Day after day, year after year, I suffered the consequences of our prideful ritual gone awry. I, too, had gained my immortality. I lingered these long centuries to serve as a warning."

"Then something occurred to change things," Wrella surmised.

"Yes," Gathion brightened. "One day, a man entered Hazen. Surely guided by the gods, he found his way to the gemstone. He removed it from the altar, and with it, the curse. I aged so rapidly, there was scarcely the chance to tell him to destroy the book containing the ritual."

"It was done," Thadius informed him.

"I am relieved." Gathion appeared comforted by the news. "Do not follow our folly. Magic and prayer are the tools of man, forged for us by higher powers. To place ourselves above the divine invites disaster."

"So after the Goblin Campaign, the stone was rescued from Hazen, not the Darkwood, like the tales say. But who freed the gem and released you from the curse?" Ryan inquired.

"I am sorry," Gathion shook his head. "I can tell you only that he was a servant of Orinn and a wizard of good heart."

"With the curse lifted, why do the ghouls stay?" Ryan asked.

"Those unfortunate souls lost their immortality and are free to leave Hazen, they simply do not realize it. After all of these years, they know nothing but hunger. They will age and eventually die out. Beware of them, for their bite will poison your flesh."

Gathion walked to the altar, and his gaze lingered on the gem. Wrella started toward him, but Thadius halted her with a hand on her arm. With a snort, she brushed him off.

"You are in possession of this mighty relic. Be warned. We underestimated its power. It can do great good. Used in arrogance, or for evil purposes, the Stone of Orinn can bring destruction."

"We will restore the stone to the Temple of Orinn," Thadius promised.

"Orinn will read your intention. If this is not so, the gem will not leave this place."

"We're being pursued by goblin warriors," Wrella broke in. "Is there another way back to the surface?"

"There is. A tunnel meant to be utilized in the event of a siege. It lies through a secret door and will lead you out into the hills, east of the city. But I caution you, move quickly and do not stray. There are other dangers besides the former citizens of Hazen."

"Other dangers?" Thadius repeated.

"You will pass the entrance to the old mines. Beneath them, there are caverns. Some say they lead to the caves that dot the hills. However, the caverns were the home of the Deep Dwellers."

"Deep Dwellers?" Ryan was almost afraid to ask.

"A race of troglodytes. They sometimes snatched away lone miners. They may still inhabit the lower caverns. Stay to the tunnel." The flame in the braziers flickered. Gathion sat back down on the marble bench. "Our time is at an end. This was my final obligation. A last warning, should the Stone of Orinn ever return to this chamber."

The High Priest and Grand Magi of Hazen stretched out on the cold marble slab. With help from Thadius, he spread the blanket over himself once again. With a parting smile, Gathion drew the cover over his head. As the last of the oil was consumed, the soft emerald glow faded and the gemstone went dark. The chamber was reduced to torchlight and the blanket settled around Gathion's still form. He was at peace.

The radiance of a single rune lingered on the far wall as goblins began to beat on the door.

# ❧ Chapter 23 ❧

At the altar, Thadius hesitated only a second before grasping hold of the Stone of Orinn. Pocketing the green gem, he strode to where the rune had materialized. He placed his palm on the cold marble stone and pushed. To their relief, the block recessed with a click and a smooth section of wall moved inward.

"The way out," Thadius presumed.

While the goblins beat on the door outside, the three slipped through the secret door. With a heave, they pushed the section of marble wall shut behind them. They followed a well-engineered corridor for a whole city block before coming to an airy chamber. A staircase of wood and stone had once staggered up the brickwork to their left. The years had rotted away the timber, and broken stones lay in a loose line of debris.

"We couldn't get back up to the city if we wanted to," Wrella observed.

"Gathion said to stay in the tunnel," Thadius motioned them onward.

They passed into a corridor twice the size of the last, which better fit Gathion's description of a tunnel used to move an army. If their luck held, Ryan reasoned, they would exit somewhere east of the city and beyond any of Torr's goblins. Though well-built in its day, the stonework had suffered over the years. Loose bricks, mortar and a layer of silt littered the ground. Among the fallen materials were the footprints of Hazen's present inhabitants. Countless tracks crisscrossed in each direction, most of them aged and hardened.

"Arrows at the ready," Thadius advised.

"Beware their bite, it will poison your flesh," Ryan reminded them of Gathion's warning.

They continued along the tunnel until their torches burned low. When they stopped to light new ones, Ryan helped take stock of their provisions. While they did, Thadius placed the Stone of Orinn into a plain leather pouch and dropped it casually into his backpack.

"We've some smoked fish, a little jerked meat, a loaf of bread and a few apples left from Askelon's stores," Ryan announced.

"Three skins of water," Thadius counted.

"Four torches and two full flasks of oil remain," Wrella completed their hasty inventory.

"We'll get out into the hills and put this city far behind us," Thadius promised. They resumed their march, and soon, the wide entrance of a passage appeared on their right, descending into pitch darkness.

"Where does it lead?" Ryan questioned.

"Definitely deeper," Wrella commented. "That must be the mines Gathion spoke of."

As they passed the entrance to the ancient mines, Ryan could imagine marching as a soldier of Hazen. He wondered if an army had ever laid siege to the mighty city and if this tunnel might have been used in a bold counter-attack. He turned at a sound from behind.

"We're being followed," Thadius confirmed.

"Goblins?" Ryan hoped.

"I'm afraid not."

"I say we lay a trap," Wrella suggested.

"We've no time," Thadius disagreed. "Let's just stay ahead of it."

The floor became rougher, dotted with more fallen stones and the remnants of heavy timbers. More ghoulish prints left Ryan worried. If they should be set upon by a band of the creatures . . . Then an almost equally frightening sight greeted them ahead. There was no exit.

Though they all saw it plainly enough, they advanced to the end to examine the caved-in area for an overlooked nook or cranny that could lead out. There was none. The roof and walls had collapsed long ago. Claw marks scraped the sloped earth, evidence that not even the ghouls had penetrated past the collapse zone.

"The old mage said nothing of this!" Wrella spat.

"He is obviously not all-knowing," Thadius replied.

"Now what?" Ryan brushed the dirt from his pants. "Do we backtrack and hope to find a way to the surface?"

"We've no choice," Thadius sighed. Ryan could hear the pain in his voice.

A loose stone clattered in the darkness and Thadius spun about. "For now, we have a more pressing problem."

"Things are going from bad to worse," Wrella mumbled.

Into the edge of their torchlight crept two ghouls. Ashen as corpses, their unnatural eyes glistened. With wicked fangs bared, they charged as if in a berserker rage.

"The left one!" Thadius yelled. Ryan dropped his torch and drew back his bowstring. All of their arrows struck the target and the gray-skinned creature tumbled and fell. Thadius called for one more volley, meant for the ghoul on the right. Only Ryan's shaft missed.

"Set to receive!" Thadius instructed. Bows cast to the side, swords were drawn and all stood shoulder to shoulder with weapons pointed directly at the charging ghoul. To Ryan's amazement, the unthinking creature did not slow. At full force, it slammed into their formation and was pierced by all three blades. With a feeble swipe, it clawed at Thadius before collapsing before them. In the next second, Wrella lopped off its head.

The first ghoul had staggered to its feet and now advanced. Thadius slashed into a withered shoulder. Wrella darted in, her lighter sword opening its belly. Dark red hair whirled as she spun, and her blade descended in a blow that ended the fight.

Wrella kicked the ghoul to make sure it was slain. "It wasn't easy to stop these two. If we should run into a pack of them . . ."

With a sense of urgency, they rushed back down the tunnel, aware the goblins could not be far away. As they neared the juncture with the old mines, their collective fears were confirmed. Tiny dots of flame waved about in the distance and faint shouts echoed.

"A battle," Ryan assumed. "They must be fighting those things."

"There are an awful lot of goblins," Wrella glowered, "and they're in our way."

With the exit barred, Ryan saw only one choice. "The mines lead to a cavern system, according to Gathion."

"Into the mines for now, we can at least get out of sight," Thadius directed.

"The caverns lead to caves further out in the hills," Ryan continued.

"The lad's right," Wrella surprised him. "Unless you think we can take on a score or more of goblins."

"If we struck tactically, ambush them here and there, we could whittle their numbers down," Thadius proposed.

"Your wound has already slowed you," she objected. "And we haven't the arrows for those tactics."

Ryan agreed.

"The mines it is," Thadius concluded. "Perhaps we can locate a path that circles back and lets us slip by Torr's warriors."

"Torr?" Wrella repeated. "Their leader has a name?"

"And quite a following," Ryan told her.

"How do you know its name?"

"It's a long story, and we don't have time," Thadius deflected.

"Fine, keep your secrets," she sneered.

They hurried into the rectangular entry, passing under massive beams that Ryan was sure were solid tree trunks. Although not as broad as the tunnel they left, it allowed two to stride abreast with plenty of space to swing a sword. After a short walk, the entrance opened into a spacious area of columns carved from the natural stone. Among the remains of enormous tables and benches, rusted tools lay half-buried in a layer of dirt and loose rock. Ryan shone his torch to see more corridors.

"Which way?"

Thadius rubbed the dust from a smooth, flat stone beside one of them to reveal a faint inscription. "*West Tunnels*," he read.

"Nothing that reads exit?" Wrella flashed a smile.

"It could lead us around the goblins," Thadius hoped.

"That's doubtful." Wrella rapped on a decayed table. "We passed no other passages since departing Gathion."

"You're right," he ceded. "But we've got to choose one."

"West is as good as any," she shrugged.

With matching frowns, Ryan and Thadius followed Wrella into the passage.

Narrowing to about six feet in width, the rough-hewn shaft began fairly straight but wound around as it descended deeper underground. It brought them into a dank and musty chamber, where evidence of digging and scraping scarred the uneven terrain. Pallid cave crickets leapt from their path and crawled across the walls. Ryan was astonished to see mushrooms half his height growing along the damp ground. His stomach rumbled.

"They're giants! Do you think they're edible?"

Thadius shook his head. "We shouldn't risk it."

Beyond the overgrown fungi, another pair of passageways branched off. Wrella absently ran her hand over the surface of a mushroom cap as they passed. Ryan noticed a large bubble rapidly form where she had first touched it. His right hand twitched involuntarily, nerves jolted by an unseen force. This time, he was sure it was a warning. It had happened in the goblin village before he grabbed hold of the shaman's staff. He had not mentioned it to Thadius, but it also occurred just before the goblin warriors had surprised them in the palace.

"Look at that," he alerted the others.

"Back!" Thadius commanded. As they retreated, the expanding bubble burst and filled the immediate area with a cloud of powdery vapor. "Don't breathe it in," he advised. They returned to the main chamber, where Thadius halted to catch his breath.

"Did anyone inhale any of the mushroom's cloud?"

"No," Ryan and Wrella both answered.

"So we've given up on the western tunnels?" Wrella questioned.

"There might be more of those mushrooms about. If one of the western tunnels has them, likely the rest will too. Let's proceed with caution."

Thadius led them toward the next opening. "*South Tunnels*," he read the inscription.

They entered a neatly cut corridor, almost ten feet wide, with a ceiling of about eight feet. The floor gently declined and rotted timber lay across their path at regular intervals, the remains of massive shoring beams. They passed several narrower side passages and stepped over rusted pieces of hardware and the remnants of flat carts.

"What could they have mined here?" Ryan wondered.

"A precious metal of some kind?" Wrella cast an eager glance about. Ryan nearly walked into her when she came to a sudden stop. An iron gate spanned the corridor ahead.

"I don't believe this!" Ryan laid hold of the thick bars. He and Thadius tried to force the ancient gate open.

"It's no use," Thadius growled in frustration. "The lock and latch are rusted together."

"Maybe one of the passages we passed will lead us . . ." Ryan's comment trailed off as shuffling noises came from the darkness behind them. Wrella raised the torch above her head.

"Something's creeping up on us." Her eyes squinted. "In fact, I think there's more than one."

"There's enough space at the top to climb over," Thadius stated.

Beyond the iron bars, roughly cut walls expanded out into the blackness. Ryan knew not what lay ahead, but if ghouls were drawing near, they did not have a choice. He squeezed his pack through the bars of the gate.

"Thadius, you go first. You'll need a boost with your wound."

Thadius shoved his pack between the bars. "No, you first. We'll be—"

"He's right, you thick-headed dolt!" Wrella seized him by the shoulders and shoved him toward the gate. "Now get up there."

With their help, Thadius reached the top of the gate. With a grunt, he pulled himself over. As he did, Wrella pushed her pack past the bars and readied an arrow.

"Here they come!"

"Quickly, Ryan." Thadius nocked an arrow and sighted. Through the bars, his missile flew, sinking deep into the chest of a ghoul. Wrella called for Ryan to hurry as she fired.

Ryan jumped and caught the top of the gate. Hoisting himself up, he threw a leg over and dropped to the ground. He grabbed his bow and snatched an arrow as three ghouls charged at Wrella.

# ❧ Chapter 24 ❧

Wrella leapt and sprang off the rock wall to catch the upper bar of the gate, inches from the ghoul's grasp. She flipped over the top and landed on her feet. Clawed hands shot between the bars, and Ryan raised his bow to fire.

"Don't waste an arrow!" she scolded. "Leave them for the goblins."

They picked up their gear and retreated from the gate. The former citizens of Hazen gnashed their jagged teeth and raked the air with their claws. Knowing their story, Ryan was genuinely sorry for them. Better to have died on the spot than to have spent untold years trapped in these hideous forms.

They discovered themselves in a chamber where stalagmites rose from the rocky floor and matching stalactites hung from above. Thirty feet past the gate came an unexpected find. Four great cauldrons sat evenly spaced in a line that spanned the width of the small cavern. The rock above was darkened by years of soot. Curious, they inspected the squat vessels.

"This was probably the chow line," Wrella guessed.

Thadius ran his fingers through a thick layer of ash. "These served another purpose. But why here? Did they need the heat, or perhaps the light?"

Ryan noticed his hand go to his side. "We should change your bandage while we can."

"Let's make it fast. I still hope to locate a passage that could let us slip past the goblins."

"Then what?" Wrella watched as Ryan unraveled the bloodstained dressing. "All the way back through the sewers? Don't you think this Torr has posted guards?"

"I don't have all the answers for you." Thadius looked tired. "Our choices are limited." He winced and grumbled as Ryan peeled away the old cloth and exposed his wound. It was no better. Despite what care they could render, there would be no real chance to heal with all the constant movement and exertion.

"Fighting that running battle is starting to sound better and better to me," Wrella replied sharply. "Come on, I'll give you a hand with the bandages, if only to save time."

Ryan pressed new bandages over the wound while Wrella wrapped Thadius' torso tightly. When they resumed their journey, they found another barrier of iron bars at the opposite end of the chamber. This gate hung askew.

"At last, a lucky break," Ryan let out.

"Beware," Thadius cautioned. "These gates were built for a reason."

"The Deep Dwellers," Wrella remembered aloud. "What did the old mage say about them, a race of troglodytes?"

"That sounds pleasant," Ryan mumbled. He could not help but note that deeper was exactly where they were heading.

The narrow passage dipped dramatically and opened into another cavern. The wink of crystal imbedded within the strata flashed like tiny stars in the night. Working their way among squat stalagmites, they halted at a jutting deposit of crystal. Thadius poured some water over it and rubbed away the dust and dirt to reveal a smoky purple color.

"Amethyst. A stone often used in magic."

Wrella drew her dagger and attempted to loosen the cluster. She succeeded in dislodging a palm-sized piece as Ryan and Thadius moved on to search the long cavern. Ryan shot her a frown.

"Why shouldn't I get a gem for all my troubles?" she scowled.

Ryan feared another dead-end, until they came across a yawning hole. The nearly vertical shaft dropped away at a steep angle into the unknown depths. Ten feet below the opening, a shelf of flat rock prevented them from seeing any deeper. Ryan peered into the hole and reconsidered the notion of fighting their way back to the surface.

"Things really are going from bad to worse," Wrella snickered. "Are we seriously considering climbing down there?"

"It's not my first choice," Thadius admitted. "We're between a rock and a hard place."

Wrella groaned.

"There were at least three ghouls back at the gate. The goblins will have suffered casualties," Ryan offered hopefully.

"I can backtrack and scout them out," Wrella volunteered.

Thadius shook his head. "I'll go."

"Not hardly," Wrella argued. "I'm faster, quieter and not hampered by a serious wound." She set out before he could protest further. "Just don't go anywhere without me."

Wrella disappeared into the darkness.

Thadius dropped his backpack. "We are re-packing."

"What?"

"Put everything of value into your pack."

"Rations too?"

"Whatever fits. Fill mine with extra clothes and such."

Puzzled, Ryan did as he requested. They finished their task and were eating their rations when Wrella reappeared. Her news was not good.

"The goblins have reached the gated cavern," she reported. "I don't know how many they lost to the ghouls, but there sure are a lot of them left."

Thadius handed her a chunk of hard bread. "Did you get a count?"

"At least two dozen. Probably more."

"What of the leader?"

"A big armored goblin? It was shouting orders. And a shaman is with them."

"That's an unfortunate complication," Ryan commented.

"Yes, and it's using magic," she informed them.

"Spells?" both questioned in unison.

"The whole cavern was lit up with a yellowish glow. Probably to blind those ghouls."

Thadius was silent. Wrella lowered her voice.

"We'll make easy targets for their archers."

"True, there isn't much cover here," Ryan added. "The stalagmites at this end of the cavern are too far apart and not big enough to provide any protection."

"We've no choice," Thadius determined. "We need to find a decent ambush point before they overtake us."

Ryan was less than thrilled by the prospect of descending further into the earth. Every leg of this journey had led them into more dire circumstances than the last. Wrella was right, he decided. Things were constantly going from bad to worse.

Thadius was first into the hole, making his way down to the rock shelf. He leaned over the ledge and shone a torch for a look into the shaft below.

"There's a steep slope, and the drop isn't far. We can make it."

"That's reassuring," Wrella muttered.

Ryan prepared to join him. "Can you see the bottom?" There was an uncomfortable pause, and he knew he would not like the response.

"Not exactly, but I'm sure it's there. There's no easy way to climb back up."

"I'm turning back," Wrella snapped. "I've had enough of scurrying around down here with the cave crickets!"

"The goblins are in the same predicament," Ryan pointed out.

"Except they outnumber us ten to one, and they have a shaman."

"Precisely why we must press on," Thadius stated.

"It's a bad choice, either way," Ryan shrugged at her. "I'll follow whatever path you choose," he said to Thadius.

Without another word, Thadius slid over the edge of the shelf and dropped to the slope below. Loose earth shifted under his weight and sent him rolling another twenty feet or so before he could stop his slide. Ryan descended to the shelf, then joined him, landing on the slope and halting his downward motion with feet outstretched before him. Both of them had scrapes from the sharp rocks, but otherwise, had landed with no injury.

"Are you okay?" Ryan asked.

"I'm still in one piece," Thadius grimaced, his hand momentarily pressed against his side. He rose and waved his torch about. They stood in a cavern where thick fingers of rock descended from above, many connecting to stout towers of stone rising from the floor.

Ryan looked to the shelf of rock above. "What about Wrella?"

"She'll have to decide for herself."

Ryan almost called out to her, when a torch dropped from above. Wrella had chosen to stay with them, and Ryan had to admit he was glad. Although he had not entirely forgiven her, she had aided them time and time again. Besides, he thought, even she deserved better than to die alone in this forsaken place.

Together, they picked their way through the rocky terrain. Overhead, the occasional vein of amethyst caught their eye, amid slender stalactites and protruding formations of stone. Before them, a passage came into view. Staggered niches surrounded the entrance, some containing rounded mounds covered by dust and streaks of mineral deposits. In one of the higher niches, Ryan recognized the macabre shape.

"These are skulls! Human skulls!"

"So that's why the miners of Hazen constructed such sturdy gates," Thadius supposed.

"Those things are ancient. For all we know, these trogs died out years ago," Wrella tried to sound encouraging.

"Nevertheless, these skulls once served as a warning to any who ventured this deep. We should keep arrows ready and our torches brightly lit," Thadius counseled.

Ryan shouldered his bow and took up both torches. He held them high in an attempt to give them as much lighting as possible. In silence, they traversed outcroppings of banded stone and climbed over boulders as they proceeded along the passage. Though he was comforted by the light, Ryan also feared it could attract unwanted attention. But perhaps Wrella was right, and these Deep Dwellers had perished long ago. Then a silhouette moved at the edge of the torchlight.

Wrella was wrong.

Shapes receded into the inky blackness, and unnerving croaks echoed as the party made their way forward. Thadius and Wrella raised their bows in unison.

"Those aren't ghouls, or they would have attacked," Wrella whispered. "Are they Gathion's Deep Dwellers?"

"The ones who snatched away miners," Ryan reminded them.

"Hazen has been abandoned for generations. Humans are only a legend by now," Thadius theorized. "They're leery. It might grant us some advantage."

Ryan noted that the creatures kept to the shadows. "Maybe they're sensitive to the light."

"Or they await reinforcements," Wrella aimed at one of the silhouettes.

"Gathion warned us they're dangerous. But don't shoot unless we're threatened." Thadius ordered.

The passage opened up and they descended a twisting trail into the largest cavern they had yet seen. Their torches flickered like candles against a vast sky of black.

It smelled of earth and water and . . . something else. Something Ryan instinctively did not like. Lending credibility to his theory, whatever these creatures were, they backed away from the light. However, they were not completely lost to the darkness, and when one did not withdraw fast enough, Ryan saw it clearly.

The pale humanoid was shorter than a goblin. Enormous black eyes blinked at them from a squashed and wrinkled face. With a mouth full of charcoal-colored teeth and little nose or ears to speak of, it was a disturbing sight to behold. It held up a skinny arm to shield its eyes and shrank away.

"Spread out a bit," Thadius instructed as they reached level ground. "Let's see what's out there before we get ourselves surrounded."

With a few strides in opposite directions, their area of illumination increased. Before them, the placid surface of an underground lake shimmered. Loose rows of giant mushrooms spread out along the shore to their left, the same variety that they had encountered in the mine tunnel, though taller by a few feet. A growing number of troglodytes were also revealed, creeping toward them down wide pathways through the forest of fungi. Many carried crude knives of black stone. Scattered among the stalagmites and jutting rocks around them, a dozen or so Deep Dwellers grunted and swayed back and forth menacingly.

The croaking increased, answered by a deep chorus that emanated from somewhere along the shore beyond the mushroom fields. Ryan worried they would soon be overpowered by sheer numbers. "There's already a crowd gathered and more are coming our way."

"And they don't exactly look friendly," Wrella agreed.

A rock struck Thadius, thrown from the field of mushrooms. More stones followed, striking Wrella in the leg and shoulder. One bounced off Ryan's armored chest.

"Enough of this!" Wrella took aim at one of the rock-throwers and let fly. A terrible squeal erupted and the Deep Dwellers dove for cover among the mushroom caps. Some continued to pitch stones.

Thadius picked up a hefty rock. With an overhand throw, he launched it into the great mushrooms.

"Rocks?" Ryan questioned. "We aren't going to hold them back with—"

But the next throw connected with one of the huge fungi. It bubbled and released a defensive cloud of noxious gas.

"Rocks!" Ryan repeated. He joined in, throwing loose stones as fast as he could. A misty cloud soon wafted between the fields and the lakeshore, forcing the troglodytes to withdraw.

"We need to move while we have the chance," Thadius set out.

They reached the lakeshore, where the still waters gave no indication as to their depth. Sightless fish darted from the shoreline in white flashes as Thadius led the way in the opposite direction of the mushroom cloud. The stones continued, thrown from those Deep Dwellers around them, though with much less frequency. Ryan was grateful for his chainmail. Wrella released an occasional arrow in an attempt to keep their attackers at bay. They did not get far before a high-pitched trill began.

"What is that?" Ryan called out. The shrill sound echoed all about as it rose to a crescendo.

"Bats!" Thadius yelled over the noise. "The mushrooms' cloud must have irritated them."

Within seconds, a mass of fluttering wings and furry bodies encircled them. Thadius kept them moving through the spinning maelstrom, and for the moment, the stones ceased.

"This is our chance!" Wrella cried out. "The bats are more of a hindrance to them than us."

They rushed along the water's edge, following well-worn footpaths that wound through patches of bioluminescent fungi. Small mushrooms glowed with a green phosphorescent light, and a stringy fungus clung to rock formations, radiating a lilac aura. As the swarming bats thinned, they were pelted with stones once again. Thadius advised Wrella to use her arrows sparingly. This she did, showing restraint and choosing her shots carefully. Yet, when she notified them that only three arrows remained, it sent a chill down Ryan's spine. Sooner or later, he reasoned, these Deep Dwellers would figure out they were out of arrows. Then the real battle would begin.

Thanks to Wrella's skill with the bow, the troglodytes learned to grant the dangerous intruders a wide berth. Few now drew near enough for an accurate throw. Ryan did not realize how long their torches had burned until their flickering light dimmed. They came to a halt at the far edge of the lake to light new ones.

"We've only two left," Ryan gave the count.

Thadius shouldered his bow and handed his arrows to Wrella. "From where have the majority come at us?"

"From the other end of the lake," Ryan answered. "Their lair must be that way."

"If those passages led to daylight, their eyes wouldn't be so sensitive," he deduced.

"And if I had wings, I still couldn't fly us out of here," Wrella declared. "So how does knowing where these underground freaks sleep help us?"

"Gathion spoke of how the caverns led to caves," Thadius said through gritted teeth. "We want to look for a passageway they avoid. It might lead us out."

"Well, it certainly seems like a long shot," she returned sarcastically. "But if it'll cost us our last arrow and use up our last torch, then by all means—"

"Shut up!" Ryan shouted. "Nobody asked you to come along. In fact, nobody would even be here, a mile under the earth, if it wasn't for you!"

A jolt shot through Ryan's hand. He froze as Wrella raised her bow and loosed her arrow.

# ❦ Chapter 25 ❧

Wrella's arrow shot by Ryan in a blur. He spun to see a Deep Dweller pitch forward. Its stone dagger clattered to the ground. Troglodytes charged them from every direction, brandishing knives of obsidian, chipped to keen edges. As another closed, Ryan slashed an outstretched arm. With a yelp of pain, it dropped the knife and vanished back into the darkness.

As fast as the creatures came at him, Thadius cut them down. His blade was a silver flash and his dagger its deadly companion. Wrella's sword whistled as she whirled full circle and left two of the troglodytes with deep cuts. Surrounded by the dead and dying, Ryan looked on with a sense of sadness. These were the poorest fighters he had ever encountered. Untrained, unarmored, and while their weapons could be lethal, they were of the most primitive construction. If only they could somehow communicate.

A pasty-skinned troglodyte leapt on Ryan. He hit the ground hard and was shocked by the weight of the short creature. Ryan let go of his sword and grappled with it to keep from being stabbed. He seized the Deep Dweller's wrists as it straddled his chest, and though he was strong for a lad of fifteen, the sharp stone knife slowly descended toward his throat.

Thadius' boot slammed into the troglodyte's ribs with a thump, sending it rolling. It scrambled to its feet and fled with the other survivors of the failed assault.

"Are you hurt?"

Ryan stood and dusted off his armor. "Only my pride."

"Not that it matters, but I'm just fine," Wrella said with a hint of scorn.

"I know," Thadius replied, holding his side. "I've seen your skill in battle."

The dim light hid the blush in her cheeks. "You look like you need to rest a minute. Then let's move out before they're back in greater numbers," she suggested gruffly.

The cavern narrowed and the ground smoothed. Ryan could tell by the pattern and discoloration in the amber-striped strata that water sometimes flowed in streams that rose past his knees. He was thankful this was apparently the dry season. The cavern ended with a yawning opening through a stone wall of slanted striations.

"There's a stink in the air," Wrella snorted.

"We finally agree on something," Thadius mused.

With a frown, Wrella stepped into the lead and thrust her torch about. "I wish I had a free hand, I'd pinch my nose shut."

Pale millipedes crawled at their feet as she led the way into the oblong-shaped opening. Barely eight feet in height, there was no room to swing a sword. Ryan could feel the walls closing in with almost every step. Further on, a trio of passages branched off. Deep Dwellers retreated from their left and right. None appeared on the path before them and Ryan suspected a trap.

"To the left, the ground rises," Wrella reported. "But there are lots of eyes reflecting back at me." With a few steps, Thadius was at her side.

"Water formed these passages," he declared. "What lies to the right?"

Ryan investigated his side. "I've got eye shine here too."

He hoped Thadius would choose the ascending path. Perhaps it might lead back up to the mines. Ahead, he could detect the stench of rotting meat and who knew what else.

Thadius studied the layers of discolored rock. "I say we follow where the water went."

"That figures," Wrella disapproved.

"Hear me out, then decide for yourselves."

"There must be a good reason why Thadius wants to pick the stinkiest route," Ryan defended. "Right?"

Thadius grunted. "Water has flown through here for countless years, creating channels in the rock and widening caverns."

"Explain it better, because I still want to go up," Wrella stated stubbornly. Ryan had to admit that he did as well.

"Over the years, water has dug deep under these hills by eroding away limestone. There's no water flowing right now—"

"So let's go upwards, where we know we'll stay dry," Wrella argued.

"Wait a minute. Since there's no water at the moment, we can follow its course, probably all the way until it had poured out into the hills," Ryan said hopefully.

"Sounds very iffy to me," Wrella shook her head. "We'll have to backtrack if you're wrong."

"If I'm wrong, you'll get your goblin battle."

"Then it's settled," Ryan accepted. "Let's not waste time."

With Thadius in front, they proceeded. Beyond a brief bottleneck, the pathway opened into a spacious cavern, where they discovered the source of the mysterious odor. Piles of refuse snaked along a deep gully, deposited by flowing water. The stench was nearly unbearable and they covered their noses with as much cloth as could be found on short notice. Red beetles and the occasional cave spider scurried about the ground.

"That's ungodly," Ryan gasped.

Thadius held a square of cloth against his face and kept them moving past the remnants of innumerable troglodyte meals. Ryan could make out bits of pelt, bat wings and the bones of fish.

"This is their trash!"

"Oh, it's worse," Wrella coughed from beneath a hastily tied bandana. "This is their waste!"

They traveled as quickly as the rough terrain allowed and at last came to the end of the cavern. In the flickering light, they examined the cavity before them, barely five feet in width and about as high.

"Single file from here," Thadius announced.

Swords drawn, they bent to enter a passageway. Despite his discomfort with the cramped conditions, Ryan was glad of one thing. They had passed beyond the stench of the troglodytes' refuse. He could hardly detect the smell as they made their way deeper beneath the earth. However, with each twist or turn, the walls seemed to grow closer together. Soon, Ryan could not chalk it up to his imagination. He crouched as he walked and could easily touch rock on either side.

"This is getting a bit narrow, don't you think?" he whispered.

"Stay calm. Things may get uncomfortable," Thadius advised.

"Too late, we passed uncomfortable an hour ago."

Ryan's uneasiness increased as the passage continued to shrink. They were forced to their hands and knees and funneled into a tube about three feet in diameter. He could not stand to crawl any further into the confined space.

"Thadius, I don't know if I can do this!"

"Control your breathing and try not to think about your surroundings."

"That's not going to happen," Ryan responded. "What if we come to a dead-end?"

"All of that water went somewhere. I have a good feeling about this," Wrella reassured him.

"You do?" Ryan asked incredulously. "Now I know I won't like this!"

"I like it no better," Thadius confessed. "I feel like a mole already. But I've noticed one thing."

"What's that?" Ryan needed some good news.

"The air is cleaner. The stink of that cavern is gone and I think it's because of air pressure from below."

"An air current?" Wrella paused.

"The air seems fresher the deeper we go. At least it isn't as foul."

"Thadius . . ." Ryan wanted to tell him of his fear yet could not bring himself to admit it aloud. Especially in front of Wrella.

"We'll go a little further," Thadius coaxed.

Even with this assurance, Ryan's heart raced. Though he had faced the undead and dark magics, this was somehow different. His pulse pounded and his breath grew short. This claustrophobic fright was not something he could grapple with or reason through. Sheer will may not be enough to overcome his increasing anxiety. "Have we reconsidered battling the goblins?"

"I know I have," came Wrella's reply.

"Wrella, can you take the lead?" Thadius requested.

"I guess so," she answered in a subdued tone.

"Slip by us, while there's still room. Then Ryan can slide by me."

Leaving her torch, she pressed past Ryan and drew up beside Thadius.

"Cozy, isn't it?" She smiled as she wriggled by him and collected his torch.

"All right, Ryan."

Carefully, he passed the torch to Thadius, who pushed it aside. Ryan squeezed by, scuffing his armor and sword hilt along the stone surface. When at last he was clear of Thadius, he breathed a bit easier.

"I could have gone by faster if you'd have let me," Ryan panted.

"It was difficult, wasn't it?"

"I suppose."

"Now you know you can handle a tight spot."

Thadius called for Wrella to lead on. Ryan kept his eyes on her torchlight. He didn't want to handle any more tight spots. He wanted this leg of the journey to end. The tunnel they crawled through grew even smaller, and he wondered how they would turn themselves around if it should become impassable.

"Anything yet?" Thadius hollered over the scrape of limbs, armor and other equipment.

"More of the same." There was a hint of trepidation in Wrella's voice.

Ryan recognized the fracture in her usually confident demeanor. It had been the same on that day long ago, when the king's men had hunted them. While it did no good to dwell on the past, it did take his mind off the present situation. He did not notice that Wrella had come to a halt until his hands fell on her soft leather boots.

"What is it?"

"Tight. Very tight," she responded. "We'll have to remove our packs and push them in front of us."

This was the last straw for Ryan. He had done well to make it this far but could not see himself inching into the earth any further. The only thing worse than inching his way back out, would be to run out of light in the middle of it all.

"I can't do this!"

To his surprise, it was Wrella who cried out.

"You're okay, Wrella. Stay calm," Thadius soothed.

"This *is* calm!" she returned sharply. "Calm enough for being buried alive under tons of rock and troglodyte waste!"

"Perhaps we should turn back," Ryan offered. "There's no telling how far we'll get before we find the way blocked or another forest of poisonous toadstools."

Thadius let out a long breath. "Very well. The decision to follow this path was my mistake . . ."

"I'm going through!" Wrella shouted.

"You always have to pick the opposite side!" Ryan admonished. "What changed your mind?"

"A breeze," she replied. "It was definitely there. We aren't far from fresh air."

The possibility of a way out lifted Ryan's spirits. His fears were temporarily alleviated and he worked to shed his pack and bedroll. "Can you see anything?"

"More darkness."

Ryan asked no more, for even that brief description of what lay ahead took the edge off his joy. Thadius and Wrella kept their torches at arm's length while nudging their packs in front of them. In this manner they proceeded, measuring their travel in inches instead of feet.

The tunnel tapered and it became awkward to raise his head. Ryan knew he could never have done this alone. Damp with perspiration, he mustered all of his will and concentrated on moving forward, like an earthworm burrowing through the soil. Nothing more than a faint glow reflected off the rock around him, caught out of the corner of his eye.

Ryan's nose practically touched the stone floor as he scooted along and he was relieved the surface was somewhat smooth. Behind, he could hear Thadius labor to keep pace. Escape was not Ryan's only concern. Thadius needed more than herbs and salves. He needed serious care and bed rest.

"We're coming up on something," Wrella's muffled report drifted back.

They were the sweetest words Ryan had heard in days, perhaps weeks. The reflected light of her torch abruptly ended. Wrella squirmed through a hole and dropped from sight. Ryan followed, passing her his pack as he cleared the mouth of the cramped tube. She set aside Thadius' gear and both helped him crawl free as well.

Though the area they occupied was little more than ten feet square, Ryan was as relieved as if they had broken through to daylight. The claustrophobic fear that had gripped him quickly passed and he stretched out gratefully in each direction. Meanwhile, Wrella donned a pack and cinched down her gear. Picking up the brighter of the torches, she stepped into a passage that continued off into the darkness.

"You should rest a bit," she said to Thadius. "I'll scout around, then have a look at your wound. We'll probably need to clean you up and put on a fresh dressing at least."

Ryan agreed. Thadius was soaked with sweat and looked haggard. Their flight had further aggravated his wound. Ryan aided with re-securing their weapons and equipment. During the long trek on their bellies, most straps and buckles had become loose. When Ryan was ready to retrieve a bandage wrapping, he discovered that Wrella had grabbed the wrong backpack.

"She took your pack by mistake," he shook his head.

Thadius grunted in response.

Ryan's jaw dropped. He suddenly remembered that was where Thadius had placed the pouch with the gem.

The Stone of Orinn was gone.

# ❧Chapter 26❧

"Thadius, she's taken it! We've got to—"

"Relax, the gemstone is safe." Thadius patted his front pocket.

Panic faded into disappointment. "So, she's made her move at last. I held out a glimmer of hope that she might somehow change."

"We could be wrong," Thadius offered.

"No," Ryan accepted. "It's why we put everything important into my pack. Your instincts were correct."

"In any case, we need to find our way out of here, and fast."

The passage they followed soon split. The flow of water had left deep fissures in the rock beneath their feet, and with no loose soil, there was no evidence as to which direction Wrella had gone. Thadius was reduced to taking his best guess, and they traversed the wider of their choices. Ryan was relieved when a faint glow came into view.

They entered the lower portion of a spacious cavern. An upper level encircled the opposite half of the cavern and Ryan could see enough to know that the cavern continued off into the darkness above. Across an underground forest of giant mushrooms, they spied Wrella. Somehow, she had navigated the overgrown fungus without alarming one into releasing its noxious vapor. She struggled to scale a sheer rock face, and preoccupied with her climb, did not notice them. Strapped to her back was Thadius' pack.

Wrella wedged her torch into a crevice and searched for the next handhold. Ryan could not see how she was going to complete her ascent. He was amazed she had gotten as far as she had. There looked to be few cracks or jutting features among the smooth stone surface. Ryan worried if Thadius could make it at all.

"Now what? Do we let her go, or go after her? She'll be twice the trouble, I'm sure."

"Wait, do you see? Wrella!" Thadius called out. "Something's moving up there!"

She turned around on a thin shelf and unshouldered her bow. "Stay away, both of you! I happen to have one arrow left. It would be a shame for you to end up with it."

Then in the flickering torchlight, Ryan saw it too. An angular, lizard-like head appeared on the ledge above her. While some details of the creature were lost to the shadows, Ryan estimated its body to be an easy six feet in length. A sharply tapered upper jaw reminded Ryan of a snapping turtle. Protruding eyes white as pearls cocked in Wrella's direction.

"He's telling the truth, come back to us."

"Not likely!" she retorted.

Before Ryan could voice another warning, the giant lizard opened its beaked maw. A thick tongue shot out and struck Wrella in the shoulder. She nearly toppled from the narrow ledge and cast her bow away to flatten herself against the sheer rock.

"Hang on!" Ryan started toward her.

"Careful," Thadius cautioned.

Wrella regained her balance, and with a grimace, pulled back against the tug of the elongated tongue stuck to her armor.

"You're not used to such big prey, are you, my scaly friend?" she called to it. Another reptilian creature crawled into sight above her as Ryan and Thadius picked their way among the tall fungi. Ryan tried again to reason with her once they reached the base of the wall.

"Wrella, please listen. Cut yourself loose and we'll catch you."

"I'm not about to lose all I've worked for!"

A second sticky tongue slammed into her from the opposite side. The impact bounced her off the rock wall, giving her a bump to the head and leaving her dangling in midair.

"Wrella, cut yourself free," Ryan urged.

"Will you risk everything to satisfy your greed?" Thadius added. "You know what the return of the stone will mean. Do you want to see the whole kingdom suffer?"

"Phah!" she spat. "What of *my* suffering?"

As the combined pull of both tongues hoisted Wrella upward, she reached out and snatched her torch from the crevice, flinging it up and over the ledge above. Taking a firm grip on both slimy tongues, she allowed herself to be lifted up the side of the sheer wall.

"Nice move," Thadius admitted.

"Thadius!" Ryan pointed. Deep Dwellers appeared on the upper level from the mouth of a passage across from them. Half a dozen of them gathered and all hefted stones.

Thadius grabbed Ryan by the shoulder. "Quick, out of these mushrooms."

Ryan and Thadius retreated through the immense caps, with less caution this time. Though careful not to brush against any, their efforts were in vain. The Deep Dwellers cast their stones, striking mushrooms all about. As they feared, the fungi bubbled and released their gaseous clouds.

*     *     *

Wrella kept a firm grip on the slimy tongues and her feet in contact with the wall. With a back-and-forth sway, she steadied her ascent. Nearing the ledge above, she release her hold on one and drew her dagger. The two creatures had converged, each reeling in its clammy tongue in anticipation of a huge meal. Clawed feet braced against stone, and milky eyeballs twisted about to get a better view of the prey each labored to reel in.

It was time to act. Her dagger severed the tongue of the larger one. The beast scurried away with a croaking cry. As Wrella rolled over the edge, she did the same for the other. Tongue flopping about, it spewed a trail of blood as it crashed into an approaching third monster. This one Wrella set upon and slew with her sword before it could use its tongue against her. She retrieved her torch and held it aloft for a look around.

Below, troglodytes targeted Ryan and Thadius as they ran. She could hear the thump of stones on the soft fungi. In a few minutes, toxic gas would fill the cavern. She turned to see a glimpse of daylight at the mouth of a distant cave. There were more of the giant lizards between her and the open sky.

Wrella hesitated.

"What am I thinking?" She mumbled to herself. She had no doubt that Thadius would deal with her harshly should she return. "Since when do I care what some self-styled adventurer with a sour attitude thinks of me?"

Her mind was set.

"See you boys in the next life!" she shouted in triumph. With a battle cry, Wrella charged toward freedom.

*    *    *

A misty cloud of foul gas wafted across the cavern. Ryan and Thadius stayed ahead of the brownish haze and retreated into the passage. Where it split, they stopped to catch their breath.

"Even if we could wait for the air to clear, how are we going to get up that wall?" Ryan asked when he could speak in a whole sentence.

"We're not," Thadius replied, "unless we can duplicate her feat of acrobatics."

"We don't know for sure if the mushrooms' gas is poisonous."

"I'm willing to bet it is." Perspiration dripped down his face, and Thadius looked worn. "We can't wait here. Torr won't give up."

"True. We've only one torch left and it won't last much longer."

Already the flames flickered low. Ryan was not eager to explore the narrower branch of the passage. What if they were forced to crawl on their bellies again? He would rather take his chances with the troglodytes and burn the shirt off his back to light the way. And it may come to that, he thought. The way the flame danced . . .

"Thadius, do you feel a breeze?"

"Yes, a cold draft."

A distant echo reached their ears.

"The goblins are crawling from the tunnel," Ryan stated.

"Let's hurry."

The other branch was more of a tall fissure in the rock, leading them deeper beneath the Lost Hills with twists and turns that kept them guessing as to their direction. They squeezed past a protruding rock formation to find themselves in a tight passage of banded rock. Ryan cringed. It ended in an angled wall that funneled down to a wedge-shaped hole.

"At least it's big enough for us to crawl into and keep our packs on," Thadius said.

Ryan was encouraged by the slight breeze. But Thadius suddenly motioned for silence.

"Wait here."

As Thadius bent and disappeared into the blackness, Ryan strained to hear any sounds of pursuit. He could make out faint shouts and imagined that the goblins had discovered the cavern of mushrooms. In another moment, Thadius eased his way back to him.

"There's another cave beyond," he barely whispered.

"Then let's get out of here," Ryan returned in a low tone.

"Something smells in there."

"Something bad?"

"Very bad. Big-and-hairy bad. I think it's a bear."

"Bear?" Ryan's eyes widened and his voice jumped an octave.

"Yes."

Goblin voices grew louder.

"So Wrella took the easy way out," Ryan mused. "What should we do?"

Thadius was silent. The torch sputtered, and this time it was not due to any air current. It was nearly spent.

"Stay close," he instructed. "Do as I do, and for Orinn's sake, don't let your armor jingle."

"I'll try," Ryan promised. They worked together to cinch every strap and buckle they could. Armor, packs and weapons were tightly secured, and Thadius placed his cloak around Ryan to further muffle the metallic links. They approached the small hole at the end of the passage.

"Toss the torch away."

Ryan did not hesitate. Though he was uncomfortable in the darkness, he did not want the bear to smell fire and wake in a panic.

"Here we go." Thadius barely breathed the words.

Thadius bent and slipped into the entry. He was instantly engulfed in blackness. Ryan could see absolutely nothing. He crawled in next, rock closing in around him. There was only the occasional creak of movement coming from this piece of gear or that. He laid a hand on the heel of Thadius' boot with every careful step, to reassure himself that the woodsman was just ahead. An odd smell struck him, quickly becoming a powerful stench, irritating his throat. Afraid he might gag or cough, Ryan swallowed hard and pressed on.

Stone walls gave way to open space. A white blur materialized in the distance. Ryan could not gauge how far, but he was sure it was daylight. Somewhere across the cave, something big breathed in a shallow and steady rhythm. Ryan concentrated on putting one hand in front of the other. Then a deep snort froze them in their tracks. Sweat trickled down his face and he fought the urge to jump up and run.

"Orinn, if this stone is really worth it, please get us out of here," Ryan mouthed a silent prayer.

A rumbling snore followed and Ryan could breathe again. Satisfied that the bear still slept, Thadius continued. Ryan stayed on his heels and was grateful for the hibernating beast's loud breath. It masked what noise they made, quiet as they tried to be.

As the level of illumination gradually increased, Ryan could make out more of the cave. Not ten feet from them, a great bear lay curled up, a mountain of dark fur. Across their path, an outstretched paw twitched. Thadius guided them around, and to Ryan's relief, a squat exit came into view. Perhaps another twenty feet and they would again see the sun.

A light flared from behind. A surprised goblin screamed . . . and pandemonium broke loose.

# ❧ *Chapter 27* ❧

The bear reacted instinctively to the intruders in its midst. Powerful claws swiped at those goblins who entered, while more pushed and crowded their way through the narrow hole. The winter den was a scene of chaos. Goblins shrieked and trampled each other to escape when they realized what they faced.

"Run!" Thadius ordered.

They darted from under an overhanging slab of stone and into the first rays of the dawn. Ryan blinked and shielded his eyes against the brightness. Below, lay a valley of amber grass and sparse trees.

"Make for the far side and don't stop!" Thadius shouted.

Ryan ran, half-blind at first as his eyes gradually became accustomed to the sunlight. He kept his head down and his legs pumping. Thadius lagged behind. Halfway across the valley floor, Ryan slowed to match his pace.

"It's not much further," Ryan said. Thadius nodded and pushed on, his breath creating heavy clouds of fog in the cold morning air.

Ryan scanned the ridge behind them and located the shelf where the bear's den lay. A group of goblins stumbled into the daylight. The creatures tripped over themselves as they fled the cave. Ryan counted six in total, including their shaman. The last goblin from the cave was larger than the rest. Ryan caught the glint of armor. Torr had somehow survived. The bear emerged next. Seeing its full size, Ryan was stunned. The animal was bigger than his horse.

"Cave bear," Thadius proclaimed. "I never thought to see one."

"I've seen one too many," Ryan replied.

The great bear loped after the goblins. Just when it seemed it would have Torr for breakfast, the chieftain lashed out with his scimitar at a fellow goblin running alongside. The unfortunate warrior tumbled and Torr raced past, leaving it to be mauled by the angry bear.

Ryan and Thadius pushed on until they crested the opposite slope. Ryan hoped that the cave bear would chase after Torr, but a pair of wounded goblins stumbled from the beast's lair, catching its attention. With a roar, it charged after them. Torr waved the surviving goblins onward. Thadius led them from the crest, then knelt to catch his breath and check his weapons.

"There's no doubt, they saw us. And there are five of them," Ryan said with frustration. "I wish we had some arrows left."

"Take a knee and relax. It'll take them a moment or so to reach us."

"Relax?"

"At least we'll be rested." He gestured to some brush about thirty paces from a lone pine tree. "Conceal yourself. When I call out Torr's name, it will be your signal. Strike them from behind. And Ryan, strike to kill."

Ryan moved to the designated spot and dumped his gear in a pile. He settled in and tried to still his nerves. Hearing goblin voices, he risked a peek.

Thadius stood near the pine. The goblins approached him with caution. Muddy and disheveled, Torr appeared otherwise unharmed. The shaman, as well as the other goblins, sported all manner of cuts and abrasions. One of the goblins had been raked down its arm by a ghoul. Greenish flesh was mottled with gray. Torr waved the warriors forward.

As the trio surrounded him, Thadius threw his dagger with deadly accuracy. A warrior collapsed, grasping its throat in an attempt to stem the flow of blood. The goblins circled him and the shaman raised a rod of adder wood. It began a chant, thrusting the rod toward Thadius. When the shaman evoked the name of its god, Thadius reeled. He shook his head and wiped his face. Torr barked an order and his men advanced.

Thadius lashed out with his sword, nearly decapitating one. He spun about and missed the other by a wide margin. He rubbed his eyes as the goblins circled. Again, Thadius fended them off. However, his counter-strikes were late and not well-placed. Something was wrong. A goblin crept around him, and before Thadius could react, it slashed his leg. Thadius fell into a sideways roll and sprang to his feet. His sword flashed in silver arcs all about as the goblins withdrew.

Torr laughed aloud. The shaman maintained its chant, the rod pointed at Thadius.

Then Ryan put it together. Thadius was blinded by goblin magic. A warrior closed in and poked Thadius in the shoulder with its spear. He shifted his defense as the other goblin slapped his opposite shoulder with the flat of its blade. They were toying with him before the kill. Ryan tensed. Where was the signal to act? Torr grunted a command and his warriors assumed a more deadly posture. As the shaman chanted, Torr started toward Thadius. Ryan's heart sank. There would be no signal. Thadius was giving him the chance to escape.

Ryan's mind reeled. Should the Stone of Orinn fall into goblin hands, Malikar and the king would have their war and launch a new goblin campaign. Perhaps Drynas or even Llerwyth might be attacked. The conflict could drag on long enough to see Darien come of age. Thadius' last words brought him back to the night in the goblin camp. He had sworn an oath to use his sword only in defense. Ryan rose. That time was now.

Unnoticed as yet, Ryan rushed the shaman. Absorbed in the spell of dark magic, it was caught by surprise. Steel pierced flesh and penetrated between rib bones. The bond with its deity broken, the shaman's spell was lost. Ryan yanked the blade free and slew the goblin with a second stroke. Torr and his warriors were poised to finish Thadius. Had he acted too late?

"Thadius!"

The goblins spun about. It was the distraction Thadius needed. His sword whistled as it came around, its arc hardly slowing as it separated a goblin head from its shoulders. Torr grabbed hold of the last warrior by the front of its coat. Using the smaller goblin as a shield, Torr charged.

Larger and stronger than most of its kind, the goblin chieftain swung the heavy scimitar with the skill to use it effectively. Thadius backpedaled as he dodged and parried. Unable to land a blow, Torr shoved the struggling goblin onto Thadius' blade. Thadius fell with the dying goblin and scrambled to escape Torr's onslaught. Despite the weight of its banded armor, Torr was nimble. The goblin landed a solid kick that sent Thadius sprawling.

Ryan bolted forward and picked up a fallen spear. He hurled it as Torr raised the scimitar. The spearhead glanced off an armored shoulder. With a snarl, Torr whipped about and set upon him. Ryan met the goblin's assault with a sturdy parry. His arm stung with the impact of metal on metal, from his hand all the way to his shoulder. Before he could launch a counter-attack, the goblin raised a long foot and kicked him squarely in the chest. Ryan flew backwards as if bucked by a horse.

"Torr!" Thadius called out.

"You're late," Ryan croaked. He lay in the grass, winded. His vision swam.

Torr rushed at Thadius anew. The former Huntsman kept the pine between them, and chips of bark flew as the goblin's strokes missed their mark. Both maneuvered for the next strike when Torr landed a weighty punch that slammed Thadius into the tree. The goblin brought its hilt down on the woodsman's wrist. Thadius was disarmed and Torr kicked him away before he could reach for his fallen blade.

Thadius rolled beside the spear Ryan had thrown. He seized hold of it and sprang, thrusting it into the goblin's abdomen. Torr staggered and dropped the scimitar. It grabbed the wooden shaft with a clawed hand and batted Thadius aside with the other. The chieftain let loose a primal howl and pulled the spearhead from its body. Torr flipped the sharp point about and loomed over a fallen Thadius.

From behind, Ryan's sword descended, cleaving flesh and bone and washing grimy armor in black blood. With a guttural growl, Torr sank to the earth, dead.

Thadius rose on unsteady feet. Ryan hurried to his side.

"Gather your gear," Thadius panted. "We've little time before the vultures give away our position."

"I don't think there's a single goblin left."

"Cave bears rarely pass up an easy meal. That goes for wolves and gods only know whatever else hunts in these hills."

Ryan scanned the land about them. To the south, he spied a distant wood line. "Thadius," he exclaimed, "we're practically out of these cursed hills! Darkwood lies within sight."

"Take the gem to Drynas," came the weak reply.

"Thadius?"

"The gem must get to Ephram," he strained.

"Not until we've patched you up. Then we'll return to Drynas together," Ryan promised. "First, we need to get away from this valley."

Ryan collected what gear he could carry and helped Thadius to his feet. "Lean on me," he insisted. "We'll walk to the edge of the hills and make camp."

Ryan perspired under the heavy burden in spite of the cold temperature. His breath left his lungs in clouds of vapor, and the frozen grass on the leeward side of the ridge crunched beneath his boots. He struggled to keep an ailing Thadius on his feet as he searched for a protected spot to serve as camp.

At last, Ryan spied an outcropping of rock. The position was well-situated, he had a good view all about them for some distance and it was protected from the wind. With the last of his strength, Ryan brought Thadius to rest in a patch of soft grass.

"Hold on, Thadius, I'll get a fire lit." Ryan gathered what nearby fuel he could find.

"There's not enough to burn all day."

"No, but we can rest and you need treatment. There's still a chance to fight the infection. Besides, you've sprouted a few new holes."

Thadius shed his shirt and unbandaged his side. Wrella's stitching had come undone and the skin was red and swollen. An ochre fluid oozed from the gash. Ryan washed the site and saw to his other wounds before cutting and pulling away the old stitches. Thadius readied a needle and thread while Ryan built a fire.

"Surely Wrella's discovered by now that her plans were all in vain." Ryan shook his head. Part of him felt sorrow for her. Wrella seemed doomed to follow a path of greed and self-destruction, regardless of the camaraderie they had shared.

"It's hard for someone to change in such a short period of time," Thadius responded.

The flames grew as Ryan added more branches. Thadius was right, it would not last. There was not enough dead wood or brush about to keep a fire burning through the night. He laid aside the ingredients needed for later. Now was the part he dreaded. The wound needed to be re-stitched. With an unsteady hand, he examined the sharp needle. Held up close, it somehow looked longer and thicker than it really was.

"Steady," Thadius tried to calm him. "You can do this."

"I've never stitched this deep."

"It's no more painful, if that's a comfort." As the curved needle neared his flesh, Thadius let out a breath. "I wish we had some strong drink."

"For you, or for me?" Ryan asked.

"A little for both," he winced.

Ryan sweated freely as he sewed under Thadius' direction. Both were soaked by the end of the procedure. Ryan applied a poultice generously, directly to the inflamed tissue about the laceration. Afterward, he made a tea, using every healing herb in their inventory that could be taken internally. He prayed it was enough.

As Thadius slept, Ryan struck out to collect the rest of their gear and as much wood as he could. Even if he accumulated enough material to burn through the night, they could not stay. With little water and less food, they needed to begin the journey south as soon as possible.

Cresting a nearby rise, Ryan spotted a cluster of trees. He set to work with their hand axe and chopped off leafless limbs with loud cracks. He thought nothing of the noise or how far it may travel until he spied horses approaching.

# ❧ Chapter 28 ❧

Ryan counted three horses and a single rider, heading straight for him. As he dashed toward camp, he recognized Jona as the horseman. He could not believe his tired eyes and halted to await the Huntsman. Jona led both of their horses and slid from the saddle to greet Ryan.

"Curse it, lad! I've been up and down this trail, hoping the two of you would somehow emerge from these hills before time ran out. I've been summoned to Ardan."

"Thadius is hurt," Ryan managed between breaths.

Jona's expression changed to concern. "Lead me to him."

They found Thadius awake, lying before the fire.

"I don't suppose you've kept my horse well-fed?" Thadius rose stiffly.

"Not as well as its owner, I'm sure," Jona replied. "I brought lunch with me, and I have medical supplies. Maybe we should unpack those first."

Ryan secured their mounts and unpacked the provisions while Jona checked on Thadius' wounds — both old and new.

"You've done a good job," he complimented Ryan.

"I was taught well," Ryan gave Thadius a nod.

"You two look like you've battled from one end of the underworld to the other. Especially you," he referred to Thadius.

"That's not far from the truth. But it was worth it." Thadius cracked a smile.

"You've recaptured the gemstone?" Jona's eyes widened.

"*We* did," Thadius confirmed, slapping Ryan on the shoulder. Ryan beamed with pride.

Jona passed out a shared meal from his rations, consisting of dried deer meat, hard rolls and boiled eggs.

"It's not much," he apologized.

"It's a banquet," Thadius declared.

As they ate, Jona inquired about their adventures. Thadius spoke of the goblin shrine and Torr's village. He said nothing of Hazen, centaurs or their trek beneath the earth. As for Ryan's suit of chainmail, he explained it away as captured goblin treasure.

Jona shared with them his written orders. Thadius furrowed his brow as he read. Not only was the Legion's outpost turned over to the earl, most of the Huntsmen in the region were to assemble at Ardan.

"This makes our task all the more urgent. The Stone of Orinn must be returned to Drynas with all haste," Thadius stated.

"We're not exactly welcome at the city gates," Ryan reminded him.

"My route to Ardan is not specified. Let me accompany you to Drynas," Jona requested. "Or at least to Aldwyn. You'll need some rest and recuperation."

"I can't argue with that," Thadius relented. "I'll be ready to ride by morning."

Throughout the frigid night, Jona and Ryan took turns at watch. Each fed the fire from their meager stock of wood and kept the coals hot to brew another batch of herbal tea. Ryan rose early to scout the area. By the time Thadius woke, Ryan had returned with a souvenir.

"Still no sign of Wrella. But I did find this. It's yours by right." Ryan set Torr's sheathed scimitar before him.

"I'd almost forgotten about it." Thadius drew the sword and Jona joined him in an examination of the goblin blade.

"See the pattern of steel and iron," Thadius pointed out.

"There's an awful lot of steel in this sword to be goblin-forged," Jona commented.

"Yes, the goblins are getting steel from somewhere. From someone."

"Bandits?" Ryan offered.

"Perhaps . . ." Thadius sheathed the curved sword and secured it to his steed. "To Aldwyn."

During their first rest break, Jona unbandaged and checked on Thadius' side.

"I don't like the looks of it," the Huntsman frowned, covering the wound before Ryan could see it.

"All the more reason for haste," Thadius grunted.

They maintained an easy gait, both for the horses and for Thadius. But with food and water running short, Thadius urged them to continue far into the night. When at last he led them into the cover of the woods, Ryan tended to the horses while Jona started a fire. An exhausted Ryan battled sleep and the cold to complete his turn at watch. He woke to find Jona gone. Thadius lay still.

Ryan jerked upright. He held his breath, waiting for Thadius' chest to rise and fall.

"Yes, I'm alive," Thadius murmured.

Ryan breathed a sigh of relief. "I'll make you some tea."

"Be sparing with our herbs," he instructed. "It's about four days to Aldwyn." Sweat beaded on his forehead.

Ryan built up the fire, and set to work. When the brew was ready, Thadius chuckled as Ryan poured him a steaming cup of tea.

"What's so funny?"

"The dire boar was a ridiculous idea."

"It's not like I had a chance to think of something better."

Thadius laughed, despite the obvious pain in his face. "But that goblin's face was priceless." He sipped his tea. "Trenn needs to examine the materials we took from Hazen. See that he—"

"We will — together."

As Ryan pondered their situation, he absently rubbed his hands together for warmth. He noted the ring on his finger, his intended gift for Arlena. He told Thadius of the incidents involving the silver band.

"It gives you a strange jolt?" Thadius repeated when Ryan had finished. "And you think it's some kind of warning?"

"It might sound odd, but it did come off of a sorcerer's shelf. It doesn't happen at every peril. Maybe if danger is close?"

"Perhaps if life-threatening," Thadius considered, "or unexpected."

After a paltry breakfast, Ryan labored to pack up their camp. At his insistence, Thadius rested to conserve his strength.

"Jona has been gone a long time," Ryan voiced.

"He's scouting," Thadius said dismissively. Yet, he felt for the gemstone in his pocket. "Now you've got me double-checking his loyalties."

"Sorry. It's just that after Wrella . . ."

"I know," he nodded.

"I guess Jona saw no trace of her."

"No. He would have mentioned it."

Satisfied, Ryan saddled their horses and extinguished the fire. Jona returned as he did so, guiding his mount skillfully between the tall trees.

"A patrol nears," he informed them. "I've barely stayed ahead of them."

"We need to get deeper into the woods and fast," Thadius ordered.

Ryan assisted him up into the saddle, then mounted his own horse. The three withdrew further into the shelter of thick oaks and alders. A mounted patrol appeared, heading west. Twenty men strong, the warriors rode past with no clue they were being observed. Ryan saw the flash of their yellow surcoats. If only they would help them in their quest! When they passed out of sight, Thadius led them back to the forest edge.

"I can't ask you to risk your position by aiding us," Thadius addressed Jona.

"We've already settled this. I'll report to Ardan, I'm merely taking a roundabout route."

Thadius grunted. "Then let's be swift."

Throughout the day, they pushed their steeds hard. Though all were hungry, weary and chilled to the bone, each resolved to press on as long as their mounts held up. The hour was late before they finally camped for a few hours of precious sleep. Thadius permitted them a fire, it was simply too cold to do without one. Ryan spent the short hours trying to warm his fingers and toes, and slept fitfully.

Thadius was slow to rise when the trio prepared to set out again. They encountered no other patrols or people during the chilly and overcast day. Thadius led them in a wide arc around to the northeast to avoid the fort that sat along the Cimrinn River. Not a mile from the old bridge where they had previously crossed, Ryan filled their water skins as Jona cleaned and dressed Thadius' injury.

"How is it?" Ryan asked.

"Better." Jona forced a smile. Ryan did not believe him. Thadius was pale and slumped in the saddle.

Jona assumed the lead and set a faster pace. They reached the rickety bridge that spanned the freezing waters of the Cimrinn River and sped southward. The town of Aldwyn still lay two days ahead. To add to their misery, the clouds increased and the temperature fell. A light snow began before dark.

Camp that night was a miserable affair. Thadius was made as comfortable as possible. Ryan coaxed a fire to life and added more wood than Thadius would have approved of. He used the last of the poultice on his wound and brewed the last of the healing tea. As Thadius slept, Ryan and Jona spoke in low tones.

"I've done all I can," Ryan confessed.

"And you've done well. He wouldn't have gotten this far without your care," Jona comforted. "It's in the gods' hands now."

"If that's the case, I prefer they do something useful," Ryan answered in frustration. How could Orinn let the man who rescued the gemstone die of his wounds?

Thadius was no better by morning. His condition worsened as the day unfolded and he rode bundled in their thick blankets. He often closed his bloodshot eyes and seldom spoke.

"We should hasten our pace, if it's possible," Jona determined when next they rested. Ryan agreed. They were in a race against time.

"What kind of care will we find in Aldwyn?" he asked the Huntsman.

"There are those who specialize in infections," Jona assured him. "However, they come with a price."

The hours stretched for Ryan. Visibility became limited as the snowfall increased and covered the trail before them. He kept his steed abreast with Thadius, while Jona rode on the other side. Both worried that a feverish Thadius could slip from the saddle. It was a welcome sight when the sky lightened in the east.

With the first rays of dawn, a line of horsemen came into view. The half a dozen riders appeared to be a hunting party. Each was dressed warmly and all carried bows and full quivers. Ryan exchanged greetings with them as they passed.

"We're nearly there," Jona announced. He was correct, for within the hour, they arrived at the town of Aldwyn.

A wall of gray stone surrounded the town, rising over twenty feet. Square watchtowers constructed of rough cut timber dotted its length in intervals, and a pair of these framed a double gate, where a squad of guardsmen stood on duty. Jona brought them to a halt and explained that they were Huntsmen in need of supplies and a healer, as one of them was deathly ill. The men on duty quickly waved them through.

"We need medicinal supplies and fresh bandages," Ryan stated.

"We'll get an inn room first, then I'll bring you what you need. I'll also find us the best healer in Aldwyn," Jona promised.

The Huntsman led them to a small but comfortable inn, where they stabled their horses and helped Thadius to a soft bed. A high fever gripped him and Ryan's fears were heightened when he realized Thadius no longer perspired. Jona left in a hurry to gather the needed items, leaving Ryan to unpack their gear. He piled their equipment in a wardrobe and fetched a pitcher of cool water.

"Waste no time," Thadius whispered as Ryan poured him a cup. He reached into his pocket and withdrew the Stone of Orinn. "Take it, and ride to Drynas."

"I'll keep it, but we'll bring it to Drynas together. Jona will find a healer and you'll be back to normal in no time."

Ryan cleaned the wound as best he could. The flesh was bright red and swollen and a putrid yellow ichor oozed from around the stitches. Ryan was relieved when Jona returned with a middle-aged man in tow.

"Gentlemen, this is Master Landon, Aldwyn's best. Good sir, your patient awaits."

With a practiced hand, the robed man inspected the wound. Thadius tensed whenever he applied even the gentlest of pressure on the site.

"I can see that this occurred days ago. How did it happen?" the healer inquired.

"A slight altercation," Thadius answered vaguely.

Landon arched an eyebrow. "It will make a difference in the treatment. I assume there was a weapon involved. Steel? Iron? Or something else?"

"It was a goblin arrow," Ryan offered.

Landon's face grew grave. He withdrew a piece of parchment and a charcoal pencil from his belt pouch. "Goblin arrowheads are often poisoned. At the very least, they are filthy. Gather these items, and I'll prepare an ointment." He handed Ryan the parchment containing a scribbled list of ingredients. At the bottom was his price. Ryan was shocked.

"We can do better than this," he said with disappointment. "Some of these herbs won't be potent enough. Some are just for pain."

Landon straightened, his brow set in obvious irritation. "Then I suggest you make him comfortable." The healer paused at the door. "And I would not delay in sending for a priest." With that, he left.

"You're not making any friends in Aldwyn," Thadius teased in a weak voice.

Jona took the list from Ryan. "I'll fill this order and we'll make a healing brew together. On my way out, I'll have the innkeeper bring up lunch."

Ryan felt drained and had no appetite. He was relieved when Jona was back with a satchel bulging with medicinal supplies. The two set to work concocting a potent poultice. After treating Thadius, Ryan sought out the innkeeper for more water and fresh cloth. Worn-out, he leaned against the long counter while he waited.

"Ryan?"

The accent was somehow familiar and he turned to see a head of white, spiky hair.

"It's Ryan, right?"

"Crispen?"

"Well-met," the bard greeted. He glanced Ryan over and shook his head. "You look as if you've crawled all the way here from Drynas!"

"I wish my journey had been so easy."

"Come and share my fare, you could do with a little nourishment."

"Really, I'm not—"

"I insist," Crispen pressed him. "I haven't forgotten how you came to my defense that night in Drynas. At the very least, I owe you a good meal."

"You owe me nothing."

"My conscience tells me otherwise."

Ryan sat down with the bard. He had an idea how Crispen could dispense with this so-called debt. There was one man he was sure could save Thadius and the bard might provide the means of getting him here. Over a hurried lunch, Ryan related to Crispen what he could of their tale. The bard listened with genuine concern as he ate, and when Ryan made his request, the musician readily agreed.

"I'll not delay." True to his word, the bard packed his few possessions and immediately left the inn.

Ryan hardly slept in the hours that followed. He tended to a pale Thadius into the night as the man drifted in and out of a feverish sleep. Ryan was praying when Jona abruptly stepped into the room and shut the door behind him. "There's a man downstairs, asking about a sick Huntsman. Are we expecting anyone?"

Ryan jumped to his feet. "Not this soon. Does he have gray eyes, scruffy beard? Is he alone?"

"He's alone, I think. I never saw his eyes."

A firm rap sounded on the door. As it swung open, Ryan and Jona drew their swords.

# ❧ Chapter 29 ❧

"Ephram!" Ryan greeted the wizard.

"In the flesh." The elderly man slapped him on the shoulder and offered a hand to a bewildered Jona.

"I received an urgent summons from a most unusual man. Spiky hair, plays a lute. Ring any bells? I whisked myself to Aldwyn straightaway." He gave Ryan a wink and his gaze fell on Thadius. "And I see I'm not a minute too soon. You'll have to thank that bard properly next time you see him."

Ryan rubbed his bleary eyes. "Ephram, Jona and I have tried . . ." He suddenly lost his voice.

Ephram patted his shoulder in understanding. He set down a worn pouch and examined an unconscious Thadius, removing his bandage with care. Heat radiated from the woodsman like a furnace. Ryan recited what medicines they had already administered. When Ephram had seen enough, he rose and ushered Ryan and Jona toward the door. "There's a bit of work to be done, and I don't need any distractions," he insisted. "However, I will need one specific item."

Ryan pressed the Stone of Orinn into his hand. The wizard nodded solemnly and his eyes met Ryan's. "Herein lies our greatest hope."

Ryan closed the door. In the moment he lingered, he could swear the soft light coming from beneath the door glowed with a tinge of green. He and Jona waited downstairs in the common room. The hour was late and the fire burned low. There were few other patrons, finishing off their last drinks. Jona added a pair of logs to the fire and they settled at a table close to the flames.

"Who is Ephram?" Jona asked. "He seems like something more than an ordinary priest."

"He's . . . not exactly a priest." Thadius trusted Jona. Ryan decided he would too. "*Wizard* is the proper term."

"How did he learn Thadius was here?"

"Yesterday, I ran into a bard I'd met in Drynas. I told him what I could about the situation and asked if he could find Ephram. He set off right away."

"You do keep interesting company."

"What of you? Will you report to Ardan?"

"I'll see Thadius on his feet first."

Ryan could ask no more of him and was thankful he would risk punishment to help them. Besides, it was good to have a loyal companion on their side for once.

Ryan and Jona spoke of Huntsmen and war, gemstones and gods, as the night wore on. Careful not to mention Hazen or centaurs, Ryan was a bit vague on some aspects of their adventures. Jona did not press him further, and Ryan wished he could have shared more. Both staved off sleep, worried over Thadius. Then at last, Ephram came down the stairs.

"Good news, we pray?" Jona stood first.

"The news, gentlemen, is good. Let's sit for a bit before you go barging in and interrupt his rest."

"So he'll be okay?" Ryan needed to hear the words.

"Yes, the fever and infection will pass."

Ryan breathed a sigh of relief and collapsed back into the chair.

"This is great news!" Jona replied. "First the gemstone, now this. We have much to be thankful for."

"Indeed," Ephram nodded. "However, about the gemstone . . ."

Ephram cocked his head and squinted an eye. Ryan and Jona traded puzzled expressions as the mage chose his words carefully.

"We shall say nothing of gems, the Lost Hills or anything else for that matter."

Ryan was dumbfounded. "Say nothing? I don't understand."

"Surely such a deed should not go without reward, or at least the proper credit due?" Jona joined in Ryan's disbelief.

"Let me clarify things. Perhaps you'll agree with us. And if you don't, we can discuss it. After all, you were part of the gem's recovery," Ephram said to Ryan.

"Us? So Thadius is in on this?"

"The Vicar of Orinn has been persuaded to hold a special service, at the Temple of Orinn in Drynas. Earl Malikar, Lord Varis, Magistrate Allen and most of the nobles in Galanthor will be present. Malikar will use the occasion to announce the king's intention to march on Ilsgaard."

"War . . ." Ryan whispered.

"Are you sure?" Jona questioned.

Ephram glanced about. "I trust my source. But if the Stone of Orinn were to suddenly reappear in the middle of the service . . ."

"Then the war is over before it starts," Ryan answered.

"Precisely," Ephram affirmed.

"It sounds like it might work," Jona said. "The Huntsman Legion would be grateful."

"Grateful that *Orinn* returned his gift to the land," Ephram reminded him with a raised finger.

"Of course," Jona accepted.

"No hero's welcome, I suppose," Ryan sulked. "On the other hand, it makes sense. Neither Thadius nor I can openly return the stone."

"And I have other orders," Jona sighed. "Besides, I'd have a lot to explain, and I wouldn't even know where to begin."

Ryan squirmed in his seat. "Ephram, have we waited long enough?"

"You have, lad, but don't—"

Ryan bounded for the stairs, Ephram's last words unheard.

Thadius' fever broke that night and his color returned. During the next few days, his condition improved remarkably under Ephram's care. Ryan and Jona restored and resupplied their missing or damaged items and equipment. Ephram had brought plenty of coin, and Ryan spared none of it to see Jona well-provisioned before he departed for the fortress of Ardan. Ryan was sad to see him go, and hoped he would see the Huntsman again someday.

After Jona's departure, Thadius shared with Ephram the papers and map collected from Hazen. As they studied the map and documents, they spoke of Askelon and the probability that there were other sorcerers in search of more than just the secrets of Arakronis. Ryan also related to Ephram his experience with the goblins' god.

"It's true," Ephram nodded, "the stone spent unknown years in goblin hands. I can imagine their god coveting such a relic, eager to see it recaptured for his people. Jaull would have them exploit its power to conquer and destroy."

"The people of Hazen didn't use it wisely either," Ryan reflected.

"No," Ephram agreed. "But don't judge them too harshly. Such power is seductive." The wizard withdrew the Stone of Orinn and each marveled at its brilliance anew. "This is an artifact fashioned by higher powers, and whether it has ever truly had an effect on the land or not, it certainly has been imbued with the amazing ability to heal."

"Ephram, it might have kept Thadius . . ."

"Alive?" the woodsman finished.

"Who knows?" Ephram winked. "The gods move in mysterious ways."

"Could there be a connection between the gemstones?" Ryan wondered. "The stone atop the Staff of Arakronis is about the same size and cut."

"You might be correct." Ephram tucked the gem away and squinted. "A stone of green, a stone of blue . . ."

"Something you've heard?" Thadius asked.

"Something I read, long ago. All the more reason to see this material safely to Trenn. There are others who can also lend their wisdom, and I'm sure we'll seek their counsel."

Ephram spied Askelon's wand. His green eyes brightened.

"This came from Hazen as well?"

"Yes, Ephram. I set it before you half an hour ago," Thadius chuckled. "Consider it a gift from both of us."

"The wand paralyzed us at first," Ryan told him. "But with a single word, Askelon also used it to slam Thadius into a wall."

Ephram studied the wand of hazel wood and the sky-blue gem set within the dragon's mouth. "The stone is topaz, and a superior specimen. Thank you both, this is a beautiful souvenir. You say you heard the command word?"

Unfortunately, neither Ryan nor Thadius could recall the exact word Askelon had spoken. As they exchanged their best guesses, Ephram picked up on the linguistical nuances.

"Of course!" he exclaimed. "Those are variations of the same word. The intensity of the spell may depend on how the verb is employed. Very clever."

"So Askelon could adjust the strength of the spell?" Ryan concluded.

"Something like that. I'll have to conduct some experiments to be sure."

Ryan retrieved his suit of chain mail from the closet. "And there is this. We're sure it is magical too."

"Magical indeed," Ephram pronounced as he inspected the armor. "No rust or tarnish on a single link."

"Impossible!" Ryan bent closer. "I must have scratched every inch of it, sliding along that tunnel on my belly like a worm."

"It's in need of a thorough cleaning and some light oil. Otherwise, this armor could have been hammered together yesterday," the wizard proclaimed.

"Perhaps therein lays the magic," Thadius suggested. "A suit of armor that mends itself."

"Extraordinary," Ephram declared.

With the examination of the Hazen materials complete, Ryan and Ephram dined in the common room, bringing Thadius his dinner after they had finished. He had scarcely emerged from the room since their arrival, and though his recovery under Ephram's supervision had been nothing short of miraculous, Thadius insisted that he should not be seen. Some days earlier, a wanted posting had appeared, tacked up in the town square. Ephram reported another copy on display at the main gates.

Ryan was glad to see Thadius launch into his dinner with an enthusiasm resembling his former self.

"Well, your appetite seems to be restored," Ephram ribbed. "If we depart tonight, we'll have time to spare before Malikar's plans unfold."

"Not to mention the fact that Askelon may be searching for us. But are you sure you're ready to travel?" Ryan asked while Thadius wolfed down the last of some broth-soaked bread.

"Mm-hmm," he nodded.

"It's settled then," Ephram agreed.

"I'll ready our horses," Ryan offered. He paused at the door. "Are you sure you wouldn't enjoy the ride, Ephram? I know you planned to return to Drynas by magic, but what if Thadius' fever comes back?"

Thadius wiped his mouth and tossed down the napkin. "Honestly, I feel much better. We'll pack our gear. Just stop by the kitchen and make sure we're stocked for the road. And no more broth, something with substance! Chicken, beef, anything with hooves! A wheel of cheese — their biggest . . ."

Thadius' ongoing list faded as Ryan descended the stairs.

Ryan saw to their provisions before heading into the stable. As he worked to saddle their horses, a pair of armed men spoke with the night watchman in lowered tones. Their horses shared a nearby stall and were still saddled. From the corner of his eye, Ryan observed the subtle hand-off of a pouch. He did not miss the faint jingle of coins as the watchman strode by, making a hasty exit and hurrying down the street.

Pretending to cinch down straps and double-check equipment, Ryan eased around his horse and started for the door leading into the inn. His heart skipped a beat when one of the men moved to block his path.

"That'll be far enough," the man warned in a gruff voice. Tattoos wrapped the bearded man's forearms, and his balding head shone in the lamplight. He hefted a knotted club, resting it casually across a shoulder. Before Ryan could draw his blade, the other man had circled around. Ryan felt the point of a sword in his back.

"Easy now." A hand stretched around from behind to relieve Ryan of his blade. He was pushed against a stall by a roguish character with short, curly hair. Ryan fought to keep his fear in check and waited for an opportunity to strike back.

"If this is a robbery, I have little coin," Ryan bluffed.

"Don't get brave or foolish, boy. This won't take long," the tattooed man said. He gave a short whistle. Snow crunched as a cart pulled by a pair of horses rolled to a stop at the stable door. Two men slid from the bench seat to join their comrades in the stable. Both bore short clubs and rope. One of them carried an old sack.

The tattooed man produced a parchment bearing a rough sketch of Thadius' face and held it up for both to see. "Landon says this is him. We ready?" He looked at each and both nodded.

Leaving the curly-headed swordsman to guard Ryan, the other three slipped into the quiet inn.

# ᏍᎧ *Chapter 30* ᏅᎩ

Though he knew the answer, Ryan asked the question anyway. "Who are you after? Maybe I can tell you if he's even still here."

"We've seen you fetching them supplies. You know who we're here for."

"So you're bounty hunters. Are you sure you've got the right man?" Ryan's heartbeat slowed as he forced himself to calm. If all he could do right now was gather information, then it was precisely what he would do.

"A dying Huntsman doesn't hole-up in a run-down inn and a fellow Huntsman wouldn't have left him to die. That's Thadius of Corin up there. When we see the "X" in his palm, there'll be no doubts. And that's a fifty kara payday for us."

"For the four of you? You only brought four?"

"We already know he's at death's door. Landon couldn't save him. That's why the old priest is here."

Inwardly, Ryan cursed Landon for his loose tongue.

The door to the inn opened. Ryan was hoping to see Thadius but instead saw the face of the tattooed man. Ephram trailed behind, his face somber.

"I'm afraid your quarry has expired," the wizard explained to the swordsman. "Your friends are collecting the body now."

Ryan's jaw dropped. "What?"

"Dead or alive, he pays the same," the curly-haired bounty hunter snickered. "Am I right?"

The tattooed man wavered a bit and leaned against a post.

"You okay?" The swordsman stepped toward his partner. In a blur, the balding head was replaced with thick, brown hair. Beard and tattoos faded.

"Thadius!" Ryan burst out.

With a yelp of surprise, the swordsman brought up his blade and lunged at Thadius. Mid-strike, he was blown off his feet by an invisible force and sent crashing through the rails of the stall beside him.

Ryan turned to see Ephram, feet planted in a fencing stance and the hazel wood wand leveled at the unconscious swordsman.

"I haven't quite got the hang of it yet," Ephram said cheerily.

"Nicely done." Thadius straightened and walked over to examine the man, laid out flat among the splintered boards.

Ryan let out a long-held breath. "What about the others?"

"Sleeping soundly upstairs," Thadius responded.

Ephram worked his magic once again, to ensure that the bounty hunter slept peacefully until someone found him in the morning. As he did, Ryan filled Thadius in on what little he had learned as he assisted with binding the man.

"I'd already ruled them out as the earl's men. He would have sent soldiers, and they wouldn't have been quiet about it. I suppose fifty kara is a respectable bounty," Thadius said with a hint of disappointment.

"I guess it was only a matter of time before some interested party found us," Ryan reasoned.

"We'll borrow their horses and the cart for the ride to Drynas," Thadius decided as they brought down their remaining gear. "That should delay them a bit, should they make the mistake of pursuing us."

"I might as well accompany you," Ephram frowned at him. "Just to make sure you stay out of trouble."

Thadius helped him up onto the cart. "Have I thanked you for saving me yet again?"

Ephram took the reins. "Let's not make it a habit. I'm not getting any younger."

With two additional mounts in tow, the trio departed Aldwyn with no further incident. As a precaution, Thadius' appearance was altered yet again, before passing through the main gate. On the open road, they rode at a steady pace. With Malikar's declaration the next evening, Thadius urged them on. He relented to only a few hours of sleep, and this at Ephram's insistence.

As dawn broke, they skirted the walls of Drynas to approach the city from the east. Having made their escape via the western gate, Ryan and Thadius both thought it unlikely that one of the guards from that night might be pulling duty there. While still at a distance, Ryan could see soldiers scrutinizing those coming into the city.

"What's our story?"

"I'm here for a hot meal and a soft bed," Thadius remarked. "What about you, grandfather?"

"Hmph," Ephram grunted. "Make that father, or I'll introduce you as my slow-witted nephew, twice removed. As for your face, we better take care of it before the gates get crowded."

"Don't forget to add a big wart. Perhaps two, in case he's become too much of a celebrity," Ryan chided.

Thadius glowered at him.

They waited for a break in the sparse traffic, then the wizard set to work. Ephram drew forth the small mirror used in the appearance altering spell, and Ryan was curious — from what he had seen, he thought the spell required the reflection of another subject. But as the arcane words flowed, Ryan had to stifle a laugh. Thadius' eyes shifted to glare at him.

"What's so funny?" Thadius wrinkled white, bushy brows at Ryan. They were so lengthy, he suddenly looked up, catching sight of them. "Ephram, what have you done to me?"

Ephram squinted at him. "It's a remarkable resemblance."

Thadius' hands flew to his face and patted weathered cheeks. "Resemblance of who?"

A wide grin escaped the wizard's control. "My elder brother. I needed a likeness I knew by heart. Quickly now, before it wears off."

To Ryan's relief, they were waved through the gates with few questions and little notice. They placed the bounty hunters' horses and cart in the care of a public stable, reporting them as lost. After all, Thadius declared, the three of them were not thieves. At Ephram's abode, Ryan unpacked their gear and tended to their horses, while the wizard and the woodsman conspired to thwart the king's plans. As Ryan rubbed down his dark bay, the animal nudged him with its nose.

"How do you always know?" Ryan pulled an apple from his jacket pocket. He tried again to think of a name worthy of the powerfully built steed. "Don't worry, boy. I'll come up with something noble."

When Thadius and Ephram joined him, the wizard smiled broadly.

"We have an idea."


The cloaked figure drew the folds of material tighter against the chill wind. He joined the throng before the temple doors and stood in the line to enter the already crowded building. With most of Galanthor's nobility in attendance, the service was expected to be packed and guards were positioned to turn people away once capacity was reached. As one of the guards stepped forward to cut off traffic, the cloaked figure barely skirted by, settling at the rear of the noisy assembly. Every seat was filled in the spacious nave and people overflowed into the aisles.

The crowd hushed as the Vicar of Orinn strode to the lectern. The gray-haired priest gave thanks to Orinn for those gathered and acknowledged the attendance of the nobles. All eyes fell upon Malikar, and the young earl forced a smile. The aged vicar continued with a prayer for the swift return of the Stone of Orinn, the very heart of the land. With all heads bowed in prayer, it was the cue for the cloaked figure to act.

"Behold, a messenger of Orinn!" Ryan's rehearsed line rang out.

As one, the people lifted their heads and gasped in astonishment. Some cried out in fear. A tall and radiant being robed in white hovered high above, then slowly descended to the altar.

"People of Galanthor, Orinn has heard your plea! What was lost has been restored to you," his booming voice echoed off the walls.

The stunned vicar reeled and dropped to his knees, along with most of the crowd. Some remained standing, too shocked to move. The angelic visitor held aloft the Stone of Orinn for all to see. The gemstone flashed an emerald green as it was placed on the altar.

"Orinn wishes peace in the land, lest he withdraw his blessing from Galanthor and its people," he warned with a finger pointed in Malikar's direction. The young earl recoiled, and his face lost all color.

With a clap that reverberated off the walls like thunder, the holy messenger abruptly vanished. As the sharp report faded, everyone spoke at once. In the confusion, Ryan slipped out to meet Ephram in the vestibule.

"Did you get Thadius away okay?"

"Worry not, lad. Thadius awaits us back at my home. Let's get out of here."

As Ryan and Ephram reached the exit, all the doors of the nave burst open. People spilled out, eager to spread the good news.

"War is averted!"

"The Stone of Orinn is returned!"

With a feeling of satisfaction, Ryan and Ephram made their way to the mage's house. True to his word, Thadius was there. Ryan was disappointed to see their horses already saddled. He had hoped they might at least stay the night. The whole city was rejoicing.

"So much for our victory celebration," he sighed.

"I'm truly sorry, Ryan," Thadius consoled. "The quicker I'm away from Drynas, the better. Especially after what happened in Aldwyn."

"No, I'm sorry. I forgot for a minute what you've sacrificed for this victory."

"Perhaps the two of you can at least stay for a cup of tea?" Ephram offered.

"We really can't . . ."

"I should mention, there's still a bit of a glow around you," Ryan grinned.

"Yes, mainly about the head and shoulders," Ephram gestured.

"But the soldiers at the gates must see this sort of thing all the time. I'm sure they'll wave us by," Ryan shrugged with exaggerated confidence.

"Okay, one hour," Thadius gave in.

While saddened by his inevitable departure from Galanthor, Ryan was comforted knowing that Thadius was safer in the Elderwood. For now, he would enjoy the company of good friends and count his blessings.


Celebrations were in full swing, and the streets crowded with people as Ryan and Thadius rode for the gates. The guards hardly gave them a second glance, and the two continued on until the sliver of a moon was high in the night sky before stopping to make camp. For the first time in weeks, Ryan slept soundly, without stirring at every unfamiliar noise. Both were well-rested when they broke camp, and Thadius looked much more like his old self. The sun scarcely cleared the top of the trees as they halted at the grove of elms that marked the southern boundary of Ryan's land.

"You're sure you won't at least say goodbye to Darien?" Ryan tried to persuade him into lingering a bit longer.

"Tell him I'm sorry, but it would put the both of you at risk. I'm a dangerous criminal, wanted by the earl."

"I can't believe this is how things turn out, and after everything we went through, especially you." Ryan shook his head in frustration.

"Still want that hero's parade? They're a lot of fuss."

"Maybe just a little applause."

Thadius chuckled and drew his horse alongside him. "Don't get a big head, but I'm very proud of you. Without your help, the Stone of Orinn would be in goblin hands." He gave Ryan a firm handshake.

"Who needs a parade anyway?" Ryan shrugged and grinned broadly.

"I look forward to your visit in the summer. Of course, we'll drop in on Trenn and his apprentice."

Ryan blushed. "Are you sure you're up to the journey? I can ride—"

Thadius stopped him with a raised hand. "Darien's probably worried sick. Get yourself home."

"May the road be good to you," Ryan returned.

"Did you ever come up with a name for your horse?"

"I haven't had time, although this old boy has earned one." Ryan patted the animal's neck.

Thadius spurred his horse onward. "How about Aladur?" he called back.

"Aladur?"

"It's from the Old Tongue."

"I like it. What does it mean?"

"Horse." Thadius already sounded distant.

"Aladur it is."

# ↜ Epilogue ↝

Balthas arrived late, brushing away the hood of his dark cloak as he settled in a comfortable chair by the fire. He did not join the others at the table. Across the chamber, Malikar berated his inner circle of advisors and aides. The earl's tirade culminated with a silver flash, as an expensive goblet crashed into the wall. Tyresian wine splashed across the beautiful stonework and those seated at the table jumped. Malikar pounded the table in frustration.

"Can somebody tell me how this is possible?"

Malikar's aides avoided his gaze and remained silent as the dented vessel spun to a stop. Of course, none had foreseen the return of the gemstone, nor could offer an explanation for the supernatural events of the evening. Even Balthas was caught by surprise.

"Get out," the young earl dismissed the small entourage. He slammed the door behind the last of them and turned to Balthas.

"And you," Malikar addressed him with an undisguised tone of superiority, "you've been little help to me throughout this whole affair! Why did the king appoint me a chief advisor who's never here?"

Balthas bent his head and replied with measured patience.

"Forgive me, my lord. The logistics required for this campaign demand my constant attention."

While the recovery of the stone may have been a disaster for the new king and his whelp of an earl, the

327

artifact's homecoming had at least one positive aspect. He and the other members of the coven knew exactly where the Stone of Orinn was, and could no doubt lay their hands upon it again.

"Not only won't the nobles support us, every temple in this stinking city is spreading this anti-war dribble," Malikar vented.

"It is a setback, my lord."

"Setback? I'd say the whole bloody thing is off!"

Balthas rose. His tall frame cast an oversized shadow that loomed over the young earl. Malikar took an involuntary step back.

"Even as we speak, plans have been set into motion. Your king will have his war. That I promise."

*The*

*End*

The *Beyond the Elderwood* series continues with

In the quiet town of Kenliren, shudders close before the sun sets. Strange sightings and frightening occurrences spread fear among the people. When a sudden disappearance draws Ryan and his companions into the mystery, they uncover an evil that will lead them on a journey, far beyond the Elderwood.

With danger growing, Ryan forges ahead on a lone quest, only to find that true friendship will not abandon him. But in a cruel twist of fate, he must sacrifice his freedom for his friends. Alone and trapped by circumstances beyond his control, it could be years before he sees Galanthor again.

As he struggles to regain his liberty, the chance arises to bring a past evil to justice. Ryan jumps at the opportunity and undertakes a perilous mission where he encounters powerful forces that will test him like never before. When the path he chooses leaves a companion facing certain death, how far will he go to save her?

Before time runs out.

*The Hand of Rhugoth* - Book III in the
*Beyond the Elderwood* series
May 2020

Made in the USA
Coppell, TX
29 October 2019